I0637436

ALIEN SUMMER

Also by Stacey S. Thompson:

Pilgrims' Moon

ALIEN SUMMER

STACEY S. THOMPSON

This book is a work of fiction. Names, characters, places, and incidents are products of the author's imagination or are used fictitiously. Any resemblance to actual events or locales or persons, living or dead, is entirely coincidental.

Copyright © 2014 by Stacey S. Thompson

All rights reserved.

ISBN-10: 0692026673
ISBN-13: 978-0692026670

THIS BOOK IS FOR STEVE

An inspiration and fellow traveler to new worlds.

CHAPTER ONE

Indiana could've been in the Mid East instead of the Midwest for all seventeen-year-old Cameron Meyer knew. The state seemed just as flat, just as remote, and just as boring as the Arab countries he had learned about in Social Studies. Although the *Hoosier State* was mantled with fertile, green cornfields instead of baked, barren deserts, he suspected both places nurtured a similar crop: conservative, intolerant people suspicious of outsiders and new ideas, with minds just as narrow, uniform, and as uninteresting as the landscape racing by outside the car window.

Cam couldn't believe Indiana was going to be his home for the summer. He'd spent weeks dreading this trip, and now it was a reality he didn't want to face. The skyline and suburban sprawl of Chicago had receded over an hour ago.

His mother was driving, her hands in the ten and two position, eyes fixed on the shimmering blacktop ahead of them. They'd mostly ridden in silence since their departure, a convenient way to avoid their frequent, painful arguments. He never knew what to say to her anymore. Every topic was a minefield for some reason or another.

It was just easier for both of them to keep quiet.

But then his mother decided to venture into dangerous territory and spoke: "You might even like Lake Tecumseh if you have the right attitude."

Cam sighed wearily. This was well-trod ground. "Attitude won't help any. Everything sucks!"

His mother's grip tightened on the wheel, but she didn't reply. After a few seconds she switched off the A/C and lowered her window halfway as if to clear the air of *everything sucks*.

Wind blasted into the passenger compartment of their old Corolla, reeking of grass, black topsoil, and rank barnyards. She inhaled deeply. "Doesn't the fresh country air smell good? You can't get that in Chicago."

He rolled his eyes. "Thank God! It smells like crap!"

Another twenty miles of silence.

They'd driven only three hours, but Cam felt as if he'd passed through an invisible time warp into another dimension. A largely unoccupied one. Nobody seemed to live in this state. Houses were widely scattered, isolated at the ends of long, country lanes. The farms extended to the horizon, with not a single soul to be seen. The roads were narrow and strangely devoid of traffic.

An exciting land of hayrides and hoe-downs, deer hunting and trips to Wal-Mart, speaking in tongues and ice-cream socials.

Of course, they'd only serve *vanilla* ice cream. Any other flavor was probably considered *too radical*.

"I wonder if we missed Route 2," his mother said. "Can you check the directions?"

Cam unfolded the Mapquest printout from Aunt Ellen that contained the directions to the lakeside cabin. "Should be coming up soon."

"Are you sure?"

"I would be if I had a smart phone with GPS."

"You're so deprived, I know. Help me look for the sign."

Cam would've been happy to miss the road. If they kept driving for several more hours and ended up in Detroit, that would've been okay with him. He didn't relish the idea of spending a summer with relatives in Lake Tecumseh, but unfortunately that was what was going to happen.

He sighed as he looked out the passenger-side window at the endless rows of corn streaking by in a green blur. It was early June, and the tiny plants looked like little whiskers on the face of the land. The whole state of Indiana was planted with boundless fields of it. Why so much? Who could eat all of it? Where did it all go? He didn't have a clue.

"Here it is," his mother said as she slowed to make a turn onto the two-lane highway identified as Indiana Route 2. A faded sign trumpeted 15 miles to Lake Tecumseh. "We'll be there shortly," she warbled, happy their destination was in sight.

"Wonderful," Cam mumbled to the window.

"It *is* wonderful. A chance to do something different. Focus on the kind of person you really want to be."

"What do you mean?"

She appeared to collect her thoughts. "I'm worried about you, Cam. I hardly know you anymore."

Another eye roll. "It's called *growing up*, Mom."

"It's more than just *growing up*. Your behavior's changed. You've been in trouble." She shook her head. "Your new friends, they're so different, and well I—"

Into the minefield again. She never missed an opportunity to rip his friends. What did she have against them? She called them *bad influences*. They were just regular guys, not bad at all. Like all teenagers, they just wanted to have a good time and to live a little. It was good to be young. Life was a party.

They had celebrated the end of junior year at Matt Silver's house. Matt's parents were out of town, and their sprawling home was a great place to have a blowout. The celebration ended badly, but it wasn't all Matt's fault. Some troublemakers from out of town had crashed the party, and Cam had brought some alcohol—dusty bottles of old booze from his father's well-stocked liquor cabinet. He thought it would add some spice to the party and make the girls friendly, but the celebration got out of control as the night wore on. Angry neighbors called the police about the noise, but not before drunken kids trashed the house and puked in the bushes. The police called all their parents, and the Silvers quickly returned from New York.

The neighborhood was still abuzz about the party.

Cam's relationship with his mother grew even more strained afterward. He never told her about the liquor, but suspected she knew where it had come from. She had been practically frowning ever since, wringing her hands over her failure to properly raise her son. She kept repeating, *if only your father were still alive*, as if it were a prayer. Cam was sick of hearing it all the time. His father never could fix anything anyway.

At the moment, his mother was droning on about his friends and his bad behavior, but Cam wasn't paying attention. He stared at the ribbon of asphalt, the road markings reminding him of the stripes of prison uniforms. "I can't believe you're making me do this," he interrupted. "I'm too old for summer camp."

She glanced at him. "You're not going to summer camp. You're visiting relatives. There's a big difference."

"It still sucks."

"Uncle Gary and Aunt Ellen are really looking forward to your visit. They have a wonderful cabin on the lake. You're going to love it."

"I hope they have cable."

She touched his knee. "For heaven's sakes, Indiana isn't the Third World."

"It sure feels that way. We've gone miles and there's nothing."

"There'll be plenty to do, like swimming, boating, and fishing."

"But I don't like swimming, boating, and fishing," Cam said sourly. Actually, he liked swimming and boating, but he wasn't going to admit it. He had never tried fishing, but that was a sport more

4

suitable for older folks.

His mother squeezed the steering wheel tighter, exasperated. "You're very lucky to get a summer vacation on a lake. I never got one when I was seventeen."

"But you're getting one now. You're going to Italy with *Frank*." Cam snarled her boyfriend's name as if it were an epithet.

"Damn it!" she swore, abruptly slamming on the brakes. The car's tires squealed as they suddenly slowed. Startled red-wing blackbirds launched like rockets from nearby fence posts.

"Jesus Christ!" Cam yelled as his shoulder belt dug into his torso. He braced himself against the dashboard with an outstretched hand.

He had pushed too far, and suspected his mother was going to go ballistic.

She stopped the Corolla on the gravel shoulder and angrily rammed the lever to *park*. She turned and glowered at him. "I can't take any more of this! I hope you're not going to act like this in front of Uncle Gary and Aunt Ellen!"

"Act like what?"

"Like a damn ten year old. For heaven's sake, Cam, grow up!"

"What did I do?"

"I'm sick of your surly attitude, and especially how you talk about Frank!"

His mother had been dating the banker for several months. He had asked her out after she had applied for a home equity loan to help pay the monthly household bills. He was divorced, drove a black BMW, and lived in Lake Forest. Cam thought he was pompous and overbearing and didn't like how he treated his mother like a dainty princess. She was over forty.

Cam folded his arms across his chest. "All I said was you're going to Italy with him. Don't be so sensitive."

"It's *how* you said it. It's how you *always* say it. What do you have against Frank? He's only ever treated you with kindness."

"He's a jerk."

5

She reached over and pinched his upper arm and shook it. "You're the one who's being a jerk! Can't you see it? Making every conversation a battle. Don't you want me to be happy?"

"Sure, but with someone else. Not that guy."

She released him and then removed her sunglasses. She wiped her teary eyes with her fingers. "This is about your father, isn't it?"

Cam remained silent although his gaze dropped to the floor at the mention of his dad. Three years ago he had fallen to his death at a construction site. An alcoholic, Cam wondered if he had been drunk at the time of the accident. If not, had he walked off the roof on purpose, to escape his unhappy marriage, his less-than-perfect son? Had it just been an unlucky accident, a moment of inattention that took the man away from him forever?

He didn't know what to believe anymore. On one hand, he hated his father with his addictions and weaknesses. On the other, he missed him deeply. Since his father's death a great vacuum hovered in his life, sucking in all light and energy, leaving him feeling lost, forgotten, and unguided. Could the hole in his heart ever be filled? How would his life be different if his dad were still alive?

Cam had been brooding for three years. Now he was good at it.

His mother took a deep breath and exhaled loudly. Finally, she said, "It's been difficult for both of us since your dad died, Cam. But we can't stay in mourning forever."

"Who says I'm mourning?"

She reached out and took his hand. "You're so much like him. He always acted just as strong, even though I knew he was hurting inside. I tried to help, but he just pushed me away."

The screech of worn brakes alerted them to a red, battered tow truck pulling aside their Corolla. A grizzly old man wearing a dusty NASCAR cap hunched over the wheel, looking as if he were one wobbly step from the Old Folk's Home. "Everything all right, ma'am?" he drawled in flat, Hoosier syllables. "You need a tow?"

Cam's mother shook her head and waved the driver by. "Just

having a chat with my son."

"You might wanna turn your flashers on," the man said, annoyed. "A lot of crazy bastards speed down this road. You want them to see you while you're chatting."

"Thank you, but we'll be on our way soon," his mother answered.

The old man tipped the brim of his cap at them and pulled away in a cloud of diesel fumes. The truck's door pictured a wrecked flying saucer containing a frowning, green alien being towed away. The caption read: *Milford's UFO Towing Service – You Crash, We Dash.*

Cam and his mother gaped at the departing tow truck until it receded into the shimmering mirage on the black asphalt ahead.

Then they both burst out laughing.

"Did you see that?" Cam asked. "UFO Towing Service!"

"And he called other people crazy bastards!" his mother said. "We must be getting close to Lake Tecumseh. Aunt Ellen said it was famous for a UFO sighting years ago."

Cam was relieved the tension with his mother had been cut for the moment. He didn't want to have another heart-to-heart about his dad or any more arguments about Frank the Bank Jock.

"Let's get going," she said, cautiously merging back onto the highway. She started babbling about Uncle Gary and Aunt Ellen and their cabin on the lake. Soon her words decayed into background noise that Cam ignored, just as he ignored the sound of the car's engine, the hum of the tires on the roadway, and the zip of the fence posts whipping past. His mind had drifted away, pondering what was to come as they traveled the last few miles to Lake Tecumseh.

Like the other roads, Indiana Route 2 was a surveyor's dream—a straight, uninterrupted line for miles. Then, not far from their destination, the two-lane highway curved gracefully before penetrating what appeared to be a tunnel of cool, emerald woods of oak and maple. They had left the harsh sun and rigid harmony of the Hoosier road grid behind. The A/C labored less in the pleasant shade as they traveled deeper into the woodland.

A large sign heralded their arrival:

Lake Tecumseh

"Where the Glaciers Left Smiles
and Aliens Like to Visit"

Founded 1838
Population 3,409

Cam suppressed a groan. *Where the Glaciers Left Smiles? Aliens Like to Visit?* What crazy place was this? He counted how long he would be stuck in the town—ten weeks total.

An eternity.

The speed limit was only 25 miles per hour. Even the Corolla's tiny four-cylinder engine was too powerful for such a slow-poke town. They drove by a Dairy Queen, a farm supply store, and a Chevy dealership on the outskirts of town. At the center old brick storefronts with diagonal parking spaces full of pick-up trucks made the place more interesting. Cam spied a drugstore, a hardware store, and a small diner where old men hunched over a counter sipping coffee and eating donuts under lazy ceiling fans.

The town was tidy and charming, but it looked too old fashioned, too wholesome, and too dull. Cam was from *Chicago*, after all. How could such a small town compare to one of the greatest cities in the world?

One storefront had a prominent sign: *Lake Tecumseh UFO Museum.* A statue stood on the sidewalk, a green alien beckoning with a three-fingered hand. A pair of frumpy tourists stood outside the museum, consulting a map.

"You should visit that museum," Cam's mother said, pointing.

"No way! I'm not some kind of Trekkie dork."

"You might learn something."

"Yeah, right." He had no interest in any of that geeky sci-fi stuff. It was useless and it certainly didn't impress the girls.

They drove by old homes with wide porches, neatly trimmed lawns, and perfectly placed flowerbeds, but the town of Lake Tecumseh was quickly behind them. No traffic signals or stop signs had slowed their trip from one side to the other. Cam swiveled his head and looked behind at the receding houses. "That was the whole town? It's awfully small."

His mother shrugged. "What did you expect?"

"This is going to suck more than I thought."

A sliver of sun-splattered blue hung behind the large oak trees like a painter's drop cloth. Cam caught only a glimpse of the lake before the road curved and stately trees blocked the view. The lakeside neighborhood was densely wooded. Houses were carefully screened by trees and large bushes; only the ends of their driveways were visible. Mailboxes marked each property and red reflectors marked each culvert. Poison ivy grew lush and green beside the road.

"Help me look for Number 4527," his mother said, clutching the Mapquest directions while peering over the wheel at the numbers on the mailboxes.

Such a large number for such a small place, Cam thought.

Number 4527 was stenciled in black paint on a rusty, battered mailbox. Beneath the number someone had written *Wainwright*. Vines curled up the post. Cam's shoulders slumped. He hoped the cabin was in better shape than the mailbox.

They turned down the narrow, gravel driveway. The tips of tree branches scraped against the car windows as they descended a small hill toward the lake. The rear of the house faced them, shoehorned between massive trees poised to crush it during the next tornado. His mother had called his uncle's property a *cabin*, but it had two stories, an attached garage, and aluminum siding. A large, white cylinder rested five yards from the house, holding propane gas. The place was definitely not a cabin, but a large and comfortable looking home.

His mother stopped the car and turned off the engine. "Wait till you see the lakeside. It's much nicer."

They unbuckled their seatbelts and climbed from the car. Cam stretched his arms over his head. He had stuffed his lanky six-foot frame into the uncomfortable bucket seat for too long. Not only had he inherited his father's height, but his looks as well. The same brown eyes, brown hair, and slim built. Cam kept his hair long and unruly, cultivating an edgy and artistic image. Most of the time he didn't shave the splotchy whiskers that sprouted on his face either. His mother hated his *bed head*, as she called it, and the unshaven look even more.

His appearance was another topic they both tried to avoid discussing.

"Hello!" Aunt Ellen called cheerfully from the opening screen door. She emerged from the house wearing a blue-checkered apron, looking like an older version of his mother. Both women had soft features and round faces with expressive, doe eyes, but Aunt Ellen was heavier. The country lifestyle had added a few pounds.

Cam hadn't seen his aunt since his father's funeral three years ago.

Aunt Ellen and his mother embraced and greeted each other warmly. Aunt Ellen held her sister at arm's length to inspect her. "Have you lost weight? You look fantastic!"

"Thank you for noticing! I joined a health club." Cam's mother placed her hand on her hip like a runway model and revolved to show off her figure. "I have a brand new life, and I've never been happier."

"That's wonderful," Aunt Ellen said. Grinning, she stepped to Cam. He hoped she wasn't going to muss his hair or pinch his cheek as she always used to do. She clearly realized he was too old for that silliness. "Hello, Cammie," she said.

He cringed. He hated being called Cammie. Everyone used to

call him that when he was a boy. He absolutely hated it. He was now Cam to everyone in Chicago. Although sometimes his mother called him Cameron when she was angry with him.

He hated that too.

He needed to set Aunt Ellen straight right away. "Nobody calls me Cammie anymore. My name is Cam."

"Oh, of course," Aunt Ellen said, her smile not fading. "Whatever you prefer. Only yesterday you were waist high playing with toy trucks. Now look at you! You're such a tall and handsome young man!"

Cam felt himself blush.

"Oh, give me a hug!" Aunt Ellen said as she enveloped him with her large arms and pulled him into a tight embrace.

Pulling away, Cam said, "Nice to see you, Aunt Ellen." Inside, he wanted to jump into the Corolla and speed away.

"We're so excited you're visiting this summer, Cam," Aunt Ellen said. "You're going to love it!" She went to the screen door and yelled into the house for her husband.

Uncle Gary emerged wearing a dirty white T-shirt and a pair of faded blue jeans, wiping his hands on a rag. He gave Cam's mother a kiss on the cheek. "Hello, Barb. How was the drive?"

"A lot of traffic on the toll road, but otherwise, okay."

Uncle Gary stepped to Cam and shook his hand firmly. "Welcome, son. It's great to see you again."

Cam recalled his uncle and father sitting at the kitchen table under a swirl of cigarette smoke. They would drink beer and tell racy jokes that Cam would eagerly repeat in school to his buddies' delight. Cam wondered if his uncle still had some good jokes. He was older now and his clothing no longer reeked of cigarettes. He must have given up the habit.

"Come see the house," Aunt Ellen said, guiding them to the door. "There's pie and ice cream."

Cam's mother patted her belly. "I couldn't possibly!"

11

Ellen grabbed her sister's arm and steered her inside. "Don't be ridiculous, Barb. Life's too short not to have a piece of pie!"

Uncle Gary smiled at Cam. "You look more like your dad all the time. I think you're taller than him now, Cammie."

Cam cringed a second time at the nickname and then promptly corrected his uncle.

They entered the house through a back porch that functioned as a collector for piles of laundry, mud-encrusted boots, and tangled fishing gear. Inside, the large kitchen had dark oak cabinets with well-worn wooden knobs. Next to the ceiling happy kittens played on the wallpaper border, rolling colorful balls of yarn. Dirty dishes filled the sink, tins of salt, sugar and flour stood like soldiers on the countertops, and a rolling pin rested next to a flat shell of pastry. A fresh-baked pie cooled on a butcher-clock table. Cam inhaled the savory aroma of apples and cinnamon, and his stomach rumbled in response.

"Sorry the kitchen's such a wreck," Aunt Ellen said, grabbing a dish towel and wiping the table. "I've been busy cooking for you. I know teen-age boys eat a lot."

Cam stepped into the large living room fronting the lake. The windows were open to emit a fresh, cool breeze. An attached, screened-in porch filled with wicker furniture looked like a tempting place to curl up and nap for a few hours. He squinted at the sparkling blue waters of Lake Tecumseh, which reflected the sunlight like a plane of mirrors. A rowboat was tied to the wooden pier.

The lake was much larger than Cam had expected. Its shores were heavily wooded, but homes and cabins peeked from the cover of the trees. Numerous piers extended into the water like giant fingers. A few fishing boats passed by, bobbing in the wake left by a speeding Jet-Ski.

As the adults chatted in the kitchen, Cam stared at the glistening lake. He should have felt relieved at their arrival and calmed by the beautiful scene. Instead he sensed something odd about the surroundings. He felt afraid, but afraid of what? The lake was bright and placid. The sky was clear and blue. Their cabin was homey and comfortable. Yet in Cam's head, an unpleasant strangeness revealed itself unexpectedly. A cold rush of nervousness chilled him, and the skin on his forearms tightened into gooseflesh. His breath quickened.

As if a door had been opened on a winter's day.

And then, as quickly as it had arisen, the subconscious fear disappeared.

What had happened?

Had he experienced a premonition? A psychic warning shot across his bow?

Shaking his head clear, he dismissed the unusual feeling as his overactive imagination. He was tired from traveling and arguing with his mother and stressed by being with his relatives for the summer. No wonder he was feeling strange.

He shrugged it off and joined the others in the kitchen for pie and ice cream. Aunt Ellen served him an extra large portion. He relished its delicious, sugary magic. His aunt was a good cook, unlike his mother who seldom did more than reheat leftovers in the microwave or order take out. He was sure to gain a few pounds over the summer.

The adults chatted about family and discussed recent happenings. Cam listened politely but largely kept out of the conversation.

After they had finished eating, Cam's mother fidgeted in her chair and glanced at her watch. "I need to go, or I'll get caught in rush hour on the Tri-State."

"Already? We've hardly had a chance to visit," Aunt Ellen said.

"I'm sorry, but Frank's taking me out tonight, and I can't be late."

Cam hated how Frank the Bank Jock ran his mother's life. He controlled her as easily as he manipulated the accounts at his bank. Why was his mother so weak and needy? She had needed his father, too. She had stuck with the man for years, even when his drinking got out of control, and he did as well. They were not happy memories, and Cam felt a dark cloud descend over him amid the kitten-encrusted walls of the kitchen.

Cam's mother stood and hugged him. "Behave yourself!"

"Yeah, yeah," Cam mumbled.

"Don't worry about him, Barb," Uncle Gary said. "We'll take good care of him."

"I know you will," Cam's mother said. "See you in August."

They filed outside, and after some more parting words, Cam's mother drove away with an exuberant wave out the driver's side window.

Why shouldn't she be happy? Cam thought. She had a romantic summer planned: elegant dinners, sailing on Lake Michigan, even a whirlwind Italian vacation. Holding his duffle bag, he watched the car ascend the driveway, the coarse gravel crackling under its wheels. His mother turned onto the main road and was gone.

At least that's over, he thought. Now here I am.

Then a strange feeling again. A sense of foreboding, and it wasn't due to his mother's departure. Something else was causing his uneasiness, something about this small place in Indiana.

He shrugged it away again, but this time it seemed to want to stay.

*   *   *

Cam's bedroom was on the second floor and decorated in crisp blue and white beach colors. A pair of French doors opened onto a small balcony, giving him a wonderful view of the green-splashed shores of the lake as June's late twilight slowly descended on the landscape.

He should have been happy with the comfortable room and beautiful setting, but he was not. Being 180 miles from home and removed from his friends, he was in an irritable mood. He felt imprisoned in Lake Tecumseh, Indiana. *Where the Glaciers Left Smiles and Aliens Like to Visit.* Cam wasn't smiling, and he felt like an alien amid the quiet, rural surroundings and the down-home cheerfulness of Uncle Gary and Aunt Ellen.

On the first day of his prison sentence, Aunt Ellen cooked barbecued pork chops, fried potatoes, and green-been casserole for dinner. Pears in lime Jell-O for dessert. Cam could hardly move after eating so much. Later he joined Uncle Gary and Aunt Ellen to watch the local news, Wheel of Fortune, and two crime shows on television.

Now he lay on the bed, reflecting on his arrival at Lake Tecumseh, watching the blades of the ceiling fan go around and around and feeling the cool breeze on his face. About nine o'clock, the long summer day had not yet completely surrendered to night.

He rose and went onto the balcony. One fishing boat slowly motored across the lake. What was the fisherman doing out at such a late hour? Cam grabbed the binoculars off the dresser and trained them on the boat.

An old man in a red-checkered shirt was hunched in the boat, his hand on the rudder of the motor. He stopped the boat in the center of the lake and swiveled his head. Unsatisfied with something, he moved the boat a few feet to the east. Still unsatisfied he then moved the boat a few feet to the west. He repeated the precise back-and-forth positioning several times before turning off the motor and looking very pleased with himself.

Viewing from the shore, Cam didn't understand why the old man was so intent on that exact location. Was the fishing better there?

And why was he on the water at his age anyway? It was almost dark. What if he fell out of the boat and drowned?

Cam continued to watch through the binoculars as the old man donned a strange-looking helmet with protruding knobs and a wire antenna. Talking to himself, he carefully adjusted the knobs and repositioned the wire antenna. He turned his head as if he was trying to pick up a signal.

Is he senile? Cam wondered.

The helmeted old man then closed his eyes, calmly folded his hands across his chest, and slowly reclined until his body was lying flat against the plank seats of the small boat.

He looked like an old corpse in a floating coffin.

He's having a heart attack! Cam thought. Clutching the binoculars, he bolted from his room and bounded down the stairs, skipping every other step all the way.

Startled, Uncle Gary and Aunt Ellen looked away from the flickering television screen. "Whoa!" Uncle Gary called. "Where's the fire?"

Cam ran to the porch and pointed outside. "There's an old man in a boat! I think he had a stroke or something!"

Uncle Gary rose and crossed to Cam. "Is it old man Milford?"

"How the hell should I know who it is?" Cam said, glancing through the binoculars. "It's some old fisherman. He's not moving! Call 9-1-1!"

"Let me see," Uncle Gary said, taking the binoculars and inspecting the scene. "Don't panic, there's nothing wrong."

"How can you be so sure?"

"It's just as I suspected. It's the right time, and that's Orville Milford's boat."

Milford? Cam recalled the tow truck with the sign on the door: *Milford's UFO Towing Service – You Crash, We Dash.* He asked his uncle if the elderly driver was Orville Milford.

"That's the same man," Uncle Gary replied as he handed back the binoculars. "This is his strange routine. Every evening about the same time he goes out on the lake and meditates or something."

"And he's real particular about the exact spot," Aunt Ellen added from the side, her eyes glued to the television. "He's been doing it for years. At first it was strange. Now it's old hat."

"Why does he wear that silly helmet?" Cam asked.

Uncle Gary sat in his recliner. "I haven't seen a helmet before, but we hardly pay attention anymore. Maybe it's one of his new inventions."

"Does he have Alzheimer's?" Cam asked.

"No, he's sharp as a tack, just a little odd. People call him Crazy Old Orville. He's a local celebrity."

"He is? For being a tow-truck driver?"

Uncle Gary shook his head. "No, because he says he had a *Close Encounter.*"

"A what?"

"Haven't you seen the movie, *Close Encounters of the Third Kind*?" Aunt Ellen asked incredulously.

Cam shrugged. "I'm not into sci-fi. It's for nerds. Plus those old special effects are so stupid."

His aunt's jaw dropped. "That movie's not old! And the special effects were incredible! I remember seeing it when it was released! I was amazed."

"Orville Milford claims to have had a *Close Encounter* with a UFO," Uncle Gary explained. "He says an alien space ship crashed into the lake twenty years ago."

"No wonder people call him crazy," Cam said.

"His stories are good for tourism," Uncle Gary said. "Once he got the UFO craze started, people jumped on the bandwagon. Lots of otherwise normal people were reporting flying saucers and little green men in the area. The Chamber of Commerce decided it was a good way to promote Lake Tecumseh to tourists, especially in the off season."

Cam pictured the community's welcome sign: *Lake Tecumseh – Where the Glaciers Left Smiles and Aliens Like to Visit.*

"The UFO mania draws a different crowd, folks who aren't boaters or fishermen," Uncle Gary said. "They come from far away. You'd be amazed how many people believe this stuff."

"You don't believe in UFOs, do you?" Cam asked.

"Of course not. It's just harmless fun."

"We even have a UFO Museum," Aunt Ellen added proudly. "It was rated very highly by *We Are Not Alone* magazine."

"I saw it on the way in," Cam said without a tinge of interest, recalling the statue of the green alien outside the front door of the small museum.

He couldn't believe Lake Tecumseh would latch onto something as ridiculous as UFOs for self-promotion. Weren't towns supposed to highlight their scenic beauty, architectural monuments, or historic battlefields?

But aliens? Flying saucers?

What an odd place.

What an even longer summer ahead.

CHAPTER TWO

To Cam, everything in Lake Tecumseh moved slowly. People weren't in a hurry to get anywhere. Cars crawled through town as if the asphalt were a layer of molasses. Shoppers lazily shuffled the sidewalks as slowly as the plodding sun crept across the sky on the long summer days. Store clerks wasted time chatting with customers while Cam waited in line behind them, seething at the inconvenience. The languid pace was endlessly frustrating, and after the first two weeks, he wondered if he could ever slow down to match the locals' sluggish rhythm. He missed the frenetic energy of Chicago.

Uncle Gary and Aunt Ellen were cast from the same mold as their neighbors. They weren't lazy—far from it—but the long days did not scream *hurry* to them either. They tackled the gardening, household repairs, and other off jobs with energy and good humor. They enlisted Cam's help and tried to instill the same positive work attitude in him, but it was mostly unsuccessful. He disliked the chores, but at least they helped pass the time.

Between the never-ending projects, which he suspected were his relatives' way to keep him busy and out of trouble, Cam spent his free time walking beneath cathedral-like roofs of tree branches shading the lanes of the neighborhood, admiring the blue lake, and swimming in its cool waters. Uncle Gary allowed him take the row boat onto the lake, which he did frequently. Cam enjoyed floating in the boat shirtless, watching the clouds drift by, and darkening his tan. While his boating gave him needed peace and solitude, strange feelings sometimes plagued him even on the calm water. He felt as if he were being watched, even when no one was in the vicinity. Sometimes he thought he heard whispers, although the only sounds were the rustling of the leaves and the screeches of the gulls flying overhead.

Cam attributed the mental discomfort to his unhappiness with being away from home, but there was something more to it than that. Was he imagining things? Was he going crazy? He couldn't figure it out. The strange feelings in his head were unexplained, unnerving, and unwelcome.

He had a lot of time to think since his arrival in Lake Tecumseh. His mother complained about his bad grades and said he had slacked off. What did she know? She was last in school years ago. Courses were more difficult now, everyone knew that. Sure, he had a couple of D's on his report card, but what did that prove? He was never going to be an Honor Roll student anyway, so why bust his butt trying? Let those A-students sitting in the front row of the classroom have that *honor*. Meanwhile, he had lots of friends and an exciting life and wasn't about to waste it with his nose stuck in dull books.

He kept reliving the end-of-school-year party because it had been the final straw between him and his mother. Everything would have been fine if the lightweights had been able to hold their liquor. Was it his fault they had drunk too much? Was it his fault they had gotten out of control? Was it his fault the police had shown up? His mother should be more understanding. Sending him away for the summer wasn't going to change anything.

The one thing that allowed Cam to keep his sanity was Uncle Gary's computer, which was in the extra bedroom downstairs, which doubled as the house office, the sewing room, and the overflow closet. Cam found it unusual his uncle kept the computer in such a crowded, uninviting place, but at least he had one.

Uncle Gary showed the computer to Cam a few days after his arrival. The gray plastic monitor and keyboard shared the table with a sewing machine, spools of thread, and fabric swatches. "We don't use it much, but it's handy for weather forecasts and stock prices," Uncle Gary told him.

"Thank God you got the Internet," Cam said, relieved.

"It's slow and freezes up occasionally, but it'll get you through the summer."

"Cool!" Cam eagerly sat at the desk and wiped the dust from the monitor with the front of his T-shirt. He pressed the *on* button and watched as the screen flickered to life. The computer was so old it practically groaned.

"No porn sites," his uncle reminded.

"Gimme a break!," Cam said with a dramatic eye roll.

The computer had out-of-date Windows software, an AOL browser, and very little memory. But the Internet was Cam's connection to the outside world. He established a new screen name befitting his summertime situation: *ExileIN17.* He thought it clever—Exiled in Indiana, age 17.

Uncle Gary and Aunt Ellen didn't understand why Cam wanted to spend so much time on the computer when the lake and woods beckoned outside. But Cam enjoyed surfing the web and instant messaging his friends back home. They were having a great time in Chicago, and he regretted missing the excitement. He couldn't wait for August so he could return and join them.

August would be the start of senior year, and he didn't know if he were ready for another year of high school. At least it would be his last. What would he do after he graduated? He had no clue where his life would take him. College seemed beyond his ability—both mentally and financially. He had no interest in joining the military. Maybe he'd try construction like his dad.

His mother was dating a banker. If he sucked up to Frank,

perhaps one day he'd get a job in his bank. Cam frowned. He didn't like that idea at all.

Cam often stayed up late killing time on the computer, long after Uncle Gary and Aunt Ellen went to bed. He didn't normally get to bed until after midnight. He didn't know what bothered his sleep— the change in surroundings, the different mattress, or just the unique noises of the old lake house—but something did. He never had trouble sleeping before, but here, in Lake Tecumseh, he was bothered by strange dreams and fitful sleep.

Usually he would no sooner drift off to sleep than be rousted out of bed in the early morning by Uncle Gary and Aunt Ellen to pull weeds in the garden, fix the porch screens, or paint the tool shed. Only his youthful stamina kept him going with so little sleep. Today he was drafted for a plumbing project, which he tackled with all the enthusiasm of a man heading to his execution.

"Damn it—I mean darn it—this part doesn't fit," Uncle Gary grimaced, his arms up to the elbows in the leaky toilet tank while assorted plumbing tools lay scattered across the blue porcelain.

"It doesn't bother me if you swear," Cam said, standing in the doorway to the bathroom, knowing little household repair projects could become nightmares. He and his mother had often tried to fix things, but that usually only delayed the inevitable call to a professional.

Gary pulled out his arms and dried them on a rag. "It's not whether cussing bothers you; it's whether it's the proper thing to do."

"You never worried about it when you were B.S.-ing with my dad. I learned a lot of good swear words from you."

"Not what I wanted to teach you, that's for sure." He carefully inspected the disassembled toilet parts, which resembled discarded pieces from a botched plumbing autopsy. "Can you go to the hardware store and get me a bigger one of these?" he asked Cam, showing him the misshapen component.

"Sure," Cam answered, picturing himself driving his uncle's Chevy into town. He extended his palm. "Gimme your truck keys."

Uncle Gary smiled. "Who said anything about driving? You can ride the bike in the garage."

Cam furrowed his brow. "Did my mother tell you not to let me drive?"

"She said you've been reckless."

"It was the other guy's fault!" Cam insisted, recalling how he had gotten rammed from behind by a jerk yakking on a cell phone. Fortunately, there had not been much damage.

Uncle Gary wrote down the name and dimensions of the part, and Cam stuffed the note in his pocket. Cam then went to the garage and looked forlornly at the ten-speed bicycle leaning against the wall.

His wheels for the summer.

With a sigh, he mounted the bike and rode toward town. As he pedaled, he felt the bright June sun warm his face and smelled the fertile aroma of the green countryside. The trees were like a giant picket fence lining the road. The houses and cottages were bedecked with flowers and surrounded by emerald green lawns. Recent rains had kept everything quite lush, but the weather pattern had changed, and the temperature and humidity were increasing. Cam started to sweat under his T-shirt.

He rode along the side of the road, just inches from the gravel shoulder, and only a few automobiles passed him on the way. The drivers were courteous, slowing and leaving a wide berth as they passed. He bristled when one car approached him rapidly from behind. Its engine rumbled with the throaty roar of excess horsepower. He looked over cautiously as a red convertible accelerated and streaked by in a crimson blur, the right wrist of the young, blond driver perched on the top of the steering wheel. The shiny Mustang sped around a curve and was quickly out of sight.

Cam sneered, annoyed at the speeding driver. He felt vulnerable riding on a flimsy ten-speed bike when a few tons of steel and plastic raced by him.

The driver of the Mustang was probably a lucky jock from a wealthy family who coasted through life with every skid greased. Cam didn't have advantages like that. His mother had little money. He didn't have a car of his own. Nothing came easily for him, especially schoolwork. Although he was in good shape, he wasn't an athlete. He had considered joining the swim team, but at the last moment, he backed out, not wanting to go to all those early morning practices.

Wondering if he were good at anything, Cam rode into the town of Lake Tecumseh in a bad mood. He passed the houses with quaint porches and entered the small business district. He leaned the bike against a telephone pole beneath the sign for *Joe's Hardware*. If he were in Chicago, he'd lock the bike, but a precaution like that seemed unnecessary in such a small town.

The door to the hardware store chimed as he entered. The shop was crammed with shelves, and the aisles were narrow. The stale air smelled of paint fumes, corroding metal, and decaying cardboard. Ceiling fans rotated slowly above.

A clerk stood behind the counter. His name tag said *Joe*. He looked up at Cam and arched his eyebrows in acknowledgment. "Can I help you, son?"

Cam handed over the note. "Yeah, I need one of those."

The clerk read the slip of paper. "Sure. Follow me." He stepped from behind the counter and led Cam to an aisle jammed with strange looking plumbing supplies. Joe grabbed a box off a hook and handed it to Cam. "You got a big project going on?"

"No, my Uncle's got the project. I'm just the *go-fer*."

"Are you visiting from out of town?"

Cam nodded. He didn't want to have a conversation with the clerk. Whatever happened to speedy service? He just wanted to get in and out and not tell this stranger his whole life story.

The clerk asked Cam where he was staying, and he told him.

"The Wainwrights are good people," Joe answered. "Regular

24

customers. You're very lucky to be here for the summer."

Cam didn't feel lucky, but he decided not to explain, fearing it would prolong the tiresome conversation. Then the door chimed as another customer entered. Cam sighed with relief at the possibility to make a quick escape. He paid Joe the Clerk and headed for the door.

"Enjoy the summer," the man called cheerfully from the counter.

Was that even possible here? Cam mused.

Bag in hand, he stepped outside. The sunlight was blinding, and he squinted against the glare. Something caught his gaze and he froze. His eyes locked onto a beautiful, young girl his age on the other side of the street. She greeted a passerby amiably, her smile a beacon even in the distance, and then walked across to Cam's side of the street. She was petite, wearing tight shorts and a white lacy blouse with spaghetti shoulder straps that accentuated her well-developed figure. Her straight, brown hair reached just to her shoulders and then curled playfully.

The girl noticed Cam staring. She flashed a smile, her full cheeks rising up. She then pulled open a door and disappeared inside a neighboring building.

Cam immediately followed after her, pausing at the entrance to read the sign overhead: *The Lake Tecumseh UFO Museum*. The statue of the green alien stood outside, gesturing with a three-fingered hand. The sexy girl had gone inside the UFO museum, so he took a deep breath and decided to check it out.

Obviously the museum had once been a small store a lot like *Joe's Hardware*. Large windows fronted the street, now obscured by racks of mounted items. Display cases divided the museum's floor, and models of UFOs dangled from the ceiling. Cam only superficially noted the contents of the museum and the absence of other visitors. Instead his gaze focused on the girl behind the reception counter, who he had followed inside.

"Welcome to the Lake Tecumseh UFO Museum," she said in a warm, country accent that Cam found very appealing. "There's a two-dollar donation, please."

Cam fished in his pocket and handed her the money.

"Is there anything you're particularly interested in?" she asked with a smile and a slight tilt of her head.

Cam bit his lower lip and turned away shyly. He was interested in *her*, but didn't want to reveal she was the only reason he had come inside. Girls didn't like when guys came on too strong. Since she worked in the museum, he would probably score points by pretending to be interested in the subject matter. "I'm just here to look around."

"Let me know if you have any questions!"

Cam smiled demurely and then shuffled to the exhibits. He furtively glanced back to the girl at the counter. She was busy writing in a ledger, looking like an angel against the light streaming through the windows around her. When she looked up, he quickly turned away, directing his attention to an exhibit titled: *Unidentified Flying Objects throughout History.*

Cam cursorily reviewed an illustrated timeline of ancient UFO sightings: Aztec gods in feathered headdresses sitting in apparent space capsules, rock paintings of beings wearing what looked like spacesuits, and giant animal figures and runways carved into the desert of Peru to signal visitors from the sky. He was amazed. It was as if people had always been looking up into the heavens, trying to explain the strange things they saw.

As he moved by the exhibits, he kept an eye on the beguiling girl. She was immersed in her work and not paying any attention to him. He was not surprised. He didn't have much confidence around girls, and why would a pretty one like that be interested in him? Disappointed, he read the displays instead and soon found himself fascinated by the information about UFOs. The stories from the Bible especially intrigued him, not that he knew much about the Bible. Was Ezekiel's wheel in the sky a revolving spaceship? Were Sodom and Gomorrah destroyed by an atomic attack from aliens?

Was the Star of Bethlehem a mother ship hovering over the Levant?

Cam chuckled at the silly stories. Maybe they were meant to be tongue-in-cheek, but he didn't know for sure. The curators of the museum took the topics seriously, and the displays were detailed, well-constructed, and riveting.

As he progressed through the exhibits from ancient history to present day, the chronicle of mysterious events suggested the continuous visitation of Earth by extraterrestrials. When the timeline passed into 1940s, the documented occurrences of UFOs increased significantly in number: Roswell, the Bermuda Triangle, Barney and Betty Hill's interrupted journey, and then, incredulously, Lake Tecumseh, Indiana.

"That's why we have a UFO Museum," the girl said over his shoulder.

Startled, Cam spun around and was face to face with his own UFO—the *Unidentified Female Object* who worked in the museum. He had become so engrossed in the exhibits; he hadn't realized she had walked up next to him. "W-What?" he sputtered, suddenly nervous she was standing so close.

She pointed to the display panel. "Who would think we'd be on par with Roswell or the Bermuda Triangle?"

Cam's tongue seemed twisted into knots. Regaining his composure, he said, "I've heard of those places before, but never Lake Tecumseh, Indiana."

She scrunched her pretty face. "Isn't that why you're here, to learn about the strange sightings in the area?"

"Not exactly. I'm staying with relatives for the summer. I saw the museum and thought I'd check it out. I'm Cam Meyer."

"I'm Lindsay Brock. My family runs this museum. Where are you from? Chicago?"

He nodded. "How did you know?"

"Your accent."

"Oh," he answered flatly, unaware he had one. He thought the

Hoosiers, on the other hand, drawled their words as if they lived much farther south. Now *they* had accents.

"In the summer, most people go to the lake instead of the museum," Lindsay said.

Cam flashed his most charming smile. "It's a nice museum, and I don't know much about UFOs."

She smiled, encouraged by his interest. She went to the display labeled: *Lake Tecumseh – Where Aliens Like to Visit.* She swept her long, bare arms across the exhibit with a dramatic flourish as if she were a model on a television game show. "Our little town is an epicenter for UFO sightings."

The panels were collections of newspaper articles from the early 1980s to the present, photos of awestruck men and women pointing into the sky, and a map of the county dotted by red X's, each mark indicating a UFO sighting.

"Do you believe any of these stories?" Cam asked, unable to contain his skepticism.

"What do you mean?" she asked, sounding perturbed.

"Aren't they just lonely people trying to get attention? How come aliens always visit out-of-the-way locations instead of landing in the middle of Washington, D.C., for example?"

"That's obvious." She lowered her voice and looked furtively around them and then whispered, "They don't really want to be seen. They're studying us."

He smiled, struck by her beauty. Her cinnamon-colored hair set off her round face and wide cheekbones like a picture frame. Almost stuttering, he said, "You believe all this E.T. stuff?"

She chuckled. "I have an open mind. I've been immersed in these stories all my life. You see, my grandfather is Orville Milford."

Cam remembered the old man who performed the nightly ritual on the lake. The man his uncle said believed he had encountered aliens years ago. "*The* Orville Milford?"

She seemed surprised. "Have you heard of him?"

"I see him every evening in his boat on the lake. He wears a silly helmet and meditates or something."

"That's him all right. He started this UFO craze," she said proudly.

"He saw a UFO crash into the lake about 20 years ago, right?"

"That's right." She pointed to a newspaper sealed beneath glass on the display panel. "Here's the original news report."

Cam took a closer look. The article was titled: *Local Fisherman Tells of Big One that Got Away.* Orville Milford was in the photo standing on the lakeshore, dressed in a flannel shirt and pointing to the water. He was 20 years younger, but resembled an old curmudgeon even then. The caption beneath the black and white photo read: *Orville Milford, Route 1, points to site of UFO Impact.* Next to the newspaper article was Orville's surprisingly detailed hand drawings of a glowing, egg-shaped object crashing into the lake.

The article was written by a skeptical reporter poking fun at the eyewitness in a town where probably nothing important ever happened. Cam began to feel sorry Orville Milford was made the town laughingstock. "So nobody really believed him?"

"Not at first, but he kept repeating the story every chance he got. Eventually, people started to listen."

"Did they ever search the lake?"

She shook her head. "No planes were reported missing from the local airports or Chaffee Air Force Base. The officials said my grandpa just saw ball lightning."

"Ball lightning?"

"A powerful electrical discharge like regular lightning. Ball lightning can be any shape, color, or size. I guess it's amazing if you see it, but it's very rare."

Cam found the young curator amazing. She was obviously very intelligent, as she provided the explanation effortlessly. He felt outclassed in her presence. Having never applied himself in school, he couldn't explain scientific phenomena as clearly as she did.

Lindsay didn't look like a science geek at all. She exuded charm and confidence and had a friendly, easygoing manner. No wonder he was so attracted to her. She wasn't like the empty-headed, stuck-up girls he hung around with in Chicago. The girls he had invited to Matt Silver's party.

"Grandpa says it wasn't ball lightning," Lindsay related. "The sky was clear."

"Why does he go out on the lake and meditate?"

She looked at her feet, embarrassed. "He's an odd fellow. Let's just leave it at that."

Cam didn't press her. If she didn't want to talk about her grandpa's strange behavior, that was fine with him. He studied the map marked with the red X's. "What about these other sightings? Any truth to those?"

"I'm investigating each one to find out. I'm writing a book about UFO sightings in the county. My hypothesis is that these sightings were triggered by my grandpa's report."

"You mean copycats? They're just making their UFO encounters up?"

She shrugged. "I'm not sure. I've been interviewing the witnesses, trying to corroborate—or disprove—their stories. There may be a psychological element, some kind of mass delusion. Once the seed is planted, anything weird or unusual is attributed to aliens."

"You must be really smart to be writing a book."

She blushed. "Mr. Russell, my science teacher, is encouraging me. It also sharpens my analytical and writing skills."

"I'm not good with either of those," Cam admitted with a shy smile, "so I admire someone who can write." He pointed to another wall exhibit: *Aliens and UFOs in Literature and Film*. "Movies are more my speed. No analysis and writing in them."

The colorful display was an examination of popular entertainment on the subject. The 1938 radio broadcast of *The War of the Worlds* started the chronology, which then progressed through a litany of bug-eyed hostile aliens before ending with the cute and hopeful extraterrestrials favored by Steven Spielberg.

"This exhibit illustrates the evolution of society's perceptions of aliens," Lindsay said.

"What do you mean?"

"You see, right before World War II, Americans were anxious about invasion and impending war. They easily swallowed Orson Wells' radio dramatization of *The War of the Worlds* as a real news broadcast. It caused widespread panic. People actually thought Martians had landed in New Jersey."

"Of all places."

"That wouldn't have happened in a less skittish time."

Cam studied the panels, which featured black and white stills of B movies from the 1950s and 1960s. He had seen many of them on the late show creature feature.

"The hostile aliens in these movies represented our fear of nuclear destruction," Lindsay explained. "While there were a few helpful aliens, such as Michael Rennie as Klaatu in *The Day the Earth Stood Still*, generally, contact with aliens led to trouble."

"So today's friendly aliens, like E.T., represent what?" Cam asked.

"They fill a spiritual void. People want to think we're not alone in this universe, that we're part of something bigger and grander than what we see. The extraterrestrials portrayed in the media now are usually intelligent and wise. They're explorers. They're saviors, protecting us from ourselves."

Watching Lindsay's every graceful motion, hanging on her every word, Cam felt as if he were an ice cube melting on a steamy summer sidewalk. Since meeting her Lake Tecumseh had gotten a lot more interesting—and a lot hotter.

The door chimed, and they both turned in unison toward the entrance. A handsome teen-ager in a sleeveless muscle shirt stepped inside. He smiled at Lindsay as he removed his sunglasses then strode to her and snatched her up in his tanned, muscular arms and planted a deep kiss on her lips. "Hey, baby," the blond interloper whispered.

Cam's softening heart froze from the blast of frigid air chilling the room due to the unexpected arrival of the stranger. His shoulders slumped forlornly. He should have realized a girl as smart and pretty as Lindsay would have a boyfriend. Not just any boyfriend, but a square-jawed, broad-shouldered guy who looked like the school's star quarterback.

Lindsay pulled away from the guy's grip and introduced him to Cam as Brian Little.

Brian shook Cam's hand. His grip was like iron. "You checking out the museum, buddy?" Brian asked.

Cam nodded weakly. The museum was not all he was checking out before Brian's arrival. Lindsay had really been his focus, but that had suddenly and unhappily changed. He forced a smile while he frowned inside. Then he recognized Brian as the driver of the sports car that had sped by him. "Red Mustang convertible, right?"

Brian glanced toward the door. "Am I being towed or something?"

"No, I saw you on the road. I would love to have a cool car like that."

Brian smiled, flashing deep dimples. "It's fast, dude."

"Obey the speed limit," Lindsay reminded.

"Yeah, yeah," Brian mumbled.

With Brian's arrival, Cam was not eager to stick around. The package in his hand reminded him of his errand to the hardware store. Uncle Gary was probably wondering what had delayed him so long. Thankful for an escape route from the awkward threesome, Cam said, "I gotta get back to my uncle, or he'll be pissed."

"Come back and see the rest of our collection," Lindsay said, pointing to the display cases. "We have reproductions of alien artifacts from throughout the world."

"Okay," Cam said as he rushed to the exit. He waved a quick

good-bye to Brian and then took one last look at the beautiful girl who had taught him more about aliens and UFOs than he was ever interested in knowing. "Nice meeting you, Lindsay," he said as he pushed through the door.

"Nice meeting you, too!" she called after him.

Outside the museum, the people and cars of Lake Tecumseh moved in their usual languid pace. However, Cam's mind was reeling and his heart was racing. He took a deep breath to calm himself as he walked to his bike, his sneakers seeming to float over the concrete. He had never met a girl as exciting as Lindsay. She was incredible. He had to have her for his own, whatever it took. He certainly wasn't going to let someone like Brian Little stand in his way.

*   *   *

Following his meeting with Lindsay Brock, Cam couldn't get the young beauty out of his mind. In the silence of the night, lying on his bed, she drifted through his thoughts like the cool breezes from the ceiling fan caressing his body. He heard the playful cadence of her speech; felt the soft touch of her skin, and tasted the sweetness of her lips.

And finally, when at last he departed the waking world, she joined him in his dreams.

But she was not the only one in his dreams. Something else lurked on the periphery, something sinister. A fleeting shadow just out of view. A dark presence waiting to reveal itself.

Sometimes, during the day, Cam experienced the same sensation and it unnerved him. At night, when his mind drifted off to sleep, the darkness was blacker, stronger, and it gave him nightmares.

In his dreams, he saw images of strange landscapes. Standing awestruck on a high promontory, slightly chilled from the night, he gazed over razor-sharp mountains of black stone. The craggy landscape extended as far as he could see. The peaks pressed against each other as if someone had taken both ends of the earth and smashed them together to save room.

Behind the tooth line of the mountains, the sun was rising. Golden rays shot skyward as the yellow orb appeared, casting neighboring clouds aglow. Using his hand as a visor, Cam shielded his eyes from the brightness of the yellow disk as it rose heavenward.

Then, something larger and unexpected emerged a few seconds later.

A *second* sun.

Cobalt blue and nearly twice as wide as its yellow brother.

The yellow and blue suns ascended into the sky like dual gods while he watched. In the combined glare, the landscape around him looked pallid and overexposed.

Cam's initial feeling of confusion at the exotic sight dissipated as the suns' beams warmed his face. He felt as if he had returned to a home faraway, but that didn't make sense. This wasn't his home. His home wasn't lit by two suns.

Whose home was it?

He looked around on the mountaintop. He was all alone yet he sensed someone, or something, was there with him. An unseen presence lurked just out of view, in the corner of his eye. He glanced toward where he thought it emanated, but nothing was there.

He shuddered, feeling afraid.

Cam awoke in a cold sweat in darkness, the sheets crumpled at the bottom of the bed. He was in his room on the second floor of the lake house. The ceiling fan rotated slowly above in the moonlight. He sat up, feeling as if he had just returned from a long journey. He rubbed his eyes in confusion and glanced at the clock: 3:45 AM.

What had he seen?

Where had he been?

Normally, a nightmare wouldn't have bothered him. He'd wake up, steel himself, and then promptly forget whatever had bedeviled him.

Not anymore. Now nightmares bothered him, because he had *the same one* every night since his arrival in Lake Tecumseh. The quirky town was immersed in fanciful stories of aliens and UFOs. And now the stories had invaded his dreams. He was having visions of alien planets.

What was this place doing to him?

CHAPTER THREE

The loud rap on the door yanked Cam awake. His eyes popped open. The bedroom was awash with morning light.

Outside, Aunt Ellen was knocking on the door. "You're going to miss breakfast!" she called, her tone a combination of motherly care and annoyance at his sleeping habits.

Cam was groggy, having suffered through another restless evening. Recurring dreams of an otherworldly landscape with double suns, one blue and one yellow, haunted him nightly while an evil portent lurked near, watching him but hidden from view.

"Eggs and bacon!" Aunt Ellen said through the door.

"I'll be right there," he called back, his voice little more than a forced croak. He rose from bed and stretched.

"Hurry up! It's nine o'clock."

Nine o'clock wasn't very late to him, but Uncle Gary and Aunt Ellen were early risers. They were usually awake at sunrise, which at this time of year was long before six o'clock. They would finish a pot of coffee between them and snack on cereal and pastries before it was time for *real* breakfast.

Cam rubbed his eyes and looked out the French doors at the lake as it came to life for the day. A pontoon boat was gliding past and a fisherman was heading toward his special spot. Speed boats and jet-skis would soon be slicing the azure waters. The lake would not be quiet for long.

He stared for a long moment, collecting his confused thoughts. He felt almost disembodied, as if he were still asleep. Finally, the life slowly coming back to him, he shuffled toward the bathroom.

He washed his face and looked at himself in the mirror. He was an average-looking guy, at least when he was cleaned up. This morning whiskers poked from his chin, and his brown hair stuck out where it shouldn't and was smashed down elsewhere. He tried to brush his bed hair into some semblance of order, but it didn't work.

To hell with it, he thought, which is what he thought almost every morning. He didn't mind looking like a rock star or an artist. A *Bohemian* he thought it was called. He smelled the bacon frying, and his stomach rumbled. He'd get cleaned up later.

While he pulled on a T-shirt and a pair of cargo shorts, the strange dreams still swished in his mind. He felt numb, as if he had awakened with a hangover.

When Cam stepped barefoot into the kitchen, his uncle acknowledged him from behind the newspaper. Standing before the stove, Aunt Ellen greeted him as she used tongs to place the crisp bacon onto paper towels. She reminded him to shave.

Cam rubbed his chin and sat down. His aunt always insisted that he shave, even if he were only working around the house. What was the point? He reached for the pitcher of orange juice and poured himself a glass and drank.

Aunt Ellen moved dishes from the counter to the table like a conveyor belt. "Scrambled eggs all right, honey?"

"Yeah, they're fine," Cam answered, always enjoying her cooking.

Uncle Gary folded the newspaper. "We're going to put a coat of stain on the pier today, so you'd better fuel up."

Cam sighed. He wanted to see Lindsay again at the UFO Museum but knew chores came first. Uncle Gary kept him busy weeding the garden, cutting the grass, and performing other tasks. And now staining the pier was added to the job list.

After breakfast, when they were all energized by caffeine and sugar, Uncle Gary said, "The UFO Festival is a week earlier than normal. I wonder why they changed it."

"That's strange," Aunt Ellen said, nonchalantly snatching the last piece of bacon from the platter on the center of the table.

"Speaking of strange," Cam said, "I've been having the weirdest dreams."

His relatives looked at one another, probably due to the abrupt change in topic. Aunt Ellen said, "What do you mean, dear?"

Cam shrugged. "Nightmares. I haven't been sleeping well."

"Maybe it's the mattress," Uncle Gary said.

"Or just being away from home," Aunt Ellen added.

"I dunno what it is," Cam said. "I have the same dream every night. It's like I'm on another planet, and there's something hiding that's trying to get me."

Aunt Ellen shivered. "Sounds creepy."

"Were you naked?" Uncle Gary asked.

Taken aback, Cam let his lips part. "No, I wasn't. I don't think."

"I hate the ones where you're naked in public," his uncle confessed.

His aunt started collecting the dirty dishes into a pile. "I hate those dreams where you show up at school, and there's a big exam, and you didn't study all year, and—"

"And you're naked," Uncle Gary added with a smirk.

She snapped her napkin toward him and clucked, "One-track mind!"

"What do you think my dream means?" Cam asked.

"Nothing!" Uncle Gary said with certainty. "All dreams are weird. They're just random firings of brain cells."

"Oh, there's certainly more to them than that," Aunt Ellen said, wrinkling her face in disapproval. "Oprah did a whole show on dreams. She had all these scientific experts as guests. Did you know common dreams have a hidden meaning? Some of the audience members kept dream diaries, and experts interpreted their dreams."

"What's a dream diary?" Cam asked.

"A notebook where you record your dreams as soon as you wake up. "That's the only time you can remember most of them, when they're fresh."

"Or they get moldy like bad cream cheese," Uncle Gary said.

Aunt Ellen stood up and hauled the dishes to the sink. "You know what I mean. Nobody remembers their dreams. They vanish into thin air. You have to write them down so they can be interpreted later."

Cam stared at the refrigerator. Although his recent dreams stuck in his head like an unpleasant odor in a kitchen, a dream diary sounded like a good idea. Maybe if he recorded them, he'd be able to make some sense out of them. It was worth a try. Perhaps the fear would go away, and he'd be able to sleep better.

After a hard day of work, the pier glistening with new redwood stain, Cam quickly showered and put on fresh clothes. He rode toward town eager to see Lindsay at the UFO Museum. He hoped he didn't miss her, since it was near closing time. The afternoon was steamy, and Cam was sweaty by the time he got to the center of town. He wished he had a car. It wasn't easy to impress a girl with only a bike, especially when Brian Little, the competition, drove around in a convertible.

Cam dismounted the bike and leaned it against a planter full of purple petunias. He surveyed the vehicles parked in the diagonal spaces but didn't see Brian's red Mustang. Relieved, he eagerly marched by the green alien and entered the museum.

Lindsay stood with two patrons inspecting the contents of a glass display case. She glanced toward the opening door and perfunctorily announced the museum was closing shortly. When she spied Cam instead of a last-minute visitor, she smiled warmly. Her gaze lingered on him a few moments longer than necessary.

Cam smiled back, sensing an attraction from her.

The visiting couple focused on the exhibit. The man was tall and distinguished looking, sporting a pair of wire-rimmed glasses. His wife was elegant in a prim and formal sort of way, and she clutched her pocketbook tightly as if muggings were a common occurrence in this part of the country. The glass case held what appeared to be a crash-test dummy.

The man tapped his finger on the glass and challenged Lindsay: "O'Grady thoroughly investigated the Air Force experiments on anthropomorphic dummies in his book, which is considered the authoritative reference on Roswell. He debunked this theory."

"A government misinformation campaign," the man's wife added. "They offered these dummies to explain the alien bodies eyewitnesses said were recovered from the crash site."

"We visited Roswell last year," the man continued. "Something weird definitely happened there in 1947, and it wasn't a bunch of dummies dropped from airplanes."

His wife nodded. "The truth will come out one day, once the public is conditioned not to panic that we're being routinely visited by aliens."

"National security," the all-knowing man said, nodding in unison with his wife.

Lindsay smiled demurely and gently steered the two tourists toward the door with the soft touch of someone used to dealing with the public at closing time. "There are multiple interpretations for what happened at Roswell. That makes the story so interesting."

Cam noted how Lindsay had tactfully refused to disagree with the two visitors. What her true beliefs were, he didn't have a clue.

"Thanks, dear, for the tour," the woman said, touching Lindsay on the forearm.

"You should read O'Grady's book," the man suggested, adjusting his wire-rimmed glasses. "Incorporate some of his research into your museum."

"That's a great idea," Lindsay said with what looked to be a forced smile.

After the couple departed, Lindsay turned to Cam and sighed. "Those two challenged everything! They didn't really listen to anything I said. They take all this stuff so seriously."

"Who wouldn't?" Cam said.

She furrowed her brow. "Are you poking fun at me?"

"No, not at all," Cam backpedaled quickly. He tried to disarm her with a smile. "In fact, I wanted to see more of the museum."

"It's closing time," Lindsay said as she flipped the sign on the exit door to *Closed*.

Cam glanced at his watch, feigning disappointment. He didn't really want to see more of the *museum*; he wanted to see more of *her*. "I was busy helping my uncle. I didn't know it was so late."

"I can stick around for a few minutes," she said with a shrug. "Did you want to see anything in particular?"

His mind sputtered trying to formulate an answer demonstrating a passion in flying saucers. Glancing down at the mannequin in the glass case, he blurted, "What's this dummy got to do with UFOs?"

She seemed pleased at his interest. "It's an anthropomorphic dummy used by the Air Force in the 1940s."

The nonsense syllables were like glue on his tongue. "*Anthro-what?*"

"Anthropomorphic," she repeated effortlessly. "*Human like.* The Air Force dropped them from high altitude to test parachutes and pilot ejection systems. People in Roswell, New Mexico may have mistaken these dummies for alien bodies."

The only body Cam was interested in was hers, and it wasn't alien. It had delightful, sensuous curves, and he longed to touch it. She was so close to him, all he had to do was reach out . . . .

She caught him staring and said, "You're not here to learn about UFOs, are you?"

Her directness caught him off guard. He gazed into her brown eyes, briefly losing track of time in their auburn swirls. He shook his senses back together and summoned his courage. "You wanna get a pop or something?" he asked, his voice cracking awkwardly.

She brushed back her hair with one hand and smiled. "I'm meeting Brian."

Cam's heart suddenly felt encased in plaster. The *brush-off.* "Oh, okay," he choked out, disappointed.

"He's my boyfriend," she added, somewhat apologetically.

Cam nodded; his eyes downcast to the tile floor.

"Do you have e-mail?" she asked as she walked to the counter. As he nodded, she scribbled on a piece of paper and handed it to him. "Here's my e-mail address."

Cam's spirits brightened. He watched her as a coy smile touched her lips. She *was* interested in him. He glanced at the screen name on the paper. *"UFOgal?"*

"Silly, huh?" She glanced at the clock. "I have to go." She turned off the lights, secured the cash register, and led Cam outside. Locking the door behind them, she thanked him for stopping by and then turned and stepped away.

Cam stood next to the alien statue and watched her walk down the sidewalk. As she turned the corner, she glanced back furtively and smiled at him before disappearing from view.

A bolt of electricity shot through his body as sure as if he had been struck by one of Orville Milford's balls of lightning. Cam couldn't wait to e-mail the beautiful girl. What would he say to her? What would she say back? He rehearsed the impending on-line conversation during the entire bike ride home.

* * *

That evening, sitting before the flickering screen of the computer, Cam didn't know what to write to Lindsay. He didn't want to be too aggressive, or not aggressive enough. He certainly didn't want to sound stupid. He carefully checked his spelling and grammar. Lindsay was a smart girl and would notice any sloppy mistakes. He composed his first e-mail to her with all the thought and precision as if he were writing a term paper on which his entire course grade would be based:

Hi Lindsay,

It was nice meeting you today. I would love to get together with you sometime when you're free so we can get to know each other better.

Cam

It wasn't very long, but composing it had taken a lot out of him.

After nervously hitting the *send* key, he waited patiently, hoping she were sitting at her computer at that very moment and would reply immediately.

To his surprise, Lindsay was on-line, too. His hopes had been realized. She sent him an instant message, and the two of them started to cyber-chat, she as *UFOgal*, and he as *ExileIN17*.

UFOgal: nice meeting u 2!
ExileIN17: what r u doing?
UFOgal: writing my book
ExileIN17: your book about UFOs?
UFOgal: yes, I'm working on chapter 8

Cam thought writing a book was impressive. He had struggled in English class and found the idea of writing for pleasure impossible to believe. Why would anyone want to spend all that time and effort to write a book?

On-line Lindsay explained she was researching the local UFO stories individually to gather material for her book.

UFOgal: u should come tomorrow and help me on my
          interviews. It'll be fun!
ExileIN17:r u sure? What about Brian?
UFOgal: he's not interested + busy with football practice

Cam grinned as he read the glowing text on the monitor. Lindsay's boyfriend wasn't interested in her hobby and was busy with football. Cam had an unexpected opening and was determined to take it. He wasn't interested in her UFO research either, but if it meant spending the day with her, he was willing to make the sacrifice for science.

*   *   *

Lindsay Brock lived with her mother in an old gabled house near the center of town. A giant elm tree, at least four feet wide, stood majestically in front. Its roots had heaved up the sidewalk like a ruptured ice flow. Cam jumped over the uneven surface and strode onto the porch. Plastic film stretched across the windows, leftover weatherproofing from cold winter winds. He eagerly knocked on the door.

Mrs. Brock answered, looking like an older version of Lindsay. Slightly taller, she was dressed in green medical scrubs. The name tag on her pocket read: *Amy Brock, R.N.*

"Is Lindsay home?" Cam asked.

"Oh, sure, come in," Mrs. Brock said, waving him inside.

The house was small but tidy. A threadbare couch was camouflaged by a well-placed throw. Lindsay emerged from the avocado-green kitchen and greeted him excitedly. She then introduced him to her mother, who was a nurse at the County Hospital.

"I'm late for work," Mrs. Brock said, darting around the living room, collecting her car keys and wallet. "Can you check on your grandfather today?"

"Certainly, Mom," Lindsay answered.

Mrs. Brock kissed her daughter on the cheek and whisked out the back door.

Lindsay sighed. "My mom's always been time challenged."

"My mom's the same way," Cam said. "Maybe it happens when you get older."

She grabbed her backpack off the recliner. "Ready to investigate the mysterious happenings in Lake Tecumseh?"

"Sure! What do you want me to do?"

She lowered her voice. "Watch my back."

His mouth gaped. "Huh?"

She chuckled. "I'm *kidding*! Let's go. We've got a lot to cover today. My goal's to complete the first draft of my book by September."

They headed toward the mobile home park, where a woman lived who claimed to have been abducted by aliens. It was a beautiful June day, with a clear blue sky and a warm sun and just enough of a cool northerly breeze to make it perfect for being outdoors.

"I don't get a lot of free time to write," Lindsay admitted as they strolled under the shade cast by the parkway trees. "The museum's only closed on Sundays and Mondays."

"Summer jobs can be a pain," Cam added, although he had never had one himself. Last year he was in summer school to keep from falling farther behind in class.

"It's the family business," Lindsay said. "My father started the museum a few years ago to cash in on the town's UFO craze."

"Has it worked?"

She shook her head. "It hardly pays the rent and electricity on the space. I guess it was just another one of his hare-brained business schemes. He was always looking for *The Next Big Thing*."

Noting her use of past tense, Cam hesitated before asking "What happened to him?"

"My parents split," she said, obviously concealing sadness. "Dad moved to Indianapolis last year."

"Sorry to hear about your parents."

"Who doesn't come from a broken home these days? My dad still owns the museum, but isn't interested in it any more. Mom's too busy at the hospital. So I keep the place going. I don't know why. Maybe because it fascinates me."

"You're doing a good job."

She stopped and picked up a piece of litter and dropped it into a trash can. "Are your parents in Chicago?"

"My mom is. My dad's dead."

She cringed at his harsh response and looked at him with empathy. "Oh, that's awful!"

"Yeah, I guess," he answered flatly, which blanketed them both in silence for some time.

The Lake Tecumseh Mobile Home Park was in a wooded area outside of town. Although the owner had planted red geraniums at the entranceway, the community appeared rather dilapidated. Stalks of grass sprouted amid the crushed gravel of the streets, and many of the mobile homes showed signs of neglect.

They approached a home that shined harshly like coffee-stained teeth in the bright sun. A calico cat lazed on the porch as they climbed the steps. "Mrs. Portman is expecting us," Lindsay whispered as she rang the doorbell.

Sylvia Portman answered the door wearing a red Indiana Hoosiers sweatshirt and a drooping cigarette in her hand. A cloud of smoke swirled around her. She looked as disheveled as the trailer park in which she lived, as if she had just been awakened from a mid-day nap. She blinked against the daylight and looked Cam over carefully.

"Ya never told me you were bringing your boyfriend," she said to Lindsay.

"This isn't Brian," Lindsay explained. "This is Cam. He's helping me out today."

Sucking a drag off her cigarette, Mrs. Portman motioned them inside. "Hurry up, I got the A/C on. Ya think I'm made of money?"

The blinds were drawn, leaving the living room in a dark gloom. A black cat brushed against Cam's leg and then hopped on the coffee table, which was plastered with copies of gossip magazines like *US* and *People* and tabloids like *National Enquirer* and *American Investigator*. Mrs. Portman directed them to sit as she stubbed out her cigarette in an overflowing ashtray. She immediately tapped out a fresh *Camel* and lit it.

Lindsay slid off her backpack and pulled out a pen, notepad, and small tape recorder. "Thanks for speaking with us today, Mrs. Portman. Can you tell us about your UFO experience?"

"It was *more* than an *experience*, young lady. It was an *abduction*."

"Of course," Lindsay said. "Please start at the beginning, in your own words."

Sylvia Portman began to recite her story, resembling a chimney as she spoke with her gravelly, nicotine-scarred voice. She chain-smoked and used her cigarettes as props, blowing smoke into the room for dramatic pauses, waving them like a maestro's baton when her story required action, and pressing them out in the ashtray to punctuate an important point.

Cam watched the woman's performance with interest but thought her story sounded robotic and rehearsed. She described her alien abduction in minute detail, including the dress she was wearing, who she was dating at the time, even the song that was playing on the radio. She had time-traveled back twenty years and no longer paid any attention to her two interviewers.

After a while, Cam's attention drifted to Lindsay, who sat across from Mrs. Portman scribbling notes on a yellow pad as the tape recorder on the cigarette-stained coffee table recorded the conversation. Since the interview struck Cam as absurd, he smiled at Lindsay, who smiled back.

Sitting on the couch like a queen on a throne, Mrs. Portman noticed their reaction. "What's so funny about being kidnapped by aliens?" she demanded angrily, stabbing her cigarette toward them.

Lindsay cleared her throat nervously. "Nothing! Please continue, Mrs. Portman. What about the spaceship? What did it look like?"

Cam leaned back into his chair and stretched his long legs. If Mrs. Portman continued at this pace, it would take another hour to hear the entire story.

Having their attention once again, Mrs. Portman looked pleased. She sucked on her dying cigarette, blowing out the smoke between her rounded, red lips. Her house was small; the polluted haze hung in the living room.

"I don't remember what their ship looked like on the outside. I must've been drugged," Mrs. Portman said. "When I awoke, I was inside on an examination table. I couldn't move at all. I was completely paralyzed!"

"And then what happened?" Lindsay asked.

Cam realized Lindsay was tactfully trying to speed up the plodding story.

"They were all around me," Mrs. Portman said. "I was naked."

Just as in a dream, Cam thought, figuring that's what Uncle Gary would have said.

"They were curious, and they touched me with their clammy fingers," Mrs. Portman continued. "I wasn't scared. I knew they wouldn't hurt me."

"What did they do to you?" Lindsay asked.

Mrs. Portman reached for her pack of *Camels*, pulled out another coffin nail, and struck her lighter. After inhaling deeply, she shifted on the couch and threw her head back. "They gave a *complete* medical examination, if you know what I mean."

"I understand," Lindsay said, nodding.

Mrs. Portman drew up her legs onto the couch and cradled them. "Remember, I was paralyzed and totally helpless. I couldn't fight them. They had their alien way with me."

"What did the aliens look like?" Lindsay asked.

Mrs. Portman stopped and blinked, appearing disturbed. She rested her cigarette on the ashtray and took a deep breath. "Hideous. Absolutely hideous. Pale, like corpses. No body hair and no clothing. Black eyes bulging from big heads."

"How gruesome," Lindsay said.

"The next thing I knew, I was back in my car, dressed, and parked by the side the road. The engine was still running, and the radio was still playing the same Madonna song."

Lindsay rested her yellow pad on her lap. "Was there any physical evidence of your encounter with the aliens, Mrs. Portman?"

"Physical evidence?" Mrs. Portman laughed, throwing her head back. "Of course there was physical evidence! I was pregnant!"

Lindsay remained calm and professional. "By the aliens?"

"Yes, the little bastards. I was sick as a dog for weeks, but then I miscarried. The doctor said the fetus was abnormal. He said it could never have properly developed, it was so . . . so . . . *deformed.*"

"How awful, Mrs. Portman," Lindsay said.

"Thank God it's over. I'll never forget it."

Lindsay rose from her chair and snapped off the tape recorder and gathered her belongings. "Thank you for your time, Mrs. Portman."

Cam stood up, eager to flee the smoke-choked house. He was thankful when he and Lindsay emerged into the bright daylight. He waited until they were out of the trailer park before he turned to her and asked, "Do you believe her story?"

Lindsay shook her head. "She's just an attention seeker."

"How do you know?"

"She was interviewed years ago, not long after her supposed encounter. I found it in the newspaper archive. Her story has changed dramatically over the years. For example, she never mentioned having an *alien baby* before."

"That part was creepy," Cam admitted. "Like something out of a bad movie."

"She's a good story teller. It'll make a nice chapter in my book. When the environment is seeded with the idea of UFOs and aliens, some people get delusional. They actually believe these events happened to them."

"Do you believe *your* grandfather saw a UFO?" Cam asked.

She looked at him sharply as if he had crossed a line. "He saw *something*. I don't know if it was an alien spaceship, but it crashed into the lake."

"I didn't mean to offend you."

She brushed it away. "Don't worry. That reminds me I'm supposed to check up on grandpa. Can we make a quick detour? He lives on the lake, not far from here."

"No problem," Cam said.

They walked to Orville Milford's cottage. Unlike most of the well-maintained homes on Lake Tecumseh, this one was showing its age, more precisely, the age of its owner. The house badly needed to be painted, and green spots on the roof indicated rotting shingles. The landscape shrubs were overgrown, nearly blocking the windows, and raspberry bushes and small trees were growing happily amid the knee-high grass.

They dismounted their bikes and looked around. "Grandpa likes it wild looking," Lindsay explained, sounding embarrassed by the appearance of the property.

They walked down the gravel driveway toward the house, passing the tow truck with the sign that read, *Milford's UFO Towing Service – You Crash, We Dash.*

Cam spied an outbuilding with a rusty weather vane of a trotting horse on its sagging, peaked roof. "What's in there?"

"Grandpa's workshop."

Cam followed Lindsay to the backdoor of the house, his hands stuffed into his front pockets. He didn't care to chat with Orville Milford. The old man was a cranky oddball who went out every evening to float on the lake and pray to his alien gods.

Lindsay knocked hard and called, "Grandpa! Open up! It's me, Lindsay!"

Cam waited for the door to open, but nothing happened. He looked at Lindsay and shrugged.

"He's a little hard of hearing." She knocked again, this time more forcefully. "Grandpa! Are you home? Come to the door!"

"Maybe he's fishing," Cam suggested.

"That's a possibility," she admitted. They followed a well-trod path through the bushes to the front of the house. A wooden pier jutted several yards into the lake, its boards rotting. A fishing boat was tied to the dock, bobbing in the wake of passing speedboats.

"I'm a little worried," Lindsay said, turning her back on the empty boat. They returned to the house, and she knocked again. When there was still no answer, she reached above the door and retrieved a hidden key. "Country people aren't too concerned about security."

"I can tell."

She unlocked the door and pushed it open. They stepped into a crowded mudroom. Fishing poles, oars, and large, rubber wading boots jammed the small space. The house smelled musty, as if the windows had been sealed for ages.

Lindsay called for her grandfather as they entered the dark kitchen. She opened the drapes to let in some light. Dirty dishes were piled in the sink, and papers and magazines were scattered across the kitchen table. "Maybe he's napping," she said, heading toward the bedrooms.

Cam went into the living room, which fronted the lake. Wooden shutters closed off the view. He opened them, stirring up a dust cloud in the sunbeams.

The house was frozen in time: the furniture, pictures, and the books on the shelves were old and outdated. The Zenith television had a twisting dial registering channels 2 through 13 only.

From behind Cam, a stern voice suddenly boomed: "Who the hell are you?"

Cam started and spun around to face a scowling Orville Milford. The wrinkled old man was dressed in a red flannel shirt that was too warm for summer. He wore an odd metal helmet, as if he were preparing to go on a motorcycle ride.

Before Cam could answer, Lindsay rushed from the hallway and hugged her grandfather. "Where were you?" she asked.

Pointing at Cam, Orville said, "Is this your new boyfriend, Lindsay? He's a little scrawny compared to the other one."

Lindsay pulled away from her grandfather and gasped in horror. "Grandpa!"

Although Orville had jumped to conclusions, Cam still liked being called Lindsay's boyfriend. Maybe he would be one day soon, if he played his cards right. Then Cam did a mental double take and caught himself. Orville had called him *scrawny*. He didn't think of himself as scrawny, but maybe he was when compared to Brian, a football player.

"Sometimes Grandpa says the most inappropriate things!" Lindsay said, her face red. She introduced the old man to Cam, adding that Cam was visiting from Chicago.

"Chicago?" Orville narrowed his eyes and examined him suspiciously. "Where the first nuclear chain reaction was initiated? Fermi could've blown the whole Midwest off the map. The idiot didn't know the power of what he was messing with."

Cam smirked, not knowing the story of Fermi or what to think of the eccentric old man.

Lindsay pointed to her grandfather's metal helmet, which had several Frankenstein-looking electrodes protruding from its surface. He looked like Snoopy ready to face the Red Baron. "What's the helmet for, Grandpa?"

Touching his head, Orville's eyes brightened. "Oh, I forgot I had this on. I was fine tuning my design." He removed the helmet and smoothed back his thin hair, which fell in wisps over his bald pate. He dug into the helmet and retrieved a smashed NASCAR cap and placed it on his head before passing the helmet to Lindsay.

She examined it carefully and then handed it to Cam. Orville immediately snatched it back. "How do I know you're not a government spy?" Orville demanded, shielding the helmet in the crook of his arm like a quarterback holding a football.

"I'm no government spy," Cam said.

"I can vouch for him," Lindsay said.

"They're watching me, I'm sure of it," Orville related in a serious whisper. His eyes darted toward the kitchen windows and the driveway outside.

"I came by to see how you were," Lindsay said. "As paranoid as ever I see."

"I was working on my signal amplification device." Orville gave a slight shake to the helmet and placed it on a side table.

"What signals?" Cam asked.

Orville seemed exasperated. "Signals from the aliens of course!"

Lindsay stepped to Cam and touched his forearm. "Grandpa thinks the aliens are trying to communicate with him."

"They *are* trying to communicate with me," Orville insisted. He looked at Cam. "Twenty years ago I was out fishing on the lake—"

Oh, brother, Cam thought. *Now I'm going to hear his kooky story firsthand.*

"It was a quiet night, except for the rock music coming from *Anderson's*—"

"That place closed years ago," Lindsay interjected.

"I was minding my own business," Orville continued, "when I heard this whistling noise in the sky. I looked up and this ball of light was coming toward me. It looked like a meteor, but was traveling too slow, like it was being piloted."

"Piloted? Like a spaceship?" Cam asked.

Orville nodded. "It came down fast, almost hitting me, and . . . boom!" He clapped his hands together loudly, startling Cam, although not Lindsay, who had apparently heard the story repeated so many times she knew what was coming. "It crashed into the lake not more than fifty yards away. Almost knocked me out of my boat. The water was bubbling and glowing strangely. The air was electrified. I watched the UFO sink to the bottom, and then it went dark."

"What was it?" Cam asked, trying to force some excitement into his question.

"An alien spaceship," Orville said matter-of-factly. "I'm sure of it. It's still down there, too."

"There's no spaceship in the lake," Lindsay said. "We've talked about this many times before, Grandpa. They searched the lake twenty years ago and found nothing."

"It's still there, because I can feel their presence," Orville said. He pointed to his temple. "Up here."

Cam almost snickered. Up there, all right. Up there where his brain cells were thinning as fast as his hair.

"The aliens are trying to communicate using ESP," Orville said. "For twenty years they've been trying, but no one listens, except me. I go out on my boat to listen to them. Their signal is so faint, but in the quiet of the evening, if I clear my mind and concentrate, I can hear them."

"What are they saying?" Cam asked.

"I can't decipher it, but they desperately want to be heard. That's why I'm working on my amplifier, to see if I can boost their signal."

Lindsay looked at her watch. "We should get going, Cam, if we want to get to the crop circles. Farmer Wesley thinks UFOs are landing in his wheat field."

Orville shook his head. "They're not landing on Wesley's farm. They're underwater right *there*." He pointed to the blue lake.

54

"We've got to go, Grandpa," Lindsay said, heading for the door.

Orville suddenly grabbed Cam's arm. "Also I hear the aliens in my dreams."

Cam froze. "In your dreams?"

"Yes. Watch out for them. They might visit your dreams, too."

Cam thought about the strange nightmares he had been having. They had begun upon his arrival at Lake Tecumseh. Was Crazy Old Orville right? Were aliens visiting him in his dreams? Cam recalled the visions of a strange, mountainous landscape and blue and yellow suns. He shuddered at the sinister presence lurking in his dreams like a shadow that refused to show itself. Apprehensive feelings bothered him, even in daytime. He had never been so skittish back home.

Cam glanced to the glistening water of the lake. Were aliens at the bottom trying to communicate with him, too?

Was he just as crazy as Orville Milford?

CHAPTER FOUR

In the evenings, Cam wasted a lot of time on the computer, which was his umbilical cord to the outside world and the life he had temporarily left behind. Lindsay was usually on-line a lot, doing research into UFOs and publicizing her family's museum. Cam added her screen name, *UFOgal*, to his *buddy list*. Every night when his computer chimed, signaling she had come on-line, his heart chimed in response. He would immediately stop chatting with his Chicago friends and turn his complete attention to Lindsay. Their friendship blossomed quickly on the Internet:

    UFOgal: hi cam. how r u?
    ExileIN17: ok. sup?
    UFOgal: nothing. slow day at the museum
    ExileIN17: I painted the garage today - boring
    UFOgal: what an exciting summer LOL
    ExileIN17: meeting u is exciting!

She did not reply immediately to that remark, and Cam began to grow concerned. He would not have been so forward to her face to face, but on the computer it was easier for him to express his feelings. But what if she did not feel the same way in return? He had been getting subtle, encouraging signals from her since they had met. The only obstacle that Cam could see was Brian. Strangely, Lindsay did not talk much about Brian in person or during their on-line discussions. Why did her boyfriend seem somewhat absent from her life?

Finally, after what seemed an eternity, Lindsay responded to his comment:

UFOgal: meeting u is exciting 2! ☺

Cam leaned back in his chair and smiled as gleefully as the emoticon accompanying her response.

They chatted longer on-line, mostly silly things of no consequence. Then, Lindsay started discussing her grandfather, Orville Milford. She was concerned he was acting stranger and more paranoid than normal:

UFOgal: he keeps talking about aliens and ESP
ExileIN17: did he finish his amplifier?
UFOgal: yeah, but it doesn't work
ExileIN17: what if aliens really r trying 2 talk 2 him?
UFOgal: that's stupid
ExileIN17: maybe u should research
UFOgal: ??
ExileIN17: u research all UFO stories, why not his? What about science? why does he get special treatment?

As Cam waited for a response, he scrolled backward and reread his earlier messages; wondering if had been too harsh with her. She loved her grandpa but hadn't investigated his UFO story as she had all the other UFO sightings in the county. She had doubted Mrs. Portman, the chain-smoking alien abductee, and she had quickly concluded that the crop circles on the Wesley Farm were fakes. Why hadn't she researched her grandpa's story of a UFO crash in Lake Tecumseh? According to Orville Milford, the UFO was still there. They needed to search the lake for physical evidence. Wouldn't that prove Orville's story? Was Lindsay simply afraid she might prove her grandpa to be crazy after all?

Finally, she responded:

UFOgal: ur right. I should research his story and see if it's
          true
ExileIN17: ok
UFOgal: can u help? I may be bias at times
ExileIN17: sure. anything to help science

They made plans to meet the next afternoon. Cam was excited about spending more time with Lindsay. If she wanted to play *Ms. UFO Reporter*, he would gladly go along. He didn't care whether they would prove or disprove Orville Milford's twenty-year-old UFO story. What he cared about was getting to know Lindsay Brock better. His stay in Lake Tecumseh seemed to be improving as each summer day went by.

*   *   *

As Cam swam under the water, a glimmer of light overhead signaled the way to the surface. He didn't have any trouble holding his breath; his lungs seemed to draw upon an inexhaustible source of oxygen. He was an ace swimmer, his muscles moving tirelessly, his mind clear and focused. He moved like a fish.

He swam toward the surface. When his head emerged into the air, he did a double-take. He was treading water in the center of a lake, but not one he was familiar with. The water was thick, like gravy, and the color of ink, even in the brilliant light.

The light of two suns.

The blue and yellow disks illuminated the placid lake, which was nestled amid a battlement of brooding mountains. The rocky boulders on the shoreline were covered by scraggly red vines. The plants looped and twisted around the rocks, and also grew skyward, resembling miniature, rope-like trees. The water—or the petroleum, whatever he was swimming in—lapped against the rocks, making a *slurp-slurp-slurp* noise.

He had visited this place before—in his dreams.

A crack of thunder awoke him with a start. He was lying in his bed, and the French doors were flapping in the gusty wind. He quickly sprung up and closed the doors as raindrops blew into the room like tiny cold missiles. Outside, the thunderstorm intensified. Flashes of lightning illuminated the swaying trees. The rain began to fall in heavy torrents, making the surface of the lake appear to boil.

Cam grabbed the pen and notebook from the nightstand. Sitting on the edge of the bed, he snapped on the light and leafed through the notebook to an empty page and began drawing.

He sketched a lake surrounded by mountains. He drew two disks to represent the blue and yellow suns. Around his crude sketch, he scribbled in the colors of the images, and then beneath the picture he quickly wrote his feelings of the dream and what he could remember about it.

The dream's colors were so brilliant; he also wrote a note to himself: *buy some crayons.*

He grasped at mental straws. Details of the strange dream were vanishing quickly.

The thunder rumbled through the lake cottage like a passing locomotive. The clock read three o'clock.

Cam flipped through his dream diary. Page after page was filled with sketches of the unusual landscapes that haunted his dreams. The drawings looked as if they had been conjured up by some drug-addled mind: towering, twisted mountains; double suns; and red vines choking the ground. Every dream brought something new.

This time it was the lake. But it wasn't a lake of water but of oil. Its surface had been thick and glistened in rainbow hues like the oily puddles in a parking lot after a rainstorm.

It was as if he were dreaming of an alien planet. All this recent talk of aliens and UFOs was obviously getting to him.

He was better at drawing his dreams than describing them in words. He barely scraped by with a C in English class. He was a much better artist.

Even so, his drawings included explanatory comments, some of them quite detailed and lengthy. He chewed on the end of his pen for a moment, and then shuffled the pages back a few entries. The odd dreams were occurring more frequently, sometimes several a night, and they were lasting longer and becoming more vivid and revealing. He never would've guessed his dream diary would be expanding so quickly.

He placed the journal on the night stand and turned off the lamp. Settling back onto the warm mattress, he sucked in a deep breath and listened to the thunderstorm beat against the house. Could the aliens be affecting his dreams, as Orville Milford had warned? Were they lurking out there in the depths of the lake, beaming their ESP signals into his subconscious, sending him mental pictures of their home planet? He had to know the answer, and perhaps Lindsay could help him find it.

*　　*　　*

At closing time, Cam met Lindsay at the museum. He watched her as she tallied the day's receipts. He loved the little habit she had of absentmindedly sticking out her tongue when she was intensely concentrating. Her brown hair fell across her face as she was looking down, and she flipped the unruly strands back with a brush of her delicate hand. Cam thought she was the most beautiful girl he had ever seen.

Frowning, Lindsay looked up. "Not too many visitors today."

Cam shrugged. "It's Wednesday."

"That's true. The weekends are busier." She closed the cash register and flicked off the lights. "Want to get a milkshake?"

"Sure!" Cam hoped he didn't sound too eager, but his excitement was hard to conceal.

At Dairy Queen they ordered milkshakes and settled into a booth by the windows looking toward Main Street. As they sat across from one another, trying to suck the thick chocolate through the red and white striped straws, they both shyly avoided eye contact. They had made plans to discuss UFO research, but something more than research seemed to hang in the air between them.

Lindsay straightened, a question suddenly popping into her mind. "Where do you think you'll go to college?"

Cam cringed. *College?* He didn't think he had a chance of going to college, given his grades. But he knew Lindsay thought it was something every seventeen-year old planned to do. "Haven't really thought about it," he answered nonchalantly, sucking on his shake.

"Well, you should. Investigate several before settling on one. Make sure you visit in person. It's a big decision."

"Where do you think you'll go?"

"Probably an in-state school, since we don't have a lot of money. I'm hoping for Purdue."

"That's a good school," Cam said. All he really knew was Purdue wasn't too far away, had a lot of engineers, and a good football team.

"I might start in pre-med. My mom's a nurse, so I've already learned a little about medicine."

Cam thought about his mother. She was a waitress. Maybe he could learn food service from her. A career as a burger flipper might be his only option if he didn't start working harder in school. Graduation was only one year away, but it could've been the next century for all he thought about it.

"Anyway," Lindsay said, signaling a change in the topic, for which

Cam was grateful, "it's going to be hard to be skeptical of my grandpa's story."

"That's understandable. He's your relative so you want to believe him."

"There must be a logical explanation for what he saw, but it's already been investigated. I don't know if there's anything to add."

Cam realized Lindsay already knew her grandfather's story couldn't be proven. She was just hesitant to switch on the bright light above the old skeleton in her family's closet. Some things were meant to remain a mystery, especially when someone could get hurt in the process.

He wanted to help, so he said, "If the UFO's still in the lake, why don't we try to find it? It would be the best way to prove his story."

"There's only one problem," she said glumly. "They searched the lake twenty years ago and found nothing. I read about it in the old newspapers. *County Fire and Rescue* thought perhaps a small plane had crashed. They searched the lake and came up empty handed."

"Maybe they missed it."

"It's a dead end. There's nothing in the lake."

Lindsay looked as if she were ready to cry. "Are you okay?" Cam asked her, reaching across the table of the booth to touch her hand, which was chilled from her milkshake.

"I'm fine," she said, smiling weakly and blinking back tears. "Grandpa's story is a family legend. Part of my childhood. When you find out there's no Santa Claus or Easter Bunny, it's not so much a shock as sadness at the loss of something magical from your life. My grandpa's UFO story is like that. I've doubted it for years, but it's still hard to reject completely. I *want* to believe in his UFO. I *want* to have magic in my life."

Cam continued to hold her hand, which warmed in his soft touch. "He *did* see something. There's still magic in that."

"Yes, but a meteor or ball lightning isn't as wonderful as visiting aliens. As a young girl, I believed aliens lived under the lake.

Grandpa would take me out on his boat, and we would listen for them together. He always said he could hear them. I couldn't hear them, but I went along with it anyway, because I wanted to believe they were there."

She took a deep breath. "After a while, I realized there were no aliens under the lake, they were just figments in my grandpa's mind. And then I was embarrassed by him and his crazy reputation, and I stopped going out on the lake with him. I'm ashamed how I acted. I probably broke his heart."

"I'm sure it wasn't that bad."

"It's only been recently where I've matured enough to accept him for what he is. He's getting up in years and won't be around forever. I want to make sure I spend time with him."

Cam nodded, not knowing what else to say or do.

Her melancholy reflection evaporated, and she abruptly pulled her hand away from his. She looked past him to the parking lot of the Dairy Queen where something grabbed her attention.

"What is it?" he asked as he pivoted his neck to follow her gaze. Outside, a red Mustang, its loud exhaust sounding like a motorcycle's engine, pulled diagonally across several parking spaces, taking up more than its share of the parking lot. The vehicle stopped and the large, blond driver emerged wearing a Number Five football jersey for the Lake Tecumseh Warriors.

It was Brian Little.

Cam frowned. He hadn't expected Lindsay's boyfriend to show up.

Number Five was accompanied by one of his football buddies, Number Fourteen. The two of them strutted toward the front door like a pair of muscular bookends, walking as if they marched on a red carpet under Hollywood lights.

"I didn't know Brian was coming here," Lindsay said flatly.

"Is it a problem?" Cam asked.

She appeared to chew on her words uncomfortably, as if she had a piece of gristle in her mouth that she wanted to spit out. "I guess I'd rather not deal with him right now."

"Isn't he your boyfriend?"

"Yes, but it's past its prime."

Past its prime. Cam chewed on that remark while Lindsay clammed up. The footballers had entered the restaurant and made a quick visual sweep of the dining room. Brian ignored the elderly couple in the back and looked directly at their table. Brian's mouth gaped in surprise upon seeing another guy with his girlfriend. He pulled off his sunglasses for a double take.

Lindsay smiled and lazily waved Brian over.

Brian marched to their booth, Number Fourteen following closely behind like a shadow.

"What's going on Linz?" Brian asked in a wounded tone.

"Nothing, Brian," Lindsay answered. "You remember Cam, don't you?"

Brian didn't even look in Cam's direction. "Yeah, yeah, I remember. What are you two doing?"

"Having a shake," Lindsay said. "You and Patrick want to join us?"

Brian finally looked at Cam, giving him a dismissive once over. Cam pleasantly nodded in greeting, but Brian's gaze was threatening instead of welcoming.

"Sure," Brian spat. "We'll join you." It was clear he was unhappy to find Lindsay spending time with someone else.

Brian and Patrick quickly got their own shakes and slid into the booth. Brian squeezed next to Lindsay and gave her a kiss on the cheek. Patrick sat next to Cam and introduced himself. His muscles were so overdeveloped, he seemed to block Cam's escape route from the booth like a heavy brick wall.

"How was football practice?" Lindsay asked.

"Brutal," Brian said. "Coach Barnes is a slave driver."

"I don't know why we have to start practice so early," Patrick said.

"Most teams get some time off."

"*Most* teams are *losers*," Brian said. "Warriors don't slack off in summer." He looked at Cam and smiled disarmingly. "Do you play ball in Chicago, sport?"

Cam grimaced. He didn't like being called *Sport*. "No, I don't."

"I didn't think so," Brian said with a condescending smirk. "A skinny guy like you'd get hurt pretty fast I'd think."

Cam felt his face grow red and his heart rate quicken. Brian Little was being a jerk, and he didn't like it. If Brian continued the needling, there might be a fight. Cam glanced at Patrick sitting next to him, his biceps bulging beneath his black and gold jersey. Cam was outnumbered and out muscled, that was clear. It would be a one-sided contest, and Cam's side was sure to lose.

Lindsay must have detected Cam's rising anger for she changed the subject. "We were talking about my grandpa's UFO sighting."

"You mean Crazy Old Orville?" Brian said.

"Please, don't call him that," Lindsay said.

"Sorry. I forget he's your grandpa. He's a town celebrity to me."

"I've investigated all the other UFO sightings in the county, and maybe it's time to put my grandpa's experience under my reporter's microscope as well."

"Come on, Lindsay," Brian said, "haven't I told you all this UFO nonsense is a waste of time?"

Lindsay looked pained by the remark. "You know I'm writing a book about this! It's important to me and the museum! Why can't you be more supportive?"

Brian cast his eyes downward. "Linz, you've got to keep perspective. What are the odds your book can actually get published? A thousand to one? A million to one?"

She set her shoulders defiantly. "The odds are *zero* if I don't even try. I've been making a lot of progress on my book. Cam's been helping me with my research."

Brian shot an icy stare toward Cam. "He has?"

"Yes," Lindsay said firmly. "He even has good ideas, like suggesting we look in the lake for my grandpa's UFO."

"Too bad it was already searched 20 years ago," Cam said. He was trying to think up some more ideas, because he liked Lindsay's praise, but nothing came to him immediately.

Brian appeared to steam. He sucked hard on his straw, as if the cold milkshake would cool his jealously. After a minute, he said, "You have the story all wrong."

"What do you mean?" Lindsay asked.

Brian smirked, relishing her attention on him. "Nobody ever searched the lake."

"Of course they did," Lindsay said. "*Fire and Rescue* did a thorough search 20 years ago. It's in the old newspapers."

Brian grinned and leaned back against the padded seat. "Have you forgotten my dad's the sheriff? He was a deputy back then. He said nobody at *Fire and Rescue* believed your grandpa had seen a UFO. They didn't search the lake. It wasn't worth the bother."

"So they lied to the newspaper?" Lindsay asked, her brown eyebrows arching in disbelief.

Brian shrugged. "They rode around in their boats for an hour or so and saw nothing. So they went to *Anderson's*, had a beer, and laughed about Crazy Old Orville."

"I told you not to call him that!" Lindsay grumbled.

"That's what *they* called him, not *me*," Brian explained. "They searched only the surface of the lake. They never sent any divers underwater. The newspaper just got the story garbled. The reporter was probably at *Anderson's* getting drunk with the rest of them. Dad still talks about it every once in a while."

"Why didn't you tell me this before?" Lindsay demanded.

Brian looked at her sheepishly. "I dunno. Maybe to keep you from getting all nuts about UFOs and stuff."

Lindsay scrunched her face, looking half angry and half intrigued. Her tongue protruded slightly as she concentrated. "Then Grandpa might be right! There could still be a UFO at the bottom of Lake Tecumseh!"

With a gurgle, Patrick finished his milkshake. "Seems stupid to me."

"Nobody's asking you!" Lindsay said. "We've got to get them to search the lake for real this time! It's the only way to find out for sure."

Brian shook his head. "A big waste of time, Linz. Do you want people to start calling you *Crazy Young Lindsay* about all this?"

She harrumphed and shuffled across the seat, trying to make an exit. "Let me out of here! This changes everything! If Sheriff Little says they never searched underwater, the UFO, or the meteor, or whatever my grandpa saw crash 20 years ago is *still there*! This could be the most exciting chapter of my book!"

"Oh, Lindsay, calm down," Brian said as he stood up and let her out.

"Don't tell me to calm down! "Tell me how we can mount an exploration of the bottom of Lake Tecumseh!"

With that she stormed out of the Dairy Queen, leaving the three boys staring at one another in disbelief in silence except for the swirl of soft-serve ice cream machines behind the counter.

Brian hammered his milkshake on the table and said, "Man, I love that girl!"

Cam wanted to say the same thing but thought the better of it.

*   *   *

After Lindsay's outburst at the Dairy Queen, Cam wondered when he would see her again. Should he phone her? Send an e-mail? Stop by the museum? Apparently, she was still dating Brian Little, but their relationship was past its prime. Cam twirled her words over his mental tongue: *past its prime*. He liked the sound of the phrase, but didn't quite know what it meant for *him*. Would Lindsay continue to see Brian? Would she dump Brian and go out with him instead? Why didn't she just come right out and say what she wanted? Why did girls speak in code? Why did they expect boys to be able to read their minds?

Cam was relieved Lindsay's anger was short lived. She continued to chat with him on line nearly every evening. *UFOgal* avoided the topics of Brian Little and the gentle inquiries from Cam about their status as a couple. Instead, she discussed the progress of her research and her book writing, and how she was planning to update some of the museum exhibits.

A few days later, when the temperature was predicted to soar into the mid 90's, Cam and Lindsay made plans to escape the heat by going to the beach. As he rode to her house, the intense sun burned. The straps of his backpack scraped against his chest. Sweat dribbled from his forehead and plastered his T-shirt to his skin. He didn't care; energized excitement tingled through his body.

Lindsay answered the door with a broad smile. "Hi, Cam."

"Hi, Lindsay." Their eyes locked for a few long moments. "Are you ready?"

She grabbed her backpack. "Yeah. It's going to be a scorcher today!" She called good-bye to her mother, who Cam spied through the door resting on the sofa with her stocking feet up and a pair of orthopedic white shoes on the carpet.

They mounted their bikes and rode off side by side.

Lake Tecumseh had one public beach, which was part of Grissom Park near the center of town. Cam had already gone there several times, as it was the nicest spot to soak up the sun, people watch, and enjoy the cool breeze off the lake. The town had preserved one section of the lakeshore for public recreation, but every remaining foot of the prized shoreline was private property. Staying with Uncle Gary and Aunt Ellen, Cam had access to his small piece of the lake, but it was lonely and boring. He much preferred being at the public beach with other people, and especially with Lindsay.

Cam and Lindsay rode the curving streets through leafy Grissom Park, passing through a gauntlet of cars parked on the sides. *The beach must be packed*, Cam thought, noting the lack of any available spaces. Picnickers had set up Styrofoam coolers and lounge chairs in the shade beneath the oak trees. Men tried to light pyramids of charcoal briquettes while the odor of lighter fluid wafted through the air.

The bike racks were just as congested with bikes as the roads of the park were congested with automobiles. "I knew we should've gotten here earlier," Cam said as he locked his bike to a small tree.

The gray sand beach was noisy and filled with people. Bodies lay like seals on blankets under the glaring summer sun. Bare skin was everywhere, some of it pasty, some of it bronze, and some of it red and sunburned. Children ran around like buzzing mosquitoes, tossing gaudy beach balls larger than they were, kicking water at each other, and using little blue plastic buckets and shovels to build sandcastles under the watchful eyes of the parents. Wading at the edge of the water, couples chatted and licked ice cream cones.

"Let's go to the far side, where there's more room," Lindsay said, leading the way.

They pressed through the thicket of sunbathers and found a bare spot and unfurled their colorful beach towels. Cam tried not to stare as Lindsay shed her clothes except for her red bikini. Her body was beautiful with generous curves in all the right places.

He felt his passion rise.

She positioned herself on the blanket. Fishing in her backpack, she caught him looking at her and smiled coyly. "Can you put some sunscreen on my back?" She handed him the bottle as she twirled away from him.

Cam smoothed the lotion over her back, tantalized by every touch of his fingers against her skin. When he had finished, she turned around and took the bottle. "Let me do yours," she said. "You don't want to get a sunburn."

Cam removed his shirt and let her apply the sunscreen. He was even more excited by her touching his skin. He wanted it to go on forever.

Once suitably protected by SPF 45, they lay side by side in the sun amid the other beachgoers. It was only Lake Tecumseh, Indiana, but Cam imagined he was on a beach in Miami, Maui or even St. Tropez. The location didn't matter; it was the person he was next to. Soaking up the glorious sunshine with Lindsay by his side, only inches away, he felt wonderful. He never would've guessed he'd meet someone as special as her over the summer.

In fact, he had stopped referring to his time away from Chicago as being in exile. His attitude had changed, and she was the reason.

Lindsay couldn't lie still like a piece of bacon on the frying pan of the beach. Instead, she watched the activities around them and talked excitedly about how to search the bottom of the lake for her grandfather's UFO. She formulated her evolving plans out loud. "The lake isn't that deep," she said, hardly in Cam's direction. Instead, she appeared to speak to the shore. "Grandpa says he knows the exact spot."

"The exact spot?"

"Where the thing crashed 20 years ago." She looked at the blue water of the lake, which was filled with bathers and boaters. "What if something is there, Cam? What if Grandpa did see an alien spaceship?"

"That would be exciting," he answered honestly. He pictured a little metal saucer lying in the sand at the lake bottom, its hull cracked from the impact and corroded by 20 years of exposure to the elements. He wondered if alien bodies remained in the wreckage. It would be a fantastic find if it were true. They'd be famous.

But he knew it wasn't there.

"We need to find it," she insisted.

He gazed at the water. A roaring speedboat rocketed by, pulling a skier over the speed bumps of its passing V-shaped wake. In the distance, the far shore appeared as a saw tooth pattern—towering trees and their interlocked vacation homes in the gauzy heat and humidity. The bucolic location did not seem like the site for a UFO investigation.

Cam remembered a TV program he had seen. "They used sonar to find the *Titanic*. Would that work?"

Lindsay sighed. "Where are we going to get something like that?"

"Could we drag a net under the water and try to snag it?"

"That wouldn't work either. We'd probably just get junk or a tree stump." She pressed her fingers against her upper arm, looking for a burn. "Am I getting red?"

"Not yet. Want some more sunscreen?"

She shook her head. "Let's get in the water to cool off. I brought a Frisbee."

"Good idea," Cam said.

They went into the lake and were instantly refreshed. They spent a long time just throwing the Frisbee back and forth while they stood in waist-high water. Some of her tosses were way off, and he had to leap to catch them. Each time he smashed into the water like a breaching whale.

He was having a great time. He wished the summer day would go on forever.

But eventually their recreation was interrupted by a shout from the shore. Turning toward the noise, Cam missed catching the Frisbee that Lindsay had just tossed. The fluorescent disk splashed into the water as if it were Orville's little UFO.

Brian Little and Patrick Frazier were yelling at them. Dressed in swim trunks, their muscular football bodies seemed designed for the beach.

Cam suddenly felt like a skinny weakling and was disappointed at their intrusion upon his wonderful afternoon with Lindsay. He longed for the anonymity available in Chicago. In a small town like Lake Tecumseh, one kept running into the same people over and over again, whether one wanted to or not.

Brian and Patrick waded into the water and joined them, forming a little circle. "How are you, Linz?" Brian asked while splashing water up on his torso, being careful not to get his perfectly styled blond hair wet.

"I'm fine," Lindsay answered. "We were just playing Frisbee."

"That sounds like fun. Toss it my way, Sport," Brian said to Cam.

Cam begrudgingly went to the floating disk and threw it to Brian. He caught it cleanly, and then threw it to Patrick with a strong whip of his wrist. The Frisbee flew over Patrick's head.

"Hey, watch it!" Patrick said. "You want me to swim to the next county?"

As Patrick splashed through the water to get the errant Frisbee, Brian smirked and moved closer to Lindsay. "I thought you'd be at the museum today."

"It was slow so I closed it for a break."

"I guess people would rather be having fun in the sun than reading about aliens and UFOs," Brian said.

Lindsay frowned but didn't respond.

"You didn't return my call," Brian said to her almost accusingly.

"I've been busy."

"No time for text either?"

Just then Patrick yelled, "Incoming!" as the Frisbee flew toward them.

Brian dived forward and caught it like a natural athlete. He held the disk triumphantly in the air. "Am I good or what?"

They tossed the Frisbee among themselves for several minutes; its movements resembled a bee flitting among a bouquet of flowers. Finally, Lindsay tossed up her arms and announced, "I'm tired of playing. I'm getting out of the water."

"It's a stupid game anyway," Brian said immediately, following after her.

The four of them reassembled on the beach. Cam and Lindsay sat on their beach towels and began reapplying sunscreen. Brian and Patrick rummaged through their bags and pulled out their beach gear, squeezing their towels right next to them in the only available free spot. Cam wished the two interlopers would leave them alone.

"Want me to do your back?" Brian said to Lindsay.

"No, I'm okay," she insisted, turning her body away from him and toward the summer sun.

Cam noticed Lindsay was making her lukewarm feelings about Brian fairly obvious. Unfortunately, the jock seemed clueless to her gentle brush-offs.

Cam tried to ignore him and relax in the sun, but Brian had a nervous energy and wouldn't shut up or keep still. At one point Brain got up from his towel, letting his shadow fall across Cam's face.

"Would you mind? You're blocking my sun," Cam said.

"Too much sun isn't good," Brian said, not moving.

Cam sat up and squinted at Brian standing before him like a shadowy pillar. "Just move, will ya?"

Brian snorted and reluctantly stepped to the side. "This is *boring*! You guys wanna get something to eat?"

"You're always hungry," Lindsay said.

Brian puffed out his chest. "I'm a big guy!"

"Cheeseburgers," Patrick added, licking his lips.

Lindsay abruptly sat up. A sudden idea seemed to shine from behind her sunglasses. "I've wasted enough time here in the sun. We need to search the bottom of the lake for my grandpa's UFO!"

"Are you still stuck on that silly idea?" Brian said.

"It's not silly!" She pointed to the water. "Twenty years ago, out there, on the other side of the lake, something crashed. We need to look for it."

"So it's a meteor or something," Brian said. "Why bother?"

"I think you can help."

"Me? How?"

"You're dad's the sheriff, and he's got diving equipment for lake rescues, right?"

Brian shrugged. "You mean like scuba?"

She nodded. "That's what we need. You're certified, right?"

"Of course!" Brian said proudly. "I'm an expert! I got certified in the Bahamas over Spring Break. We dived all over these cool coral reefs."

Lindsay stood up excitedly and began collecting her belongings lying scattered around her blanket. "Borrow the scuba gear and meet us in the morning at my grandpa's house. Bring your family's pontoon boat. That'll be perfect for our expedition. Grandpa will show us where the thing crashed, and you can dive and look for it."

"You want me to steal the county's scuba gear to look for a UFO?" Brian asked. "That doesn't sound like you, Linz. You're all rules and regulations and stuff."

She smiled. "We're not *stealing*. We're *borrowing*. We'll have it back in a few hours I would think. They'll never miss it."

Brian scratched his chin. "I like this side of you. A little edgy."

"Don't be ridiculous. This is for science."

"All right. Patrick and I will figure out a way," Brian said, confident in himself and relishing his indispensable role.

"Are we leaving?" Patrick asked, rising to his feet. "Are we getting burgers?"

Cam stood up, not wanting to miss out on Lindsay's adventure. "I can scuba dive, too."

Brian smirked. "You can?"

"Sure, I had some classes in school. It's not hard." Cam had taken some scuba lessons, but he was hardly experienced. But Brian didn't need to know that.

"We can be dive buddies then," Brian said.

"I want to find out what's in the lake, too," Cam said. "This is going to be an incredible adventure." He smiled at Lindsay. She was outwardly pleased by his supportive response to her call for action.

"Do you think we'll find anything, Linz?" Brian asked.

She stuffed her blanket and gear into her backpack. "I don't know, but we need to solve this mystery, and the answer is at the bottom of this lake!"

CHAPTER FIVE

In the glaring sunshine, Cam, Lindsay, and Orville Milford stood on the pier, watching the pontoon boat slowly approach. Its blue-and-white checkered canopy shaded rows of seats. The boat plodded toward them at a geriatric pace, looking more appropriate for a festive family dinner cruise than a search for a lost UFO.

Wearing only red swim trunks and dark sunglasses, Brian Little stood at the wheel. Patrick Frazier reclined in the adjacent seat, a cold drink in his hand and his large, bare feet propped lazily on the side of the hull.

Cam folded his arms across his chest. He wasn't happy Brian was joining them, but Brian had the pontoon boat and the scuba gear. They couldn't go UFO hunting without his assistance.

Cam shuffled his flip-flops across the rough boards of the dock, still not believing they were attempting to find a twenty-year-old alien UFO hiding at the bottom of Lake Tecumseh. He had never expected he'd be involved in an amateur *Discovery Channel* expedition, but that was before he fell under the charming spell of Lindsay Brock and her oddball Hoosier town. Lindsay was excited about the impending search and how it promised to solve the riddle of her grandfather's UFO sighting. Cam was excited just to spend more time with her.

Orville fidgeted as the boat grew near, as if the memories of his fateful night years ago were swirling around him like the annoying lake midges. He turned to Lindsay and said, "When they searched before, they found nothing. Said I was crazy. Said I imagined things. I imagined *nothing*. That UFO's still down there, I'd bet my truck on it."

Lindsay smiled and said, "We want to find out for sure. We're going to use scuba."

Orville poked toward the water with his stick-like forefinger. "I can tell you exactly where it is, too. It hasn't moved in twenty years."

"It's a big lake, how do you know where the UFO is?" Cam asked.

"A sixth sense," the old man answered confidently. "I clear my mind and feel my way subconsciously. Maybe I detect their vibrations, or their brainwaves or something. I can tell when I'm over the exact spot."

Even if Orville had some uncanny mental ability, or just a good memory of where he was when he saw the UFO, Cam doubted they could find anything underwater in such a large lake. Their quest seemed foolhardy, but the day promised to be fun nevertheless.

The pontoon boat pulled alongside the pier. Clean and well maintained, its rear was full of scuba supplies, which were scattered over the floor as if they had been unceremoniously dropped there in a heist. Brian killed the motor and called out to them in greeting. Patrick raised his glass in their direction and then took a sip.

Brian looked Cam over. "How are ya, Sport?"

"It's Cam."

"Whatever, Sport."

As Cam seethed, Orville leaned in to whisper to him: "I never liked that kid. He's just like his arrogant father, the sheriff, the one who made me the town laughingstock."

Patrick put down his glass and threw a rope to Lindsay. She tied it around the post to secure the boat to the pier. She turned to Brian and asked, "Your dad doesn't mind you using the boat today?"

"Not at all," Brian said, puffing out his bare chest. "He knows I'm responsible. He'd love me to go into law enforcement, too."

Lindsay looked at the scuba gear. "Did you have any trouble getting this stuff?"

"I told you I could do it. I just have to get it back before too long."

She smiled and clasped her hands together. "We're ready then. Let's go find the UFO!"

"If there's something down there, we'll find it," Brian said. "It can't be too hard. The lake's no more than forty feet deep."

Orville set his jaw and looked worried. "Are you sure about this?"

"What do you mean?" Lindsay asked.

"Maybe it's not such a good idea to disturb them. They've been down there for twenty years. Who knows what we might stir up?"

She patted his arm. "There's nothing to worry about, Grandpa."

"Are you guys getting on board or what?" Patrick said, jiggling the ice cubes in his glass impatiently.

Lindsay climbed into the pontoon boat and sniffed suspiciously in Patrick's direction. "Is that alcohol?"

Patrick grinned and took a sip. "It's a good luck toast for a successful UFO adventure. And maybe I'll get a nice tan, too."

Lindsay shook her head in disapproval and then sat in the bench seats in the rear. Cam and Orville joined her in the shade under the canopy. Brian started the engine while Patrick leaned out and untied the rope from the post, spilling a few drops of his beverage as he did so.

They departed from the pier at cocktail hour speed, which was probably as fast as the pontoon boat could move. Orville's overgrown lot slowly receded and became just a green jumble of trees, his house barely visible among the leaves. Cam spied Uncle Gary's house, marked by the little balcony off the second story guest room. From there Cam had watched through binoculars as Orville floated in his boat for his evening meditation.

For a weekday, Lake Tecumseh was busier than normal. The weather was brilliant, and the humidity, for a change, was bearable. People had come out in droves to enjoy the sun-kissed day, probably playing hooky from jobs and responsibilities. Several powerful boats were pulling water-skiers, and one boat was dragging a screeching young girl in a rubber raft, her long pigtails kiting in the breeze as if she were a jet pilot on the water. Despite the presence of others, the lake's hundreds of acres provided enough room for everyone. No one paid any undue attention to the colorful pontoon boat slowly motoring across the lake.

Orville yelled directions at Brian, guiding him to the supposed crash site. As they entered the target area, the old man ordered him to slow down. Orville studied the vicinity intensely for a moment, closed his eyes and concentrated for a few breaths and then said, "Ten yards to the right."

"OK, Gramps," Brian said, as he twirled the steering wheel. The boat turned and slowed.

Eyes still closed, Orville continued to focus. "A little forward, then about five yards to the left."

Brian rolled his eyes at the additional command but did as directed.

The boat settled into position about a hundred yards from the shore. They all watched as Orville meditated. He opened his eyes and smiled slightly. "This is the place."

Brian turned off the engine. "Are you sure?"

"Of course I'm sure," Orville responded defensively, scratching the hair underneath his cap. "Can't anyone feel the energy except me?"

The young people looked at one another with blank expressions and shrugs. Cam didn't feel Orville's *energy* either, but he had felt other strange sensations since coming to Lake Tecumseh.

Patrick tossed the anchor over the side with a splash. The chain clinked before the lead weight hit bottom. "Let the adventure begin," he deadpanned. He rattled his drink again, but only melting ice cubes remained. "Time for another!"

Brian stepped away from the wheel and joined them in the rear where the blue scuba suits, air cylinders, and other diving accessories were stacked. "Let's not waste time."

Lindsay nodded. "I agree. You and Cam should suit up."

"What exactly are we looking for?" Brian asked. "Is it a saucer or something?"

"It's not a saucer," Orville said. "It's about six feet long, egg-shaped, and it glowed when it crashed. It's probably covered with mud now."

"If there's anything there at all, Gramps," Brian said.

"That's what we're here to find out," Lindsay reminded. "I don't like mysteries."

Brian sorted through the masks, snorkels, fins, and other diving paraphernalia. He turned and looked at Cam, one side of his mouth rising in a mischievous smirk. "Are you sure you're comfortable diving, Sport?"

"Don't worry about me. I'm almost certified, you know."

"Well, good for you," Brian sniffed as he started passing items to Cam. "Be careful with this stuff, or my dad will kill us."

Cam examined the gear, which looked practically unused. There wasn't much recreational use for wetsuits and air cylinders in Indiana, unless one wanted to watch carp, snakes, and snapping turtles underwater.

Cam kicked off his flip-flops and pulled off his t-shirt, feeling rather exposed in his swim trunks. He was not big and muscular like Brian and Patrick, but he had a slim, well-defined physique and narrow waist, one that came easily for a seventeen-year old.

Brian looked Cam over, as if comparing himself to him. The dismissive look he returned indicated he felt he had the superior body of the two. Lindsay was inspecting the diving gear and not the two strutting young men.

"What's this?" Lindsay asked, holding a heavy black belt.

"That's a weight belt to stay submerged," Brian explained.

She nodded and put the belt to the side and then retrieved what looked like an oversized watch with three separate dial-shaped displays and several buttons. "And this?"

Brian carefully took the device from her. "Take a class, Linz. It's a dive console, with pressure and depth gauges, even a compass. It's very expensive."

"Oh, okay," she said, a little peevishly.

Cam and Brian both donned blue neoprene diving suits and assembled their gear as the others watched intently.

"Do you really need to get all *Jacques Cousteau* like that?" Patrick drawled.

Brian removed his sunglasses and handed them to Patrick. "This lake's spring fed, and the water's cold. We need insulated suits."

Cam pulled the neoprene hood over his head—an unpleasant sensation, like rolling a giant condom over his entire body. At least he would be warm. He had no idea how long they would be underwater and wanted to be prepared.

Cam was unfamiliar with some of the coldwater gear, and Brian, unexpectedly, assisted him in getting dressed and explaining procedures. Cam realized Brian was knowledgeable and helpful; unfortunately, he kept calling him *Sport*.

Brian gloated at being the scuba expert, especially in front of Lindsay. After a few minutes, both boys were outfitted from top to bottom in hood, wetsuits, and gear. They each wore vest-like buoyancy control devices and had air tanks on their backs. Suitably attired, horribly weighed down out of the water, they stared at one another, their masks resting on their foreheads and their snorkels dangling from their chins.

"Are you ready?" Brian asked.

"Sure thing," Cam answered confidently. He had always enjoyed scuba and wished he had kept up with the classes, especially since his grandparents had footed the bill. Unfortunately, he had lost interest for some reason and abandoned the hobby. His mother often said he had a short attention span. He momentarily wondered if that were true but then dismissed the thought and started checking the functioning of his gear.

"I hope you find something. Wouldn't that be great?" Lindsay said excitedly.

"It's down there, no doubt about it," Orville said, fanning himself with his cap. He wore a long-sleeved flannel shirt but somehow didn't connect his sweltering to his inappropriate clothing.

Cam slid his feet into a pair of fins, lowered his face mask, and inserted his mouthpiece. Brian resembled a mirror image in blue neoprene looking back at him. The two explorers were ready to venture into the underworld.

"Good luck," Lindsay said with a smile.

Brian turned his back to the water and sat on the edge of the boat and gave Cam a *thumbs-up* sign. He then executed a smooth back roll off the boat, splashing into the water with a loud plop. He immediately surfaced and moved out of the way, making room for Cam's entry.

Cam did likewise, perching himself on the fiberglass edge of the boat and performing one last check of his gear before pushing himself backward and slicing into the water.

Buoyant, Cam suddenly felt fifty pounds lighter than he had on the boat. The wetsuit was an effective insulator against the water's cold. He felt only a mild chill as he bobbed next to Brian.

Brian jerked his thumb downward, signaling Cam to submerge.

They both sank below the water, leaving a rising trail of bubbles.

Cam quickly got accustomed to the scuba gear, which was much better than he had ever used before. He thought how the county taxpayers were buying top-of-the-line supplies for *Fire and Rescue*, to sit unused most of the time.

He looked around the underwater realm. The water was speckled with light for just the first few feet below the surface, beyond which darkness the color of mud ruled.

Brian snapped on a powerful flashlight, and Cam did the same. Their beams did little to penetrate the hidden world, which was peppered with dirt, sand, and the floating detritus of organic matter.

They traded *thumbs-up* signs, indicating their exploration was ready to proceed. Flippers flapping, they descended deeper into the inky pitch, which was rescued from complete, utter blackness only by the formidable candlepower of their flashlights.

A school of small, silvery fish darted away, and a snake—or an eel—Cam couldn't be sure—bolted in surprise as they approached. Cam looked at his dive gauge. They were just fifteen feet below the surface, and already it felt as if he were swimming through the atmosphere of an alien planet.

Orville was certain this was the site of the UFO crash, so theoretically all they had to do was go straight down. The alien ship, or whatever it was, should be just below the boat embedded at the bottom of the lake.

They found the anchor chain from the boat and followed it downward like the dotted line on a treasure map. They reached the end quickly. The gray muddy bottom was featureless except for scours left by small lake creatures and a furrow carved by the anchor.

Cam checked his gauge: thirty-five feet deep.

He shined his light over the bottom, which resembled a desolate moonscape. Except for tiny floating particles and a few curious fish, nothing was in view. He reached down and scooped up a glove full of mud. No wonder people didn't scuba dive in Indiana. There was nothing to see. The bottom of the glacier-sculpted lake was even more boring than the glacier-sculpted landscape above.

A tap on his shoulder alerted him that Brian was swimming off to the right to explore further. As his partner swam away, Cam followed after him. A faint, ghostly umbra surrounded their halogen lights.

Cam swam a foot or two above the muck, scanning around him with his flashlight. The journey was like penetrating a horribly dark cave, where nothing was visible except in the surrounding small bubble of illumination. He could be heading directly toward an old tree stump and wouldn't know it until he cracked his head open. He slowed, keeping his free arm outstretched, gingerly feeling his way forward with his fingertips. The coldness began to seep through his thin gloves. Ahead, the glow of Brian's flashlight gradually dimmed.

Swimming forward at a snail's pace, Cam touched something solid and stopped immediately. He focused his light beam on his find. About five feet long and halfway buried in the muck, he discerned a cylindrical shape. The object was the same mud-encrusted color as everything else in the lake, as if it had rested on the bottom for decades.

Was this Orville's alien spaceship?

Cam's pulse quickened. The gurgles of rising air bubbles from his snorkel grew louder. He carefully touched the dirty surface of the object but had little tactile sensation through his rubber gloves. He felt a protruding lip or ridge that was too uniform to be natural. It must have been manufactured. He swam to its end, which, unexpectedly, was open. Surprised by Cam's intrusion, a large, bottom-dwelling fish popped from the partially mud-filled cavity and darted away.

Cam realized his find was a rusty metal drum, not a UFO.

Disappointed, he swam away from the corroded barrel. He then realized he had lost sight of his dive buddy. Apparently Brian had kept swimming ahead after Cam had stopped to inspect his find. Cam gazed through the darkness but could see nothing, not even a faint glow of Brian's flashlight. How could he have moved away so quickly in such a short time? Had Brian surfaced without telling his buddy? That was bad form, every diver knew that.

More likely, the darkness was just too thick to see where Brian was. He could have been just a few yards away and Cam never would have realized it. They should have stuck together.

He thought a moment about what to do. He decided to search for a few more minutes, hoping to run into Brian. He swam in a methodical, sweeping pattern, illuminating the dull bottom with his flashlight. He saw neither Brian nor anything of interest and decided to give up. Whatever Orville had seen twenty years ago had either vanished into the thick mud or had been a figment of his imagination all along. Lindsay was sure to be disappointed that there was nothing at the bottom of Lake Tecumseh and her grandpa deserved the moniker, *Crazy Old Orville.*

Strangely, without warning or provocation, Cam suddenly felt afraid. Nothing was wrong with his equipment, and nothing was in view to precipitate such a sudden emotion, but he panicked. The sensation of fear washed over him strongly and deeply. He felt the hair rising up on the back of his neck and curdle through his veins.

He glanced around the murky, impenetrable water. Nothing had changed in the last few seconds.

What was happening to him?

He floated in place, the anxiety intensifying as he tried to rationally counter the mindless panic gripping him. He fought the creeping paralysis, which seemed to be coming from outside him as much as from inside him. Were Orville's aliens nearby after all? Were they touching his brain, implanting panic to drive him away from their underwater lair?

He wanted to get to the surface immediately but steeled his resolve not to surrender to irrationality. Nothing was wrong. He was sure of that. He had to keep his wits about him.

Feeling as if he had corralled the sudden panic attack, Cam calmed himself and tried to breathe normally. He was suddenly aware of the pressure of the tons of water above him. He could feel the tremendous weight in his ears and against his skin. Even the coldness seemed more intense, despite wearing the exposure suit.

He looked around for Brian again, but he was all alone in the darkness.

He resumed his slow scrabble over the muddy bottom, his composure and confidence returning. He had only gone a few yards when he suddenly froze.

In his mind's eye he saw a specter pop into his consciousness as if a new, frightful memory had suddenly implanted itself in his brain.

The image in his mind resembled a drawing from a geometry class: something almost spherical, but its surface was actually an interlocking array of small triangles. The triangles fit together perfectly to form a pointy, balloon-like solid. Cam remembered such things were called polyhedrons, but he couldn't tell how many sides the object had. Sixteen? Twenty? Twenty-four? A knobby, long tube extended downward from the polyhedron. The tube split into six smaller ones that flailed out like the legs of a spider and moved. Their motion was not the steady stride of a muscular animal or the graceful flip of a fin. Instead, the legs rhythmically curled and unfurled in a creepy, insect-like manner.

The movement of something best left undisturbed.

A fear enveloped him, induced by the frightful image inside his brain. His mind was being invaded, but from where and by whom?

Or worse yet, was it his own mind now attacking him? Was the appearance of the spider-like apparition the latest salvo in the growing battle against insanity he had waged in his head since his arrival at Lake Tecumseh?

Not only was Cam seeing the image in his mind, he was *feeling* it. The green, geometric *thing* hovered in his brain as if it had ensconced itself there. What the hell was it? Why did it suddenly appear now in his head, when he was deep underwater?

He shuddered, trying to clear his thoughts and dissipate the unwelcome vision. The green spider-thing was still in his mind, seemingly beckoning him with its tiny, stick-like legs.

Cam instinctively realized the creature was one of Orville's aliens, and it was trying to communicate with him.

The alien *creature*—Cam was certain that's what it was—wanted him.

It was *summoning* him.

He pictured the six-legged alien holed up in its spacecraft, buried in the mud somewhere nearby. Its mental signals reminded him of the innate ability to discern one's name in a stranger's whispered conversation, or the instant understanding of a familiar English word amid the babble of a foreign tongue.

What was wrong with him? Was he suffering from a lack of oxygen?

He fiddled with his regulator and checked his air gauge. Everything was working properly. He must be hallucinating. Why was he so afraid?

Looking up, hoping to see the surface, his feet seemed stuck in the muddy bottom, even though he was not even touching it. He was practically paralyzed by the alien image etched into his mind, like the memory of a horrific car accident that looped over and over.

A polyhedral head. A straight, tube-like body. Six spider-like legs.

Cam no longer wanted to search for the UFO. He needed to ascend to the surface as fast as possible before the panic completely overwhelmed him. He disconnected the weighted diving belt and let it drop to the bottom. He then opened the valve to the air bladder of his buoyancy control harness. As he rose upward, he kicked his flippers to move faster.

He rose quickly, and in spite of the panic, he remembered to exhale as he made his emergency ascent to prevent a lung rupture as the pressure decreased. Although the distance was not far, the pressure at the bottom was about twice that of the surface.

He kicked faster, using all his strength to ascend. When he saw sunlight, his spirit improved.

He burst to the surface in a panic, with flailing arms. He quickly removed his mouthpiece and sucked in the atmosphere as if he had been deprived of oxygen his entire life.

Thank God he was no longer down there.

Lindsay saw his distress. "Cam! Are you all right?"

He caught his breath as he treaded water and his eyes adjusted to the sudden brightness. Thankfully the image of the alien creature evaporated from his mind. He pulled his face mask up over his head and wiped the water from his face. "I'm OK," he blurted, spitting out water.

He had lied to her because he wasn't ready to discuss an illogical panic attack caused by a mental image of an alien creature. He needed to take a few moments to compose himself.

The sun's rays warmed him as he floated and collected his senses. The pontoon boat floated peacefully. He heard the distant roar of speedboats and squinted at the sunshine reflecting off the water.

Everything seemed perfectly normal.

"Where's the other kid?" Orville asked, leaning over the railing.

Cam spun around, looking for Brian. "He hasn't come up?"

"No," Lindsay answered. "You better go down and look for him."

"I told you this wasn't a good idea," Orville said. "Nobody ever listens to me."

Cam looked around, searching for a trail of bubbles from Brian. The passing speedboat had stirred up a large wake that obscured all signs of the diver below.

"I'll go get him," Cam said. He felt guilty for surfacing without his diving partner, but he had trepidation about going back underwater. He reached up to lower his mask just as Brian suddenly surfaced next to him.

Brian pushed up his mask and removed his snorkel and glared at him, displaying no outward sign of fear or anxiety. "There you are! I lost you down there. Why didn't you follow me?"

"Why didn't you wait for me—?"

"Some dive buddy you are!"

Cam swam toward the boat and sighed with exhaustion—more mental than physical. He had screwed up and knew it. He shouldn't have surfaced alone. Brian was justified at being angry with him.

Brian continued to berate him as they hung on the side of the boat together.

"Never mind about all that!" Lindsay shouted. "Did you *find* anything?"

Cam wiped the water from his face. "Nothing. Just an old metal drum. There's nothing else down there."

"Are your sure?" she asked.

"There's nothing but mud," Cam said disappointedly.

"*I* found something," Brian announced proudly.

Cam turned to him, treading water. "What? What did you find?"

Brian grinned. "You gotta trust the expert. If you hadn't surfaced, you would've seen it, Sport."

"Seen what?"

"The UFO. I found it."

*   *   *

Clad in scuba gear, Cam and Brian floated beneath the surface, illuminating the *Unidentified Flying Object* with the halos of their flashlights.

Cam was disappointed. Based on Brian's excited description, he had half-expected to find a disc-shaped craft with landing gear and a pair of antenna protruding from its glass dome. Perhaps alien bodies would be strewn across the gray mud. Instead, what they swam above resembled a large, misshapen boulder with a snagged fishing line undulating from one side. No alien bodies were in view.

Interestingly the mud-encrusted object stood out starkly on the featureless bottom, appearing as if it had fallen into place ages ago. Approximately five feet long and vaguely egg-shaped, it was not surprising Brian had christened it Orville's UFO. The old man had provided an identical description of the glowing object he had seen crash into the lake twenty years earlier.

Cam didn't think Brian's find was any more interesting than the rusting drum he had found on the first dive. Only Brian was a better story teller than he was. He had gotten Lindsay and the others all excited. She had pumped him for descriptive details and quickly concluded the object was probably the remnant of a meteor. She quickly formulated plans and sent the two divers back underwater with additional supplies.

She planned to raise the meteor to the surface.

Wanting to please her, Cam had donned the scuba gear a second time. Nearly forty feet below the surface once again, he was worried about a second panic attack. Anxiety began to well up in his chest, and his heart rate quickened. Even in the cold water, he was perspiring under his wetsuit. Determined to keep his emotions under control this time, he focused on the task at hand, hoping the concentration would prevent a recurrence of his frightful earlier experience.

Brian floated nearby, holding coils of nylon rope. Cam clutched a large, yellow package—an inflatable raft from the pontoon boat. It was Lindsay's idea: They would attach the raft to the meteor with rope, inflate the raft with air, and its buoyancy would lift the meteor off the bottom and raise it to the surface. Then they would haul the meteor to shore for a scientific examination.

Ingeniously simple, Cam thought. He liked how Lindsay's mind worked. She was never out of ideas. She was always figuring out a new way to do things, calculating an alternative viewpoint to express. Although they had known each other for only a short while, she was the only girl who had ever challenged him to think bigger and more broadly, to use his brain to its full extent. No girl had ever inspired him that way before.

Brian signaled for him to assist in securing the rope to the meteor.

Cam moved closer to his partner until they were both in a swirl of exhaled air bubbles gurgling from their regulators.

Brian began unfurling rope, which floated in the water like a lengthening tentacle. Cam put the packaged raft on the lake bottom and placed a rock on top of it like a paperweight to keep it from floating away. He then grabbed the end of the rope and moved toward the meteor. He wondered how they were going to get the rope around the thing, as it looked like it weighed five hundred pounds and had rested on the bottom for centuries.

Cam touched the rock-like object with his free hand, his gloved fingers squishing through the coating of mud to press against a hard, unyielding surface.

A strange sensation suddenly shot through him and made his hand recoil as if he had touched a hot stove. But the object wasn't hot; it was as cold as everything else in the lake. And the sensation wasn't a physical one; it was a *mental* one.

His mind felt as if it had been bit by a force emanating from the meteor. He couldn't describe it further; it was no more than a prick.

Cam blinked his eyes beneath his facemask, trying to make sense of what had just happened. Was it the start of another panic attack?

He looked at Brian, who was attempting to secure the rope around the object. Brian was touching it all over the place and was apparently not experiencing any unusual sensations.

Cam decided he was just nervous. He reached out again and cautiously touched the meteor. This time he felt nothing. No unexpected flinching. No mysterious mental prick. He was relieved and took a deep breath.

Running his gloved hand over the surface, he wiped off the coating of mud from a small area. No shiny metal gleamed beneath to betray an alien manufacture. Its surface resembled the warty outside of a cucumber more than anything.

It probably was just a meteor, but with the mud and darkness how could they know for sure? That was why Lindsay had insisted they examine the object on the shore. The scientific method required hands-on analysis.

As Cam and Brian worked around the object, their motion stirred up the gray mud until they were swimming in a dirt cloud like the inside of a giant, flushing toilet bowl. Amid the swill, visibility became so poor they could barely see each other. Practically face mask pressed to face mask, they communicated like mimes. They relied on their sense of touch as they groped around the object, trying to secure the rope.

Combining their strength on the narrower end of the egg-shaped rock, they lifted it a few inches upward. Brian slipped the rope around it and fastened it tightly. He gave Cam a *thumb's up*. Now they needed to affix a second length of rope to the other end. Unfortunately the heavier end of the meteor was embedded deeper in the mire. Despite their straining, they could not budge the object. They would have to dig it out.

They scooped away the soft mud with their hands. The digging made visibility worse. Cam couldn't wait to get out of the cloud of fine particles. He felt claustrophobic as his field of vision shrank. The pressure of the water above him seemed to increase in tandem. Again, he tried to focus. He tried to modulate his breathing.

Easy, steady breaths.

The discipline helped check his growing sense of unease.

Finally they had removed enough mud to expose the end of the meteor and tie the second rope around it. Unattached at one end, each rope undulated in the current like underwater stalks of bamboo. Now it was time to connect the rubber raft.

Cam retrieved the yellow package, and they fastened the deflated raft to the free end of the floating ropes. Then Brian held his breath and removed his regulator, releasing a swirl of bubbles. He attached his hose to the filling nozzle of the raft. The rubber raft expanded with air, blossoming underwater like a giant, unfolding yellow daisy.

When the circular raft was completely inflated it revealed four seats, indentations for cup holders, and a pair of artificial palm trees with brown trunks, green leaves, and plastic coconuts.

Cam was amused and wanted to laugh. A party raft for four people to lounge in comfort!

The colorful raft looked like a tropical apparition amid the swirling dirt, and it strained tightly against the nylon ropes, trying to pull itself to the surface.

Yet the meteor did not budge from the bottom.

Cam was disappointed. Despite Lindsay's assurances, the raft didn't have enough buoyancy to float the meteor to the surface. They needed to help dislodge it from the paste-like muck. He and Brian grabbed the meteor and rocked it back and forth. They were soon obscured by even more suspended sediment.

Growing tired, Cam wondered if Lindsay had any other ideas.

Then the meteor gradually began to rise from the bottom as if it were a woman being levitated by a magician. Cam looked at Brian and saw a surprised look behind his goggles. They slapped their palms together in an underwater *high five*.

Success!

They steadied the meteor as it was slowly hauled upward. The nylon ropes were stretched taut beneath the rising, air-filled tropical raft. Would their makeshift harness hold against all the strain? Would they get the meteor to the surface in one piece or would the ropes break and send the object back to the bottom, even deeper into the mud?

The meteor slowly ascended, and their luck held. Brian's well tied ropes remained fastened, and the rubber raft did not rip apart. The divers followed after it, leaving the noxious dirt cloud.

When Cam and Brian broke the surface, they saw the excited faces of Lindsay, Orville, and Patrick staring at them from the pontoon boat. The yellow raft floated nearby, its two plastic palm trees bent inward by the weight of the object suspended below.

"Did it work?" Lindsay shouted. "Is the object attached?"

Brian lifted his face mask over his blond hair and removed his snorkel. "Stand back! UFO coming aboard!"

Lindsay and Patrick cheered. Orville stood nearby, a scowl on his wrinkled face.

Cam beamed at Lindsay. He liked seeing her so excited. He was excited all of a sudden, too. Perhaps it was just relief from completing the dive without incident. More likely it was from seeing Lindsay so energized by their find.

So what if it was just a big rock looking like a muddy potato? Lindsay acted as if it were a chest of pirate treasure.

She grabbed a rope and tossed it to the two divers. "Let's haul it to shore!"

Cam and Brain submerged and secured the tow line to the meteor, which was suspended beneath the rubber raft. Afterwards Brian climbed into the pontoon boat to pilot it to the pier. Cam stayed in the water to help guide the meteor.

"Go slowly," Lindsay cautioned. "We don't want to lose it."

"No problem," Brian said with a wink as he started the motor. "This boat only goes slowly."

As the pontoon boat motored toward Orville's house, Cam swam with the raft, one hand resting on its rounded side, the other testing the ropes. They were under a lot of strain so he yelled for Brian to go slower.

Brian throttled back the motor.

Their expedition was an unusual sight—a pontoon boat pulling an inflatable party raft with a scuba diver hitching a ride on its side. Nevertheless no one paid the explorers any attention.

Just as their boat got to the end of Orville's decrepit wooden pier, the inflated raft suddenly wrenched.

Lindsay turned back, alarmed. "What happened?"

"Kill the power!" Cam yelled, realizing what had happened. As the water got shallow near the shore, the object hanging beneath the raft had struck the bottom.

Brian turned off the engine. The stern of the pontoon boat was parallel to the end of the pier. The yellow raft was elongated like a surrealist painting.

"What's wrong?" Lindsay asked.

"We hit bottom," Cam said. "What are we going to do now?"

"Grandpa's tractor!" Lindsay said without missing a beat. "We'll tow it to shore."

Orville scowled. "You should leave that UFO be. You don't know what you're messing with."

"Don't worry, Grandpa," Lindsay said. "We've come this far, we can't stop now. This could be the greatest scientific discovery ever! Let's get your tractor."

"It's low on oil," Orville reminded.

"It'll be fine," she said.

The tractor was an old Sears model meant for lawn and garden use. Lindsay insisted on driving. They removed the tow rope from the pontoon boat and attached it to the tractor's hitch. Both Brian and Patrick joined Cam in the water to help pull the object to shore.

Lindsay sat in the tractor's seat, which was worn and cracked, revealing its decaying foam padding. She looked back at the three boys in the water, who clung to the tow rope. "Are you ready?" she asked.

"Slow and steady!" Cam shouted back.

"Let 'er rip!" Brian yelled.

Lindsay revved the tractor's motor. Its big rear tires spun on the grass, digging deep ruts in the sod. The tow rope went taut. The boys dug into the bottom with their feet to keep their balance and added their strength to the tractor's.

The tractor moved forward, slowly pulling the object toward the shore.

"Keep pulling!" Brian shouted.

The knobby top of the object broke through the water, resembling the back of a surfacing crocodile.

They boys continued to strain with all their might until the muddy meteor rested on the grass. Water dripped from its exterior in little rivulets, forming a gray puddle.

Lindsay turned off the tractor and raced back to inspect the discovery. The four of them slowly examined the find with a mixture of surprise and disappointment.

In the bright sunshine it didn't look any more substantial than it had lying like a piece of discarded junk on the dark lake bottom. It was a large, brown rock with a warty, uneven surface. One end was slightly narrower than the other, giving it an egg-shaped appearance.

Brian removed his wetsuit and strutted proudly. "The mystery of Orville's UFO is solved!"

"It's just a big rock," Patrick said. "Not an alien spaceship."

Cam agreed it wasn't anything special, but Lindsay acted as if she were an archeologist finding a long forgotten Egyptian tomb. She circled the object, touching its wet, dirty surface and inspecting every irregular bump and crevice as if her fingertips were reading Braille. "This is amazing!" she said breathlessly.

"Is it a meteor?" Patrick asked.

"A *meteorite*," Lindsay corrected. "That's a meteor that's crashed to the earth's surface."

"Whatever," Patrick dismissed with a hand flap. "I hate science."

"This meteorite is from outer space and may be millions of years old!" Lindsay said.

Brian posed next to the object, puffing out his bare chest, his arms extending like a TV model. "Maybe I'll get my picture on the cover of *National Geographic* for discovering this meteor!"

"*Meteorite*," Lindsay said with exasperation. She turned to her grandfather. "Is this what you saw crash into the lake twenty years ago?"

Orville had been strangely quiet while they inspected the find. He walked around it, concentrating, and then took off his cap. He scratched his head. "No doubt about it. That's what I saw. It hit the water glowing like a nuclear reactor."

"It's no longer glowing," Patrick said.

"It's cooled off after all these years," Lindsay said. She grinned and gave her grandfather a hug. "I always knew you saw something real, and now we know what it was!"

Orville replaced his cap and shook his head. "Listen to me, you foolish kids! Put this thing back in the lake right now! Nothing good will come from this!"

CHAPTER SIX

From the outside Orville Milford's workshop showed the same age and neglect as his house. The peaked roof was bowed in the center, decaying leaves clogged its rusty gutters, and small trees sprouted from the crumbling stone of the foundation. Cam suspected one strong gust of wind could bring the whole sagging structure crashing down.

Inside the workshop resembled Doctor Frankenstein's laboratory. The square space was a crowded chessboard of motorized saws, grinders, and drills. Metal-working and wood-working machines jockeyed against one another like opposing soldiers. Manila curls of wood shavings and the gray grit of ground metal littered the concrete floor like the debris of battle. The walls were paneled with brown pegboard holding orderly rows of every conceivable tool. Shelves and bins organized boxes, crates, and glass jars. Semi-finished projects were scattered over every workbench.

Under the garish florescent light, Cam, Lindsay, Brian, and Patrick stood in a circle examining the meteorite resting on the table in the center of the room. Orville stood behind, a distant gaze on his face, his hand absentmindedly rubbing the stubble on his chin.

Cleaned of its coating of gray mud, the meteorite was large, ovoid, and greenish-brown. Small perturbations dotted its surface like warts. Black streaks ran from one end to the other.

They had moved it inside because Lindsay wanted to examine their find according to proper scientific protocol and believed her grandfather's tools would be useful. Brian hoped to model for newspapers and magazines and thought the windowless workshop was perfect to protect their exclusive story. Patrick, as always, went along with anything Brian said. Orville just wanted the thing hidden from view, his paranoia having grown more intense since the meteorite was brought to the surface.

Cam was an innocent bystander because he, unlike the others, had no agenda. However he shared Lindsay's enthusiasm, looking over the meteorite, wondering what they were going to do next: scientific examination or photo shoot?

Patrick sighed. "Is it going to *do* something, or what?"

"Like conquer the world? Turn us into zombies?" Brian said, at which both he and Patrick laughed.

"Don't be silly!" Lindsay scolded. "This is a scientific find, not some stupid movie."

"It's all pretty *stupid* to me now," Brian said. "Let's call the paper and get our photos taken with the thing. What are we waiting for?"

Lindsay shook her head. "You'll get your chance. First I want to do a proper scientific assessment. This meteorite may be left over from the formation of the solar system. It could be billions of years old."

"Wow," Cam said. "That's really old."

"I learned about meteorites in science class," Lindsay said. She ran her hand along its black markings. "These scorch marks are evidence of its fiery entry through Earth's atmosphere." She then scratched its surface with a fingernail. "Strangely, it doesn't feel like iron. Most meteorites are made of iron."

"Did you learn that in science class, too?" Patrick asked.

"As a matter of fact, I did," Lindsay said. "You were probably smoking in the boys' room during that lesson."

Patrick pulled a pack of Marlboros from his pocket and hammered them against his palm.

Orville immediately snatched the cigarettes out of the boy's hand. "No smoking in my workshop!"

"Whatever, Gramps," Patrick snorted. "Give me back my lights!"

Orville reluctantly returned the red-and-white package. "There are flammable solvents in here. Do you wanna burn the place down?"

Patrick rolled his eyes as he headed for the door. "I'll be outside."

"Delinquent," Orville said under his breath as Patrick exited.

Lindsay grabbed a tape measure. "Help me get its measurements."

Cam and Brain stepped forward to assist at the same time, bumping elbows. Brian gave Cam a sharp look. "I can do this," Brian said.

Lindsay smiled and gave Cam the tape measure. "Do it together." She grabbed a yellow notepad from the workbench. "I'll take notes."

Cam and Brian measured the length and width of the meteorite and reported the numbers to Lindsay, who wrote them on her notepad as the tip of her tongue protruded from her soft, pink lips. "I wish we had a scale to weigh it," she said.

"I guess about 200 pounds," Brian said. "I think I lifted about 150 and Sport here lifted about 50."

"I lifted my share!" Cam protested.

"Bull!" Brian said.

"You two cut it out," Lindsay insisted. "I'm trying to work here. The meteorite's probably hollow or it would weigh much more."

Cam and Brian glared at one another while Lindsay continued her examination of the meteorite, making detailed observations that she promptly recorded on her notepad.

After a few minutes, Brian yawned and leaned against the counter. He grabbed one of Orville's ratchets and twirled it around absentmindedly, making an annoying *click-click-click* sound.

The old man snatched the ratchet away. "Don't play with my tools!"

"Sure," Brian said with a smirk as Orville replaced the ratchet on its pegboard hook.

Lindsay paced around the meteorite. "Mr. Russell should look at this."

"Who's Mr. Russell?" Cam asked.

"My science teacher," Lindsay said. "Don't worry. He's cool."

Orville frowned. "I don't want no science teacher poking around here. He'll probably try to convince me this ain't an alien spacecraft!"

Lindsay touched his arm kindly. "Now, Grandpa. This isn't a UFO. It's a meteorite. It's what you saw twenty years ago, remember?"

He pulled his arm away from her. "It's not just a rock! It's alien! It's got strange powers!"

"Grandpa, please calm down."

Cam looked at the meteorite, wondering if it were responsible for his underwater panic attack, his strange feelings, and his unusual nightmares. It didn't seem likely. It was a large, dull, lifeless rock.

"Mr. Russell knows all about astronomy," Lindsay said. "He can help us with our analysis."

Brian was fiddling with a long rasp, acting as if he were using it to file his nails. "Let's call the paper. It's not too late to get into tomorrow's edition."

"No reporters," Orville said, frowning. "No strangers around here. We need to keep this secret."

"Why are you so paranoid?" Brian asked.

"I'm not paranoid," Orville insisted, cocking his shoulders back. "People have been watching me for years, ever since I saw the UFO."

"Mr. Russell can keep a secret," Lindsay said.

"You're such a teacher's pet," Brian added acidly.

She grimaced. "I am *not*. There's nothing wrong with being a good student. That's something you wouldn't know anything about, Brian. Mr. Russell's a great teacher and we need some expert advice." She looked at Cam. "What do you think, Cam? Don't you think a science teacher could help us?"

"Definitely! We can use all the help we can get."

"Great! At least someone around here is interested in science," Lindsay said while glowering at Brian. She looked at the wall clock next to the dust-covered AM radio. "It's been a busy day. I'll get Mr. Russell to come over tomorrow to help the investigation"

"It's just a rock," Brian said. "What's there to investigate?"

"There's something strange about this meteorite," Lindsay said, "and Mr. Russell's smart enough to help us figure it out."

*   *   *

The clock's LED display was washed out in the bright sunshine streaming through the French doors of Cam's bedroom. He shaded the numbers with his hand to make out the time. Nearly eleven o'clock.

He had overslept. He was supposed to meet Lindsay and Mr. Russell at the workshop an hour ago. What had happened to him? Still in a mental fog, he kicked off the sheets and sat on the side of the bed. His bare feet ruffled paper on the floor and kicked a pen toward the dresser.

His dream journal.

He was exhausted from tossing and turning all night, haunted by more strange dreams. He had recorded them in his dream journal, including the nightmare with the six-legged spider creature. He had seen the same creature during his panic attack while diving in the lake.

Cam went to the shower, letting the hot water wash away the grime in his mind until he was thinking clearly again. He quickly dressed and took one last look around the room. Spying the dream journal on the floor, he grabbed it and stuffed it into his backpack. Lindsay thought highly of Mr. Russell. Perhaps the science teacher could help him, tell him he wasn't going crazy.

A black SUV with a personalized license plate reading SCI TCHR was parked next to the tow truck when Cam arrived at Orville's. A yellow sticker on the SUV's windshield read *LTHS – Staff.* Mr. Russell must already be inside the workshop. Brian's Mustang was not in sight. He and Patrick had apparently found something better to do, and Cam was thankful for their short attention spans.

He leaned his bike against the workshop. Its wooden double doors were closed, so he knocked. After a moment, Orville asked suspiciously from inside who was there.

Cam identified himself.

"Are you the kid from Chicago or the Sheriff's smart-ass son?" Orville demanded.

At least he wasn't the only one who thought Brian Little was a smart ass.

Lindsay told her grandfather to stop being difficult and open the door. The old man did so, peeking from behind. His eyes darted left and right across the overgrown surroundings of his yard. "Are you alone?"

Cam nodded and Orville motioned him inside, holding the door ajar barely enough for him to squeeze through.

Lindsay and Mr. Russell stood by the meteorite. "Cam!" she said, her face brightening. "You're late! What happened?"

"Sorry, I'll explain later," Cam said, sliding off his backpack and depositing it on the bench next to a row of old mayonnaise jars filled with various nuts, bolts, and fasteners.

Lindsay introduced him to Mr. Russell, who was younger than expected, perhaps about thirty. He didn't look like a science teacher either—not bald and frumpy, no shirt pocket stuffed with pens and pencils, no stooped posture from reading thick textbooks or squinting through microscopes. Mr. Russell was tall, slim, and stood arrow-straight. He had a full head of coal-black hair. He was dressed in khaki shorts, a blue Polo, and sandals. He looked rather cool for a teacher.

The teacher smiled warmly when he shook Cam's hand. His grip exuded strength and confidence. He had a commanding presence in the workshop just as he probably did in the classroom. "Nice to meet you, Cam."

Cam grunted a response. He should have been more articulate, but he was never smooth with introductions—not like Lindsay, who performed such things effortlessly. "What have I missed?" Cam asked. "Fill me in."

"Actually, we were just getting started," Mr. Russell said.

Orville nervously adjusted his NASCAR cap and stood with his hands on his thin hips, staring at the meteorite. "I detect a change in this thing. The aliens are up to something in there."

"Oh, Grandpa, don't be ridiculous," Lindsay said. She turned and smiled at Cam. "Mr. Russell was telling us about erratics."

"Erratics?" Cam asked.

"Glacial artifacts," Mr. Russell answered. "Large boulders embedded in glaciers and transported far from their origin. They don't resemble typical rocks from the area. That might explain why this rock looks so odd. It's not from around here."

"That's for sure," Orville said. "It's from outer space."

"Not necessarily," Mr. Russell said. "The northern half of this state was scoured by glaciers 15,000 years ago. The ice sheet scooped out Lake Tecumseh, deposited rich topsoil, and left behind odd rocks in strange places, such as this one."

"So you think this rock might be from Canada?" Cam asked. "Why can't it be a meteorite?" He glanced at Orville. "After all, we have an eyewitness that it fell from the sky."

Orville nodded his head, looking satisfied at the recognition. "I saw it hit the lake twenty years ago. It's as plain as day in my memory. I was fishing in my boat, when—"

Mr. Russell interrupted, preventing Orville's launch into yet another dramatic recounting of his experience. "An object this size would've made a tremendous impact crater, something like a small atomic explosion. You wouldn't have lived to tell about it."

"It came down on its own power," Orville added. "It wasn't a shooting star striking the lake like a bomb."

Lindsay looked at Cam with a half smile of amusement. She was exasperated at her grandfather's fantastic stories.

Mr. Russell rubbed his chin thoughtfully. "What we need are scientific facts."

"That's why I asked you to come, Mr. Russell," Lindsay said. "We should know what this rock is before we alert the media. Is it a meteorite or a glacial erratic?"

"Or something else completely unknown," Orville said.

Mr. Russell studied the object and then turned his attention back to the three of them as if they were his students. "Well, let's start with the meteorite theory. What do you know about meteorites?"

"They're rocks from outer space," Lindsay said eagerly. "There are three main types depending on their composition: stony, stony iron, and iron meteorites."

Mr. Russell smiled. "Very good, Lindsay." He ran his fingers over the object's surface. "There's no glassy fusion crust, which forms due to the friction with Earth's atmosphere. So I don't think this is a stony meteorite."

"What about the iron type of meteorite?" Lindsay asked.

Mr. Russell turned toward Orville. "Do you have a magnet in here, Mr. Milford?"

Orville scowled. "Of course I got magnets. I use them all the time to pick up the damn little bolts and stuff that always roll away when you're fixing something." He went to a drawer and fished out a small magnet attached with duct tape to a wooden ruler and handed it to the teacher.

"Thanks." Mr. Russell took the makeshift tool and approached the large egg-shaped object on the center table. Everyone moved in closer to get a good look. "If it's made out of metal, the magnet will be attracted to it."

The science teacher had a gift for showmanship, probably honed from years of experiments in front of students. He held the ruler end and slowly and steadily moved the magnet end toward the rock. When the magnet finally met the meteorite it was as if he had brought together two inert pieces of wood. No repulsive or attractive forces were detectable.

"There's no ferromagnetism," Mr. Russell concluded. "The magnet would've stuck like glue if it was composed of iron or nickel."

"Let me see," Lindsay asked. Mr. Russell handed her the magnet and she repeated the experiment with similar results. "You're right. There's no magnetic attraction at all."

"That proves nothing," Orville dismissed as he snatched the magnet and ruler combination and dropped it into the drawer and slammed it shut. "I didn't say it was a meteorite. It's something else from outer space. I saw it come down."

"No offense, Mr. Milford, but there's no way we can prove this object is what you saw twenty years ago," Mr. Russell said.

"You think I saw ball lightning, too?" Orville challenged.

"I didn't say that. We just can't prove the connection. I think this is a glacial erratic, an odd rock that was lying for thousands of years at the bottom of the lake until you hauled it to the surface."

"What about the scorch marks?" Lindsay asked, referring to the black streaks resembling Indian war paint.

"Probably from an ancient forest fire," Mr. Russell said.

"It's not very heavy," Lindsay said. "How do you explain that?"

"Maybe it's hollow, like a geode with a crystalline interior," Mr. Russell said.

Lindsay sighed. "A glacial erratic isn't as exciting as a meteorite. We certainly won't get any media coverage now."

"Brian will be very disappointed," Cam said. "He was already planning his own reality TV show."

"It's still an interesting discovery," Mr. Russell said. "We can run a series of geological experiments to determine what kind of rock it is."

"How do we do that?" Lindsay asked.

"I need to get some materials from the science lab," Mr. Russell said. "First we'll categorize its hardness on the Mohs Scale."

Cam snickered. "You mean Moe did something other than beat up Larry and Curly?"

Lindsay didn't appreciating the joke. "Cam! We're trying to learn something here."

"Sorry. Everyone's just so serious."

"Science *is* serious," Mr. Russell said, smiling, "but it can also be *fun*. The Mohs Scale is a way to categorize the relative hardness of a mineral by scratching it with other materials of known hardness. Since it takes a harder material to scratch a softer one, a specific hardness value can be assigned."

"Interesting," Lindsay said. "Will I learn about the Mohs Scale senior year?"

Mr. Russell nodded. "Yes. The scale goes from one to ten. The higher the number, the harder the mineral. Number one is talc, which is very soft, and number ten is diamond, which is the hardest mineral known to man." Mr. Russell then recited from memory the sequence of ten minerals comprising the scale.

Cam sighed. The day was beginning to feel too much like science class. He had no interest in the minerals making up the Mohs Hardness Scale. If he ever wanted to know, he'd use the Internet. Why memorize when you could *Google*?

"I'll get my geology kit from the lab," Mr. Russell said. "It's got all the standard minerals."

"Wait a minute," Lindsay said. "Grandpa, don't you have a diamond-tipped drill bit?"

Orville furrowed his brow. "In that package by the drill. Why?"

Lindsay went to the bench and grabbed the power drill and installed the drill bit. "You don't have to leave, Mr. Russell. We already have diamond right here."

"A diamond drill will cut through about anything," Mr. Russell said. "A diamond's four times harder than the next mineral down on the scale. This won't tell us how the rock ranks in hardness."

"But it's a start, and I'm eager." She donned safety goggles and plugged the drill into a heavy-duty extension cord and approached the object and revved the drill as if it were a race car waiting at the starting line.

"Don't touch it!" Orville shouted.

Lindsay froze. "Why not?"

"We should leave it alone! We should put it back in the lake!"

"We're not doing that," Lindsay said. "We worked too hard to bring it here." She revved the drill and poked its diamond-coated bit against the rocky object and leaned in with all her strength, her pink tongue protruding from between her lips.

The whine of the power tool filled the shop. After a few seconds, smoke poured from the straining drill. Lindsay pulled back and dropped the drill on the bench. "Whew!" she said, waving her hands in the air. "It overheated!" She removed her goggles and crouched to inspect the hole in the rock. She frowned.

"What is it?" Cam asked.

"It didn't even scratch it!"

"That's impossible!" Mr. Russell said. "The only thing a diamond can't scratch is something that's harder—like another diamond!"

"What?!" Cam said. "Another diamond?"

"That can't be true!" Lindsay said. "Look at the size of this thing. It must be a million carats!"

Mr. Russell touched the object, shaking his head. "I don't think it's a diamond, exactly. It's just harder than a diamond. This doesn't make sense."

Orville smirked at the teacher. "Of course it does. It's alien. Constructed of some advanced material far beyond our technology."

"Constructed?" Mr. Russell said with a shake of his head. "It wasn't constructed, Mr. Milford."

"Then how do you explain it?" Orville asked.

"I can't," Mr. Russell admitted.

"We've discovered something really special," Lindsay gushed. "This is going to get a lot of publicity!"

"We're going to be rich!" Cam said, his eyes glistening. "Maybe I'll be able to buy a car with the money—something really fast!"

"This will be great for my college applications!" Lindsay said. "I might get into the Ivy League with a discovery like this under my belt! I can't wait to post it on *Facebook!*"

"Now, kids, don't get all excited," Mr. Russell said. "I wouldn't be spending your earnings yet."

"You're right," Lindsay said. "We need to think logically."

Mr. Russell glanced at his watch and headed for the door in a hurry. "Uh-oh, it's time for my Driver's Ed class. Today I show accident videos from the State Police. You know, to scare young drivers into some common sense."

Lindsay grimaced. "Oh, Mr. Russell!"

Mr. Russell paused at the door. "I wouldn't IM, e-mail, tweet, post, or announce to the world what you've found until you have more scientific facts."

"Yes, of course," Lindsay said.

After a cheery good-bye, Mr. Russell left. Cam listened to the gravel crunch in the driveway as his SUV departed.

Lindsay circled around the rock. "Wow, I don't believe it! This thing's harder than a diamond."

Cam moved to her side. "What do we do now?"

"I guess we wait, like Mr. Russell said. If this *is* harder than a diamond, it's going to be big news."

"Do you think we'll get on TV?"

"I'm positive! TV, Internet, everywhere! This is going viral!"

Orville interrupted their excitement, handing Cam his backpack. "Put this somewhere else, kid, it's blocking my tools," he grumbled.

Cam wanted to tell the sour old man off, but as he took the backpack he remembered he had placed his dream journal inside. "Oh, I forgot to show Mr. Russell this!"

"What?" Lindsay asked.

He unzipped the backpack and pulled out the notebook. "My dream journal."

"For recording your dreams?" Lindsay asked, intrigued. "I didn't know you did that."

Cam shrugged. "My dreams have been rather interesting lately, I guess. I thought it would help to write about them."

She reached for the journal. "May I take a look?"

He was afraid he'd be opening a door into his soul that he was not quite ready to share if he gave the journal to her. What if she thought he was crazy? What if she saw his drawings and read his notes and feared he was a psycho? He didn't know what to think of the troubling images that tore through his mind each evening. What would she think?

Lindsay smiled at him coyly as she gently tugged on the journal, her eyes the color of cinnamon. Instinctively, his grip relaxed and she took the notebook.

She leafed through the pages, studying them intensely while remaining expressionless. Then she turned to the page with the sketch of the six-legged, spider-like creature with the faceted, faceless head. Her eyes widened with astonishment.

Embarrassed, Cam let his gaze drop to his feet. Suddenly the wood shavings on the shop floor became more interesting to watch.

"What is this?" Lindsay asked, holding the journal open on her lap to show the drawing of the creature.

"I dunno. Something from my dreams. Do you think I'm crazy?"

She shook her head. "No, of course not! You're just having bad dreams. I wouldn't worry about it."

"But what do they mean?"

She wrapped one arm around him. "Nothing! Maybe you're just stressed about being away from home. Who can figure out their dreams anyway? Aren't they just abstract images that make no sense?"

Now she sounded like Uncle Gary. In any case, he was relieved she was being supportive and nonjudgmental. He didn't know what he would've done if she had responded negatively to his dream journal. He stood next to her, feeling comforted by her light touch.

On the other side of the shop, Orville watched them with a sneer and wagged his finger as he approached. "Keep your hands where I can see them! This is a workshop, not a make-out section of a movie theater."

Lindsay rolled her eyes and pulled away. "Oh, Grandpa!"

Orville stopped next to them and glanced at the drawing of the six-legged creature in Cam's open dream journal. "That's a crazy picture," he said, pointing.

Cam didn't like Orville using the word *crazy*. Cam was feeling pretty sensitive at the moment.

"Don't make fun of him," Lindsay said.

"I'm not making fun," Orville said, wiping his wrinkled hands on a rag. "I've seen that thing, too."

"You have?" Cam asked, blinking.

"Sure. All the time," Orville said. "I'll show you. It's outside."

"What? Outside?" Cam blurted. He suddenly broke into a cold sweat. He hated facing the six-legged thing in his mind, and now Orville was saying it was outside?

Had his imagined monster come to life?

How could it be?

CHAPTER SEVEN

Orville excitedly led Cam and Lindsay outside the workshop. "It's this way," he said, beckoning them to follow him into the woods.

Cam didn't know where Orville was taking them, but it had something to do with the strange, six-legged creature that Cam had drawn in his dream journal. Where had Orville seen the drawing before? What was he going to show them? Cam's steps were sluggish. Orville and Lindsay were both ahead of him.

Like intrepid explorers of the Amazon, they marched through the overgrown woods down a narrow dirt path while bending leafy branches out of their way. After going a dozen yards, they stepped into a sun-splashed, grassy clearing.

Cam froze.

An abstract sculpture stood before him, about as tall as a man. Constructed of a mish-mash of corroded metal pieces, the artwork was a three-dimensional image of the six-legged spider creature from his nightmares!

The construction's legs were long metal rods, each bent inward to form rudimentary knees. Its tubular body was a rust-streaked, old metal cylinder. Its complicated, almost-circular head was fashioned from triangular slices of tin welded together.

Orville raised his arm toward the sculpture and said proudly,

"What do you think of my creation?"

Lindsay stood with her mouth agape. "I didn't know you were an artist."

"I didn't either until recently. "I just built this two weeks ago."

Cam was in disbelief that Orville had constructed a three-dimensional facsimile of the same creature from his dreams. He approached the sculpture slowly, shaking back nervousness while taking in the detail of its construction. He counted 20 pieces of tin comprising its head. Although he couldn't properly draw the polyhedral head in two dimensions in his dream journal, he knew 20 was the right number of sides in three dimensions.

Cam also knew Orville had accurately depicted the creature without eyes, a nose, or a mouth. The creature had no face, and although it moved like a living thing, it more properly resembled a geometric pattern fabricated by a machine.

"This looks like what you drew in your dream journal," Lindsay said to Cam.

"It's *exactly* like it," Cam said, running his fingertips across the metal, trying to understand the strange connection he apparently shared with Orville.

"What a coincidence!" Lindsay said.

"How can you say that?" Cam said. "What are the odds he'd build a sculpture of the same thing I sketched in my dream journal?"

"Maybe it's something from a TV show that just stuck in your minds."

"I don't think so," Cam said.

"What else could it be?" Lindsay challenged as she folded her arms across her chest. "ESP? A mind meld between the two of you? There's no scientific proof such things exist."

"Nor aliens, but your whole town exploits them for profit regardless," Cam retorted.

She stepped back, her brown eyes boring an unfamiliar harshness into him.

He realized he had snapped at her without reason. He felt unnerved and exposed by the revelation that he and Orville shared the same bizarre image, that they were joined by some kind of unusual psychic connection. At loss for an explanation, he was frustrated.

"Let's calm down and collect our senses," Lindsay suggested, revealing her usual grace once again. "We're just edgy."

"I'm sorry," Cam said. "This is just too weird."

Orville took off his cap and scratched his head. "ESP—that's what it is. I see this creature in my mind when I'm out on the lake. The aliens are sending me ESP signals."

"For what purpose?" Cam asked.

"I don't know," the old man answered. "But I felt compelled to build this model. Like they directed me to do it."

"You put a lot of work into it," Lindsay said.

"I just welded and bolted together some junk lying around," Orville admitted. "It was hard to assemble the head though, with all those angles and surfaces. It took a lot of welding."

"I can tell," Lindsay said.

"It's a picture of one of the aliens from inside their spaceship," Orville said.

"Oh, Grandpa. We didn't recover an alien spaceship, just a rock. There are no aliens inside beaming ESP signals to you."

"You should be careful," Orville insisted, "Treat these aliens with *respect*. For 20 years I've treated them with respect, because I know they're dangerous."

"You're being dramatic," Lindsay said.

"You think I go out on my boat every night for fun? No, I go out to placate them. I let them talk to me. It calms them down when they enter my thoughts. That's *respect*. You kids are willy-nilly about the whole thing, but you don't know what you're doing."

"What do you mean?" Cam asked.

"You've hauled them to the surface. What's going to happen

now? What if you've angered them?" Orville pointed to the metal sculpture. White streaks of bird droppings coated the head. "What if you've angered *that*?"

Cam felt a chill shudder through his spine.

Lindsay reached out and gently touched Orville's sleeve. "You're all worked up. Let's get your medicine."

He shrugged away. "I don't need no medicine!"

She cupped his elbow and led him away from the sculpture. "Come on, let's go."

Lindsay and Orville stepped from the clearing. Cam remained a minute longer, staring at the metal monstrosity. He felt as if he were staring at one of his nightmares come to life.

Upon arriving at Orville's house, Lindsay immediately sat the old man into his favorite chair in the living room facing the sparkling blue waters of the lake. While Cam opened the blinds to let in light, Lindsay crossed to the kitchen. She returned with a medicine bottle and a glass of water and handed them to her grandfather. "You're not supposed to get excited."

Orville swallowed the pill and took a sip of water. "I'm not excited," he insisted while drumming his fingers on the armrest.

Lindsay smiled. "Mom told me to keep an eye on you."

"Yeah, yeah," he grumbled, leaning his head back and closing his eyes.

"Why don't you rest while I chat with Cam." She left her grandfather's side and joined Cam in the doorway. "Let's go back outside."

Cam was happy to be out of the musty house into the fresh summer air. "Is he going to be all right?" he asked, blinking into the sunlight streaming through the tree leaves.

Lindsay brushed back her brown hair and smiled. "He's fine. He just needs to take it easy. I worry about him. It gets especially bad this time each summer."

"Why?"

"Because of UFO Days. They start next week, you know."

Uncle Gary and Aunt Ellen had talked about the festival, which was structured around Lake Tecumseh's notoriety as a supposed target for extraterrestrial spacecraft and alien visitations.

"The emphasis on UFOs gets Grandpa worked up," Lindsay explained. "After all, his sighting started the craze 20 years ago."

"Imagine that," Cam said.

"Last year the mayor tried to convince him to be the Grand Marshal of the parade. He said no. He thought they'd make fun of him."

"What do you think about his sculpture?" Cam asked, gesturing in its general direction. "I think it's like my nightmares. Those images don't come from *inside* my head. They feel like they come from *outside.*"

"ESP? Now you sound like Grandpa."

"You think I'm crazy, too?"

As soon as Cam added the *too*, he knew he had made a horrible mistake.

A dark cloud fell upon Lindsay's previously bright face. Her perky, bow-shaped lips pursed into a nasty frown. She turned away from him in a huff. "I don't think my grandpa's *crazy!*" she snapped. "After all you've learned, I thought you'd be more sensitive!"

"I'm sorry. I didn't mean that." He wanted to reach out and hug her so badly, but she stood with her back toward him.

She grabbed the handle to the screen door. "I'm going inside. I'll see you later."

The screen door slammed as she disappeared into the house, leaving him alone.

What he said was stupid, but why were girls so difficult? One slip of the tongue and he got in trouble. Talking to girls reminded him of walking through a cactus-crowded desert. A magnificent, beautiful landscape, but every step was perilous. One false move, one slip of the tongue, and one got pricked by sharp thorns.

And boy did he just get pricked.

What was wrong with him? Why couldn't he think before he spoke?

He mentally kicked himself. He deserved it.

*   *   *

After his argument with Lindsay, Cam wasn't his normal self. He liked the girl a lot, and didn't want her angry at him. He considered calling her to apologize again, but knew he should let her cool off a little.

So he moped around the house and tried to busy himself with other things.

Uncle Gary and Aunt Ellen hosted a barbecue for neighbors, and though Cam was in a surly mood, he forced himself to be sociable. The juicy spare ribs, tangy cole slaw, and buttery corn-on-the-cob made it a little easier for him to hang with the adults for a few hours. They ended the event watching the sun set over the lake, which finally had turned peaceful after a long summer day of noisy boaters and skiers. The tranquility was short lived, as swarms of mosquitoes soon emerged from the woods, forcing everyone inside.

Approaching midnight, Cam sat in front of the computer, wondering if he should IM Lindsay. He kneaded his knuckles with his palm and decided to wait.

Maybe, if he were lucky, she had calmed down and sent him an e-mail. He checked his mailbox, but it was empty.

He sighed. He should just go to bed, but he wasn't sleepy. Plus he wasn't ready for more strange nightmares. Instead, he played on the computer, wasting time.

He watched some You-Tube videos then lazily surfed the Internet, his eyes growing bleary from the silly and inconsequential information he found.

Eventually he ended up in a chat room devoted to UFOs. He

didn't recall how he had gotten there; it was as if his computer mouse had moved on its own power like the tear-shaped game piece on a Ouija board.

For some time he read the back-and-forth dialogue on the UFO chat room screen, amazed by the strident participants debating government cover-ups, alien abductions, and cow mutilations. The site was like a national psychiatrist's couch, a safe place where people bared their souls and received support from like-minded people.

Cam found the chat room rather amusing, picturing lonely geeks in far-off cities tapping away at their keyboards, spouting their personal UFO theories like the revealed gospel.

He thought about the rock they had retrieved from the bottom of Lake Tecumseh. After all that anticipation and work hauling the thing to the surface, it was just a big, warty, green rock.

He didn't find it too interesting; except for the possibility they might get their photos published in the newspaper. However, Lindsay and Mr. Russell were excited about the discovery, discussing whether it was a meteorite or a glacial erratic. They had performed experiments and concluded it was as hard as a diamond. That discovery, Cam admitted, was curious.

Meanwhile, Orville continued to mumble his warnings about the danger of messing with something they knew nothing about.

The postings in the UFO chat room had grown stale, and none of the participants seemed very interested in any of the topics. Cam thought his story was worth discussing. If he embellished a little, he would get the UFO enthusiasts excited. The sci-fi nerds would have a late night thrill debating something new. He wanted to perk up their Mr. Spock ears.

With a mischievous smirk, he typed into the public forum:

ExileIN17: we fished a UFO out of lake tecumseh

Certainly this would trump the other stories on the message

board.   At least his tale was partially true.   None of the other members of the forum had actually found a UFO.   Of course, only Orville Milford really thought the rock from the bottom of Lake Tecumseh was a UFO, but the disembodied screen names out in Internet-land didn't need to know any better.

A minute passed before someone responded:

KlaatuJr: but you should have seen the one that got away

Bad joke, Cam thought.   For some time he had watched *KlaatuJr* bullying others on the message board with his superior attitude and poor humor.   Apparently it was now Cam's turn to be the victim. Unperturbed, he typed a response, which precipitated a cascade of others to chime in:

KSUchick3: where the hell is lake tecumseh?
ExileIN17:   Indiana
KlaatuJr: figures . . .
Jim0710:   what does it look like?
ExileIN17:   like a rock, size of large barrel
KlaatuJr::   not too exciting. maybe it *is* a rock
KSUchick3: why do u think it's a UFO if it looks like a rock?
ExileIN17:   cuz it crashed into lake 20 years ago. I have an eyewitness
KSUchick3: it's not a UFO it's a meteor
KlaatuJr: No a meteorite. didn't u learn in school? duh.

So Lindsay wasn't the only one who split hairs about *meteors* and *meteorites*.

The conversation on the message board continued in a similar vein for several minutes.   Cam tried to explain what they had found, attempting to spice it up to no avail.   In truth it was a rather dull discovery.

Nevertheless *Jim0710* and *KSUchick3* were excited, ranking Cam's discovery in the same category as stories about crop circles, maniacal alien physicians, and overnight trips to Vega.

But *KlaatuJr* flippantly dismissed everything Cam typed. Cam grew weary of defending himself from *KlaatuJr's* annoying attacks and exited the UFO chat room, feeling exhausted by the vacuous exchange.

Unfortunately almost all chat rooms left him feeling the same way, whether they were devoted to UFOs or not. Something about the medium brought out the worst in people. Bullies thrived in its anonymity.

In any case, the diversion had made Cam tired, and he was now ready for bed. Before turning off the computer, he decided to send Lindsay an e-mail. It was short, just a note to say he was sorry and he hoped to see her soon. He figured that was the best thing for him to do.

He then went upstairs to his bedroom, pausing to glance through the French doors to the lake outside. Its waters were placid and empty, appearing like a black pool in the darkness. He wondered if Orville Milford had made his nightly pilgrimage to commune with the aliens, even though they had fished the mysterious UFO from the lake.

Perhaps now Orville's vigil would be over the rock in his workshop. At least no one would have to worry about an old man on the lake all alone.

Cam sat on the corner of the bed and glanced at his dream journal on the night stand, positioned for another night of data entry. He hoped he didn't have nightmares again, but they always came anyway.

* * *

Aunt Ellen sat at the kitchen table, humming softly as she snapped green beans into a glass bowl, a bright square of sunlight illuminating the tile floor next to her. Cam stopped to kiss her forehead as he headed for the backdoor.

"Where are you going in such a hurry?" she asked, looking over the top of her glasses, a mannerism Cam thought added about 20 years to her age.

"Me and Lindsay are going to Midgeville."

"*Lindsay and I*," his aunt corrected. "And Midgeville? Whatever for?"

He paused at the refrigerator and pulled out a cold soda. "A man there claims UFOs fly over his farm all the time. I'm helping Lindsay's research for her UFO book."

She cast him a sideways glance as she rhythmically snapped the beans. "Stay out of trouble."

He said goodbye and bounded out the door, excited Lindsay had invited him. She had not stayed angry for long. As he rode his bike toward her house, he resolved to *think first* and *speak later*. He hoped he could keep his resolution. It was so easy to slip up.

She was waiting when he rode up, her bike leaning against the porch steps. "Hi, Cam!" she called with a cheery wave.

"Hi, Linsday," he said, feeling awkward. "I'm sorry about—"

She brushed her hands across the air. "Don't worry! I know you didn't mean it." Her eyes locked on his for several charged moments. Then she glanced away and mounted her bike. "Are you ready for a long ride? About ten miles?"

"Sure! I'm happy to help."

"At least you're interested in this stuff. Brian thinks it's stupid."

Cam didn't like her mentioning her boyfriend, but at least she was criticizing him. She had referred to her relationship with Brian as *past its prime*.

He hoped to learn more during their bike trip. Maybe she liked him instead of Brian, for the clues were there. Did he have a chance with her? He needed to find out, but he had to wait for the right moment to begin such a sensitive discussion.

Think first and speak later, Cam reminded himself as they set out.

They rode through town and then cut through Grissom Park. Preparations were being made for UFO Days. An orange mesh fence marked the boundary of the festival grounds, which consumed the open grass of the softball diamonds and most of the main parking lot. City workers, carnival ride operators, and food vendors were busy setting the stage for the town's biggest annual festival amid the *beep-beep-beep* of backing delivery trucks. A huge red and white striped tent was being erected in the center of the activity.

"Wow! Look at this!" Cam exclaimed, never expecting a small town would invest so much effort. His pedaling instinctively slowed as he gawked.

"It gets bigger every year!" Lindsay gushed. "Look at the Ferris Wheel!"

The wheel towered over the park and the other thrill rides: a *Merry-Go-Round*, a *Tilt-A-Whirl*, a large, black *Octopus*, and others less familiar.

"This festival's a really big deal, isn't it?" Cam said.

Lindsay nodded. "There's a dance on Saturday. They crown the honorary Space King and Queen. It's called the UFO Dance."

"You're kidding."

She grinned. "No, it's for real. They've done it for years."

The two of them left Lake Tecumseh behind and pedaled through the farmland toward the tiny hamlet of Midgeville. The intense sun beat down on their backs as they traveled westward. The corn was taller than Cam, forming a green gauntlet on both sides of the road. The crop had grown quickly since his arrival in Indiana.

A few battered pick-ups passed by, but otherwise they had the blacktop to themselves. They rode in silence for several minutes until Lindsay said, "Let's take a quick detour." She abruptly turned off the road onto a dirt path leading toward a line of trees in the distance.

Cam followed behind her. "Where are we going?"

"You'll see."

The trail had deep ruts from previous bikers, which the summer sun had baked into permanent scars. The ride was jarring, and weeds brushed against Cam's bare legs as the trail narrowed as they penetrated deeper into the thickening woods.

The trail terminated at old railroad tracks slicing through the overhanging trees.

Lindsay dismounted her bike. "We'll walk from here to the secret place. Kids go there to hang out."

From the look of the tracks, the railroad hadn't been used in years. Weeds grew between the rusty rails, the creosote timbers were cracked and decaying, and saplings sprouted from the coarse stone bed.

Cam and Lindsay left their bikes and walked atop the rails, balancing themselves like acrobats on high wires, seeing how far they could go before falling off. She was much better at it than he was. He suspected his balance was off since he was distracted by such an intriguing, beautiful girl.

She commented sadly that trains no longer ran through the area and that history was being lost and no one cared. "Across the country, thousands of miles of track are falling into ruin, being sold off, and plowed under. What will we do when we run out of oil and need to use this infrastructure again?"

He didn't answer, not knowing what to add. He loved that she was such a deep thinker, fascinated by how her mind worked. She was much more interesting than the girls he had known in the past. They all seemed so shallow compared to Lindsay.

"Here's the special place," she announced.

A trestle carried the railroad tracks across a deeply cut stream. The bridge's sides were old, heavy iron and splattered with colorful graffiti. Nearly sixty feet long, the trestle was hidden by the encroaching woodland.

"I never would've guessed this was here," Cam said, amazed.

They walked onto the trestle bridging the creek and leaned their elbows on the side and looked down into the water.

"That's Deer Creek," Lindsay said.

Deer Creek was shallow and flowing lazily in the ravine. Bubbles of froth spun in an eddy, perhaps chemical residue from the fertilizers and pesticides applied to the fields upstream. In spite of the pollution, a pair of startled mallards took to the wing upon their arrival.

Cam looked at the metal sides of the bridge, which were tattooed with graffiti messages both innocuous and profane. "Lots of people have been here over the years."

"To drink or do drugs or something."

"Why are we here?"

She looked at him coyly and shrugged. "I thought you'd like to see it."

He studied her. The sun dappled across her beautiful face, illuminating her clear, smooth skin. She averted her eyes and spun away from him, focusing on the corroding metal scrawled with initials of old lovers, some worn and faded; others bright and new.

He followed her gaze to a pair scratched inside a large heart:

B. L. & L. B.

Brian Little and Lindsay Brock!

He clenched his teeth. Brian and Lindsay had been here previously, carving their love into the iron, adding their initials to others from past decades.

Why had she brought him to this *secret place* to gaze upon her initials eternally connected to those of another boy? It seemed almost cruel of her.

But just as the storm clouds coalesced in his heart, a bright beam of sunlight was projected toward him. Looking at the initials, Lindsay said forlornly, "I should try to scratch them out or something."

He blinked. "Huh?"

She turned her back on B. L. & L. B. and faced him. "Those initials—Brian and me. What was I thinking when I did that? It was so stupid!"

"Huh?" he grunted again, unable to formulate any words.

She sighed and looked into the blue sky. "I don't want those initials there anymore! I broke up with Brian."

"You did?" The storm clouds in his heart evaporated.

She looked down onto the floor of the trestle, which was littered with decaying leaves and a layer of brown dust. "It no longer made sense. We're too different."

"I'm sorry," Cam said, which was a bold-faced lie but seemed to be the appropriate thing to say.

She looked up at him and smiled. "Don't be! I'm not!"

He sensed she was not being entirely truthful, that she was forcing a happy face. He decided to allow her the masquerade.

"Brian may be handsome and have a great body, but all he thinks about is himself," she continued, wringing her hands. "He's not interested in the meteorite, the museum, or my UFO research. I need someone who shares my passions."

Cam stood silently, not interested in the description of Brian or the details of the break-up. But he was happy that it had occurred. And she knew he was interested in her UFO passions.

Belatedly he realized she may have mentioned the UFO Dance for a reason. Maybe she wanted him to ask her. He needed to summon his courage. He needed to express his interest.

But before he could muster the strength, she said, "My girlfriends said I was dumb for breaking it off just before the UFO Dance. They said Brian and I made such a cute couple that we might win Space King and Space Queen."

"And you threw *all that* away?" he said, the sarcasm seeping into his voice.

"I sure did! I'm going stag with my girlfriends."

He wished he would've acted faster, but she was the type who moved quickly with her plans. She was ambitious and well organized. He was disappointed, but at least she wasn't going to the dance with Brian.

"The breakup's a good thing because I need to focus on getting my book finished," Lindsay said. Her grin faded to a slight smile, and she stepped closer to him, watching him intently. Her eyelids fluttered. "But I don't know if I can focus."

"Why not?"

"Someone else has my attention now." She kept her stare fixed on him.

She truly *was* interested in him.

He moved closer until they were almost touching on the railroad trestle. He leaned in, and as his eyelids slowly closed, he saw hers doing the same. Their lips touched, and he felt electricity charge through him. He tasted her sweet breath, smelled the floral aroma of her hair, and most of all, felt the tingling pressure of her body against his.

He wrapped his arms around her back and squeezed her closer. Her body folded to conform perfectly to his, as if they were designed to fit together as one. They embraced for several moments, relishing the magic.

Their *First Kiss*.

He wanted to stay in her embrace forever, but in tandem they loosened their grip and gazed into each other's eyes. Her pupils were like pools of swirling chocolate, and just as sweet.

She spoke first. "I've wanted to do that for a long time."

He took a deep breath. "Me, too."

His world was spinning. After collecting his swirling thoughts, he whispered, "I really like you, Lindsay."

"I like you, too."

They fell into each other's arms again and kissed passionately beneath the dappled summer sun of the leafy *secret place*.

Doves cooed on the wing. Cicadas whined in the trees. Deer

Creek gurgled beneath them.

Cam had never realized he would encounter such wonder in Indiana.

* * *

Cam practically floated over his sneakers when he arrived home after spending the day with Lindsay. Leafing through *Good Housekeeping*, Aunt Ellen watched him with a knowing look, pleased that he was so happy.

Uncle Gary was too absorbed in the Colts game on television to pay any attention.

After his relatives went to bed, Cam eagerly went to the computer. He told his Chicago friends what had happened, how he had kissed Lindsay. They were excited for him, but they were occupied with their own social lives and weren't too interested in what was happening in far-off Indiana.

He was about ready to turn off the computer when it announced: *You've got mail!*

Hoping it was from Lindsay, he clicked the mailbox icon. He was surprised by the subject line:

Sender	Subject
MeganC@americaninvestigator.com	Your UFO

Who was *MeganC*? An unfamiliar screen name. She had not been one of the sci-fi nerds on the UFO message board mocking his posts. Perhaps she had been a silent observer.

Like forbidden fruit, the message tempted him. Opening an unsolicited e-mail from a stranger was risky, potentially unleashing an embedded virus. But it wasn't his computer, and surely Uncle Gary knew the importance of installing virus protection software.

Intrigued, Cam opened the e-mail and read:

ExileIN17:

Your story about the UFO you found is very interesting. I would like to interview you about it. Please call me toll free at the number below as soon as possible.

Megan Conrad
American Investigator Magazine

Cam read the message a second time, his mouth hanging open limply. A New York City address and phone number. Had he really been contacted by a reporter? And she wanted to interview him?

Was this legit?

He replayed the silly discussion on the UFO message board, trying to recall exactly what he had revealed about the object from the lake. He had embellished the story, wanting to make it sound interesting, especially because *KlaatuJr* had been so insufferable.

Cam had emphasized the find's alien nature, repeatedly calling it a UFO. What else had he said? He couldn't remember. And now, a New York reporter had contacted him. What should he do?

He did a *Google* search on *American Investigator Magazine* and located their corporate website. The tabloid specialized in fanciful stories like *Face-lift Disaster of the Stars*, *I married Hitler's Clone*, or *Half-Man Half-Fish Caught off Corsica*. He had seen the magazine in the supermarket check-out line many times. Like a terrible auto accident, its garish headlines were often impossible to ignore.

Megan Conrad was one of the magazine's star reporters. Her professionally-posed photo revealed an attractive woman in her early thirties, with a coiffed, no-fuss corporate hairstyle, and a rather serious, although pleasant expression. Beneath her photo was a list of credentials and publishing credits. Her specialty was the strange and paranormal, with an emphasis on UFOs and aliens.

No wonder she wanted to interview him.

He printed the e-mail and turned off the computer. He stepped into the living room and looked out the windows at the quarter moon hanging above the glistening surface of the lake.

Why shouldn't he call Megan Conrad? She had asked him to call her as soon as possible. It was a toll-free number. What harm could there be? Perhaps this was his one chance for fame and fortune.

He snatched the portable phone from the table next to Uncle Gary's recliner and punched in the number.

The phone rang with no answer.

Cam pictured Megan Conrad's empty Manhattan office. It was late at night, and her voice mail would probably pick up any second. What would he say? Would he sound like an idiot?

Better yet, he should probably just hang up—

Then, before he could disconnect, the line clicked and a woman answered. Her voice sounded almost like a recording. "Megan Conrad," she announced.

Speechless, he was suddenly aware of the loud chirping of the crickets outside.

"Hello? Hello?" Megan Conrad asked, annoyance creeping into her voice. "Is there anyone there?"

"Uh...this is Cam Meyer."

"Cam Meyer? Cam Meyer?" He could almost hear the cards shuffling in her mental deck. "Do I know you?"

Feeling like an idiot, Cam remembered she only knew him from the message board. "My screen name's *ExileIN17*. You sent me an e-mail, remember. About a UFO?"

"Oh, of course." Her voice softened. "I'm glad you called. I'm a reporter for *American Investigator Magazine*. I write a lot of stories about people's experiences with UFOs, and I was interested by what you said on the M.B."

"M.B?

"Message Board." She chuckled almost imperceptibly. "I thought all seventeen-year-olds knew this stuff."

"How do you know how old I am?"

"You said so in your posts. Plus your screen name is a dead giveaway."

Megan Conrad apparently paid close attention to the seemingly vapid exchange on the message board. Maybe that was the mark of a good reporter.

"Do you believe all that stuff I said?" Cam asked.

"Are you saying you made it up?"

"No, of course not."

"I didn't think so. I can sniff out a lie, even on the Internet. It comes with being a reporter, I guess. Why don't you tell me everything you know about your discovery?"

Cam quickly rehashed Orville Milford's 20-year-old story, their expedition to retrieve the object, and a description of the rock they had found. This time he did not embellish; nevertheless, Megan Conrad listened attentively.

When Cam had finished, he excitedly asked, "Are you going to do a story on it?"

There was a pause on the line. "To be honest, there's not much of a story there. Although it's mildly interesting, it won't sell newspapers, kid. We need an angle."

"An angle?"

"You know, something that really gets people's attention. All you've got is a moldy 20-year-old story about a fisherman and a UFO, and teenagers and a big rock."

It certainly didn't seem interesting the way she described it.

"What we need is a curse," she said breathlessly. "Perhaps one by one the unwitting discoverers slowly die from freak accidents?"

He swallowed. "That's not true. Nothing like that's happened."

She sighed loudly. "That's too bad."

"What?"

"A curse would make a good story out of it, kid. Well, thanks for calling me."

He felt his chance for fame and fortune slipping through his fingers like grains of sand from Lake Tecumseh's beach. Lindsay and the others would be disappointed when they learned he had spoken with a reporter from New York and had been unable to convince her to feature them in her magazine.

He had to come up with something fast before Megan Conrad hung up the line. He thought quickly, wondering what he could do to keep her interest.

"Wait a minute," he said. "There's something else."

"A curse?"

"No, not exactly. But I've been having these recurring weird dreams."

"Dreams? Dreams don't sell papers."

"But these dreams are different. They started when I came to Lake Tecumseh. And Orville Milford, the old fisherman, is having them, too."

"What do you mean?"

"We're both having the same dreams about some kind of creature. We think it's connected to the meteorite."

"Creature? Can you describe it to me?"

"Sure. It's got a big, glowing head and a long stick-body with six spider legs."

"Is it a spherical head like a ball or something else?"

"No, not like a ball. It's got twenty, flat sides. Like facets of a diamond."

Megan Conrad was suddenly silent on the line.

After a moment she asked, her voice sounding worried, urgent: "You're in Indiana, right?"

"Yeah. Lake Tecumseh."

"I have a trip to Florida, so I can't be there till the weekend. I've got your number off my caller ID. I'll call you when I get there."

"You're coming here?" His pulse quickened. He was going to be interviewed after all.

"I'll be there next weekend."

Fame and fortune were coming his way.

The reporter paused; he could hear her sucking in a lungful of air. "There's one other thing," she said. "You've got to keep this quiet. No chatting on the Internet about your find or this *creature*."

"Why not?"

"I'll explain later. In the meantime, leave that meteorite alone and be careful. Don't mess with it. Understand?"

Her vague warning sounded just like Orville Milford's.

"Sure," he mumbled, not knowing why she was being so dramatic.

She abruptly said goodbye and hung up. The dial tone buzzed in his ear as if the crickets on the lawn had moved inside the house.

He stood frozen, replaying the conversation in his mind.

Why had Megan Conrad sounded alarmed?

Why was she coming to Indiana?

And why had she warned him about the meteorite?

What did the reporter know that he didn't?

CHAPTER EIGHT

An oppressive dome of tropical heat had stagnated over Indiana, and the temperature was in the 90's. The hot blanket of air sucked moisture from the millions of corn stalks as if they were tall green straws, depositing more unwelcome humidity into the stale soup of the Hoosier atmosphere. While the corn loved the Caribbean warmth, the people prayed for cooling thunderstorms or an influx of high pressure from Canada. According to *The Weather Channel*, the heat wave would not break for several days. The upcoming UFO festival was certain to be uncomfortable.

The unpleasant weather did not prevent Cam from being with Lindsay. Standing in her grandfather's hot, windowless workshop, she provided a cheery perspective: "It's always hot in July, but summer doesn't last long, so I won't wish it away. Before you know it, it'll be winter and everyone will be complaining about the snow and cold."

Cam didn't want to wish summer away either, now that he had met Lindsay. He still reeled from kissing her at the old railroad trestle in the woods outside of town. He couldn't stop reliving that magical, unexpected moment.

They had a wonderful time biking to Midgeville, and he was happy to be with her again. He wanted to embrace her, kiss her sweet lips, and tell her he wanted to be a couple.

But at the moment Lindsay was all business. She clutched a digital camera and rotated around the rock, crouching to take photos from every angle. She insisted on calling the rock a meteorite, even though Mr. Russell thought it was a glacial erratic. She believed her grandfather's account of seeing the rock crash into the lake 20 years ago, but Mr. Russell was skeptical of the story.

Cam found Lindsay much more fascinating than the meteorite, and infinitely more beautiful.

She concentrated intently as she took multiple photos, documenting the discovery as professionally as possible. A bikini top peeked from the open folds of her white blouse. She wore cut-off denim shorts and sandals with little daisies on the top. She was dressed for comfort, due to the heat. In the unventilated, stifling workshop, her face glistened with perspiration.

She straightened and looked at Cam, furrowing her eyebrows. "Do you think it looks different?"

"What do you mean?"

"I don't know. It's changed color a little bit, hasn't it?"

"No, it still looks the same. It just dried out."

She stared at the meteorite. "Yeah, I'm sure you're right." She grabbed his arm and pulled him toward her. "Let's get a pic of us with the thing! I'll use the timer."

She placed the camera on a wooden box and carefully adjusted its aim toward the meteorite where Cam was standing. She then activated the timer and jumped into the image, wrapping her arm around his waist.

He loved the feel of her body. He squeezed her toward him, and they both smiled like proud discoverers as the camera snapped a photo.

Neither one of them moved apart right away. Cam reached out and cradled her head between his hands and kissed her. The warmth of her lips was like an inferno compared to the heat inside the workshop.

After a few seconds, Lindsay pulled away. "Let's get out of here. It's too hot."

"It sure is," Cam drawled, beaming at her.

She stowed the camera in her backpack and they exited. She locked the door behind them and hid the key in a bird house dangling from the limb of a nearby ash tree.

"I want to check on Grandpa. He doesn't have A/C," Lindsay said.

They walked through the overgrown yard to the backdoor of Orville's house. Gnats buzzed annoyingly around their faces, energized by the heat. Orville's tow truck was parked in the driveway, and his boat was tied to the pier. The old man had to be inside the house.

Lindsay knocked loudly and yelled, but there was no answer.

"Let's go in," she said, pushing open the screen door and stepping inside. Cam followed behind her.

She froze when she entered the sweltering living room, and Cam bumped into her back.

The old man sat in a ratty wingback chair, its armrests denuded of upholstery. His eyes were closed and his head lay tilted to one side. Drool seeped from the lower corner of his open mouth. His hands were folded in his lap in a peaceful repose.

"Grandpa?" Lindsay asked.

The man didn't move.

"Grandpa?" She repeated, her cracking voice barely above a whisper. Her tone was one that would be used in the presence of the dead.

Orville didn't stir. He looked like a reclining scarecrow in his red flannel shirt and long pants.

Lindsay turned to Cam, her brown eyes wide and upwelling with tears.

She didn't have to say anything: she thought her grandfather was dead. Cam instinctively hugged her. He held her tightly, periodically stealing a nervous glance at Orville's unmoving body.

Together they stepped gingerly toward the wingback chair.

Tears running down her cheeks, Lindsay leaned in to get a closer look at her grandfather.

She reached out to touch his face—

Suddenly Orville snorted and jerked upright. His eyelids popped open like snapping window shades.

Startled, Lindsay jumped back, emitting a small shriek.

Orville right arm sprang to attention in a robotic manner.

Cam saw the old man was holding a pistol. The weapon must have been cradled in his lap, but now it was pointed directly at them!

"Holy crap!" Cam exclaimed.

"Grandpa!" Lindsay yelled. "What are you doing?"

Unblinking and stiff, the old man's glassy eyes stared forward, as if not registering anything. He gripped the pistol so tightly, his fingers were turning white.

"Grandpa, put the gun down!" She stepped forward, but Orville's right arm twitched so she froze in position. She tapped her torso with her forefinger. "It's Lindsay! Don't you recognize me?"

"He's in a trance or something," Cam said.

Resembling a scarecrow sliding from its post, Orville suddenly sighed and relaxed in the chair and lowered the pistol. He then wiped his mouth with the sleeve of his shirt and placed the gun on the side table as if nothing had happened.

"Grandpa? What's wrong? Why didn't you recognize me?" She embraced him and then she and Cam helped him stand up.

The old man was confused and unsteady on his feet. His eyes darted around the room nervously, as if he were trying to make sense of his surroundings—surroundings that should have been instantly familiar to him.

After a moment collecting himself, the gauze seemed to lift from his eyes. "I don't know what happened," he finally said, sounding as if he were searching his befuddled mind for an explanation.

"Just take it easy for a moment," Lindsay said.

Soon Orville regained his balance and could stand on his own. Lindsay went into the kitchen and returned with a glass of water. She sat him back into the chair and sat next to him on the threadbare armrest, gently stroking his gray hair as he drank the water.

"What happened, Grandpa? Do you feel all right?"

"I feel fine," Orville said, sounding a little offended. He placed the empty glass on the table next to the gun. "I don't know what came over me. I must've dozed off."

"Don't you remember anything else?" Lindsay asked.

He shook his head. "No, nothing."

"When we came in, you didn't respond," she explained. "When you woke up, you didn't recognize us and pointed that gun at us! I was scared!"

"Oh, I'm sorry, dear."

She kissed him on the cheek and looked at the weapon on the table. "Why did you take a nap with a gun in your lap? That's dangerous! You could've hurt somebody!"

"It's for protection," Orville said. He lowered his head and looked toward the window nervously. "Strangers are snooping around."

"What strangers?" Cam asked.

"In the woods, watching the place with binoculars. Sometimes they drive by slowly in their car."

"Oh, Grandpa, why would they be snooping around this place?"

"Because of the UFO you kids took from the lake!"

"You think they want to steal it, take credit for its discovery?" Cam asked.

"I don't know what they want," Orville said. "But they know it's here, and they're interested."

Lindsay sighed. "Nobody knows about the meteorite except us."

"And that teacher," Orville added. "Maybe he blabbed. Never trust egghead teachers."

"You're just paranoid," Lindsay said as she patted him on the head. "Now about this gun. It's too dangerous to have it around the house. You might hurt yourself."

"I've been around guns all my life, young lady. I know perfectly well how to be safe."

"But you were not yourself. You were confused and didn't know what was going on around you. I'm worried this might happen again."

"I need a gun to protect myself! I'm not giving it up!"

"I'm going to tell Mom," Lindsay said firmly. "She'll come over and take the gun away for safekeeping."

"She and I will have a talk about *that*," Orville said defiantly.

Lindsay shook her head in resignation. "We're leaving now. We'll check back later."

Cam and Lindsay were no sooner outside the house and mounting their bikes when she sighed. "He's never been confused like that before. Did you see that blank look on his face? It was like he wasn't even there."

"He was out of it, that's for sure," Cam said.

"I'm worried about him."

He didn't know what to say. Perhaps Crazy Old Orville shouldn't be living by himself any longer. With his gun, he could be a menace to any visitor knocking on his screen door. From the tortured look on Lindsay's face, she was grappling with the same thoughts.

They bicycled down the long gravel driveway, which was like a shaded tunnel beneath the overarching maples. When they emerged onto the road, a four-door white sedan was parked on the shoulder.

Unusual because no one ever parked on the road in this section of Lake Tecumseh.

The car suddenly pulled away, kicking up a cloud of dust. Two men were in the front seat. The vehicle sped away and quickly disappeared around the corner.

"That was weird," Lindsay remarked. "I wonder what they were doing."

"Probably taking a leak or something," Cam said.

She shot him a questioning look. "Do you think they were Grandpa's spies?"

"Oh, come on. Nobody's spying on him."

"That was too much of a coincidence. What if someone did blab about our find? Maybe Brian or Patrick?"

She let the question hang in the sultry air as they rode away. The black asphalt bubbled like hot magma in the baking sunlight, snapping under their bike wheels.

What if someone blabbed, Cam thought.

A stone formed in his throat as he recalled his chat on the UFO message board. *He* was the one who had blabbed about their find, not Brian or Patrick.

Cam had typed the whole story on the Internet for the entire world to read. The more he recollected the on-line exchange, the larger the stone in his throat grew. He had reported the site of the discovery—Lake Tecumseh, Indiana. He had described the 20-year-old story of the fisherman and his UFO. Anyone could have searched old newspaper editions for articles identifying the eyewitness—Orville Milford. A simple search and his address would be easily known.

And on top of all that, Cam had also talked with an unknown reporter from New York named Megan Conrad. He knew nothing about her or her true motivations. She had said she was arriving on the weekend. Perhaps she had sent a pair of reporters in advance to investigate their discovery? Or was she a mysterious government investigator looking into UFO sightings and conspiring to cover up the existence of aliens?

The unexciting reality was that they had not actually found a

UFO. There were no aliens involved at all. No reason for a government cover-up.

Cam realized he was letting his imagination run away from him. It all seemed too far fetched, like something out of that old TV show, *The X-Files*.

But Megan Conrad had warned him to be careful. Why had she done that? What was there to fear?

He considered telling Lindsay about the message board discussion and his conversation with Megan Conrad. But he felt ashamed and foolish for breaking her trust.

Also there was no UFO, no aliens, and no strange men spying on Orville Milford, for God's sake. And Megan Conrad worked for a low-brow tabloid, not the NSA, FBI, or CIA.

He tried to calm himself by thinking about something else as they rode side by side.

The summer day lay before them, long and unhurried. He was with a wonderful girl whose kisses felt as if they came from the sun itself. He would tell her everything later, not wanting to spoil the moment they shared.

*   *   *

The countdown to *UFO Days* was a heady time for Lake Tecumseh as the town prepared for the influx of visitors. In spite of the heat wave, flowerboxes were freshened with perky petunias, the annoying potholes on Main Street were repaired, and the lampposts were bedecked with colorful banners of smiling, antenna-headed aliens imploring folks to *join the fun.*

The retired snowbirds had returned from Florida, and the wealthy families from Indianapolis and Chicago had arrived to vacation at luxurious second homes—which they called *cottages*—that sat unused most of the year.

Lake Tecumseh suddenly seemed full.

Day tourists, packed shoulder to shoulder into their minivans and SUVs, sat in the traffic congestion on Main Street while pulling their boats and jet-skis. Cam could almost hear their grumbling as he biked past them.

His destination was Lake Tecumseh High School, a one-level, sprawling, modern building. The grassy football field for the Warriors was on one side while the gymnasium and a largely empty parking lot were on the other.

He parked his bike and went inside the gym, knowing Lindsay would be there. She had asked him to help with the decorations for the UFO Dance, and Cam did not want to miss the opportunity to be with her.

The gymnasium of LTHS was a vast, echoing space, and it seemed even larger with the moveable bleachers rolled into their retracted positions. In the center of the basketball court Lindsay stood holding a clipboard, surrounded by the Student Council and other volunteers. Off to their side, beneath the scoreboard for the Warriors, were stacked boxes and crates filled with bunting, ribbon, and other party ornamentation.

The circle of people stopped speaking and parted like petals when they saw Cam. Lindsay, the flower within the group, was all brown hair and smiles when she spied him approach. Her round, pretty face brightened as if it had been struck by a beam of heavenly light. "Cam! I'm so glad you could come to help!" she chirped, stepping toward him and giving him a hug. Her clipboard scratched against his back.

He wanted to kiss her but felt her nervousness about a display of too much affection in front of the other students.

Amid the gauntlet of staring eyes, Lindsay was focused on the job ahead. "The UFO Dance is only three days away!" she reminded Cam. She waved to her friends and quickly rattled off their names to him—a forgettable series, just like Mr. Russell's geologic Mohs Scale.

Unexpectedly, Brian Little and Patrick Frazier were in the crowd of volunteers. Cam's complete attention since his arrival had been riveted on Lindsay, and he had overlooked the two football players.

Cam tried to freeze the smile on his face but was unsuccessful as Brian approached with his typical muscular swagger.

Cam didn't want a confrontation with Lindsay's Ex. It wasn't his fault Lindsay had dumped Brian, but Cam sensed immediately Brian was not happy.

"I didn't know you'd be here," Brian said harshly.

Cam shrugged. "I thought I could help."

"The dance is a *school* function, and you're not even a student. Only students should be allowed to decorate."

"That's right!" Patrick chimed, ever the follower.

Brushing by, Lindsay overheard them. "Don't be ridiculous! We need all the help we can get."

Chastised, Brian scowled and backed away. Since news traveled fast in small towns, perhaps he had already heard of Lindsay's newfound interest in Cam.

Lindsay was in charge of the volunteers. Studying her clipboard for a moment, she looked up perkily, exuding team spirit like a cheerleader. "Let's get started! Follow me!"

She marched the group around the court, gesturing to the future sites of the refreshment stand, the photography booth, and the stage platform for the crowning of the Space King and Queen, while referring to her carefully drawn diagram. She was a born leader, and Cam followed with the others, amazed by her poise, her energy, and her attention to detail.

"We're going to transform this gym into the best dance floor ever!" she crowed to the excited volunteers.

She assigned decorating chores with the aplomb of a CEO: those responsible for the streamers, those responsible for the bunting, and those responsible for mounting the various UFO-themed decorations.

She assigned Cam and Brian the task of setting up tables and chairs in the precise positions specified by her diagram.

Cam was excited about helping, but didn't like being paired with Brian. Why had Lindsay grouped them together? She was usually so good at making decisions.

Nevertheless he decided to make the best of the afternoon. Lindsay's enthusiasm was infectious and had rubbed off on him.

But not on Brian, who seemed downtrodden. He plodded to the furniture storage room with his head held low and his feet shuffling like a robot whose batteries were running low.

The storage room was next to the auditorium and was filled with dozens of folding tables and chairs stacked in neat piles. Cam and Brian each grabbed an end and lifted a table and marched toward the gym.

Cam was in the lead and had to walk backward. He tried to avoid eye contact with Brian.

"Linz broke up with me," Brian announced. "Can you believe it?"

Cam had been hoping the job would be completed in blissful silence. He tried to sound surprised: "She did?"

"She said we were too different. I don't think we're too different at all. I'm into sports and she's into her sci-fi crap. So what? Can't we be different and still get along?"

Cam carefully guided the table around the corner of the corridor. He could now hear the excited voices of the volunteers working in the gym. "Maybe it wasn't meant to be."

"Dude, it was good while it lasted," Brian said, smirking.

They entered the gym and set up the table. Patrick was on a ladder, draping colorful paper streamers over the court. Lindsay was supervising from below, making sure the spirals of each sagging streamer were perfectly positioned.

Brian and Cam both gazed at her longingly for a moment, and then retraced their steps through the locker-filled hallway back to the storage room.

"She's really busy this summer, you know," Brian said as they lifted a second table from the stack. "She spends all her time at the museum or writing her UFO book. She didn't have much time for me at all."

"Plus she's really interested in the meteorite," Cam said, feeling his T-shirt already stick to his sweaty skin.

"What a bust that turned out to be. It's harder than diamond, but so what? An actual flying saucer would've been better!"

On their third trip Brian said, "She'll come back to me when things quiet down. When the festival's over, and she's done with her book, she'll realize her mistake."

Cam didn't reply, not wanting to imagine the possibility.

They entered the gym. After propping open the table's legs and setting it up, Cam silently counted how many tables remained to be hauled.

Too many.

Not only was he feeling like a worker ant, he was tired of Brian's incessant talking.

When the job was finally done, and all the tables and chairs had been hauled from the storage room, Cam and Brian reassembled in the gym next to Lindsay, expecting to get another assignment from her powerful clipboard. The gym was quickly being transformed for the big dance.

Unexpectedly, Brian wrapped his arm around Lindsay's shoulders and cooed into her ear, "Are you sure you don't want to go to the dance with me? It's not too late to reconsider. We'd make a great Space King and Queen."

She shrugged away from him. "It's over, Brian! Don't you understand?"

"But Linz!"

"I'm going with my girlfriends!"

"You don't need to baby-sit them," Brian said. "You're in a different league. You're pretty enough to have a date."

Her eyes flashed lightning bolts. "How dare you insult my

friends!" She stormed away, joining the students on the other side of the gym.

"Real smooth," Cam said, not able to help himself.

"I'll ask Amanda, then," Brian said. "She's really hot. That'll make Linz jealous, especially when we get crowned Space King and Queen!"

Patrick stepped up, carrying a cardboard box of decorations. "I'm tired. Can't we take a cigarette break?"

"Sure," Brian said. He turned to Cam. "Wanna join us?"

Cam had never smoked before, but the idea appealed to him for some reason, like forbidden fruit. He was on his own this summer, so wasn't he entitled to make his own decisions? His mother was in Italy with Frank the Bank Jock. Maybe a few puffs would be fun.

But before Cam could respond, Lindsay ran up in a panic, clutching her cell phone.

"Lindsay, what is it?" Cam asked, concerned.

"It's Grandpa!" she blurted. "He said something was happening with the meteorite! We've got to get there right away!"

"I can drive," Brian said. "Follow me!"

The four of them raced out of the gymnasium to Brian's red Mustang convertible, which was parked diagonally across two parking spaces. The clean car gleamed in the bright sunlight. Brian motioned Lindsay to the front passenger seat while Cam and Patrick climbed into the cramped rear seats.

Brian started the car, which vibrated with a powerful rumble. Before Cam even had his seatbelt buckled, Brian accelerated through the parking lot with a squeal of tires, pressing Cam into the seatback.

The Mustang rocketed like a bullet into a gap in the traffic on Main Street.

"Brian! Slow down!" Lindsay chastised, striking Brian on the arm.

"Oh, sorry," Brian said with a smile, decelerating slightly. "It's got a lot of power."

Brian's quick start had caught the attention of a parked police car.

The patrol car's lights flashed on and it pulled after them, its siren blaring.

Cam turned to look behind. The cop was motioning with his left hand for Brian to pull over.

Brian looked in his rearview mirror. "Dammit," he mumbled as he slowed to a stop on the side of the road.

"Now look what you've done!" Lindsay yelled. "We don't have time for this! We've got to get to the meteorite!"

"Nice going, hot shot," Cam said, poking Brian in the back of the neck.

Lindsay frantically punched numbers into her cell phone. "Now Grandpa's not answering!"

A police officer stepped to the driver's door. He was a large, swaggering man with a protruding gut. He wore mirrored sunglasses and had a gun holstered on his belt. His expression was stern until he recognized Brian. Then he shook his head slowly. "Brian, I've told you before to be careful," the cop said. "Just because you're the sheriff's son, doesn't mean you can be reckless."

Cam clenched his teeth. He knew where this traffic stop was heading—Brian would get off scot-free. The police officer wouldn't give a ticket to his boss's son.

Brian bobbed his head and smiled disarmingly at the cop. "Sorry about that, Fred. I won't do it again," he said contritely, flashing an innocent smile.

"Main Street isn't a racetrack. You better slow down," the cop said. "You're not getting another chance."

"Yes, sir," Brian said.

Brian and Patrick retained their calm composure until the cop had returned to his squad car and pulled away with a friendly wave. Then the two of them broke out laughing like a pair of hyenas.

"You're so lucky!" Patrick said. "That was the second time he pulled you over this week!"

Brian grinned. "Am I cool or what?"

"It's not funny!" Lindsay said. "This isn't some game! Just get us there safely, please."

They arrived at Orville's house in one piece, and Brian parked next to Orville's tow truck. As they climbed out of the Mustang, Cam was relieved to stand straight again. The tiny back seat of Brian's muscle car was uncomfortable for anyone with knees, and sharing it with someone as big as Patrick made it even worse.

The door to the workshop was locked. Knocking, Lindsay yelled, "Grandpa, open up!"

Orville opened the door and scanned their faces carefully. "What? You brought the whole gang?" His pistol was stuffed into the waistband of his trousers.

"I told you to put that gun away!" Lindsay said.

He motioned for them to come inside. "Hurry!"

The four of them entered the workshop and immediately surrounded the meteorite, which rested on the table in the center. A foot-long, hair-line crack had appeared in its side, and a black liquid had oozed from the fissure, creating a small puddle on the table that dripped onto the wood shavings on the floor.

"Incredible!" Lindsay exclaimed, inspecting the crack. "Did you do this?"

Orville crossed his arms across his chest. "I didn't touch it. I came in here a few minutes ago and saw that it had split open. You told me to call if anything strange happened."

"I also told you to get rid of that gun!" Lindsay said.

They circled around the meteorite trying to get a better look at the large crack.

"What's this black slime?" Brian asked. "It's leaked all over the place." He reached out to touch the puddle of glistening liquid, but Lindsay smacked his hand away.

"Don't touch it!" she said. "We don't know what it is."

Momentarily startled, Brian backed away. "It looks like oil to me."

Cam recalled his dreams of a strange place with yellow and blue suns. In them he had swum in a lake of a thick, gooey liquid.

A lake of oil.

Once again, an unexplained connection linked his dreams with the meteorite. He rubbed his right temple. Grappling with the mounting coincidences was giving him a headache.

"Are you okay, Cam?" Lindsay asked.

"I'm fine. Just a slight headache."

With a puzzled expression she carefully examined the fissure in the rock and the oily liquid staining the table and floor. "Perhaps the temperature difference between the cold lake bottom and the hot workshop caused the crack to form along a pre-existing structural weakness."

"But you said it was as hard as diamond," Cam reminded.

"Even a hard substance can have a stress fracture," Lindsay said. "This oily liquid is what's most unusual! I don't know what kind of glacial erratic or meteorite would have a liquid center. I can't wait to tell Mr. Russell!"

Cam was happy she was excited. He only wished his headache would go away. It had quickly intensified since their arrival at the workshop. Was his proximity to the meteorite the cause?

They chatted enthusiastically about the rock until an unexpected sound reverberated through the workshop, startling them to immediate silence:

Crack!

Cam looked at Lindsay. "What was that?"

"I dunno," Lindsay said, "but it was loud."

Crack!

Brian punched Patrick. "Did you cut the mustard again?"

Patrick shook his head. "It wasn't me! It came from the rock!"

Their nervous eyes all darted to the rock.

Crack!

A bead of black slime formed at the bottom of the widening crack and then dripped to the table with a small splash.

A second teardrop of slime emerged immediately afterward, as if it were being squeezed from the inside.

Crack!

They stepped farther back, keeping their eyes fixed on the rock.

The original hairline fissure had enlarged to nearly a quarter inch gap. A black, gooey interior was visible. An acrid odor belched forth, like diesel fumes from a truck.

They stood in silence, watching the object slowly split open.

"What's happening?" Lindsay asked, her jaw slack.

"It's hatching," Orville said.

Crack!

CHAPTER NINE

Crack!

Inexplicably, the knobby, egg-shaped rock was splitting open as Cam and the others watched with amazement mixed with fear. Black oil dribbled from the widening gash in the object's side, and the fracture now extended more than halfway around its circumference.

Lindsay furrowed her brow. "I wish I had my camera with me to document this!"

Orville pulled a gun out of his waistband and checked the ammunition. "I knew it was a mistake to haul this thing in here!"

"Whoa, Gramps!" Brian exclaimed, jumping back a step upon seeing the weapon.

Lindsay grabbed her grandfather's arm and forced the gun down. "Put that thing away! Do you wanna hurt somebody?"

"But it's hatching!" Orville said.

"Meteorites don't hatch!" Lindsay yelled.

"This is creepy," Patrick said. Then he dramatically hummed the theme from *The Twilight Zone*.

Brian shoved Patrick away. "Stop that, you idiot!"

"Look!" Lindsay said, pointing. "I can see something inside!"

Crack!

The fracture in the rock broke open wider, and a slop of black goop was expelled onto the table like a push of excrement. Solid, round balls were suspended in the disgorged oil like meatballs in pasta sauce.

"Gross!" Brian said. "What the hell is that?"

The released spheres were each the size of a golf ball. Coated with thick, black oil, they slid across the table amid an ever-enlarging inky puddle.

One sphere rolled to the table's edge, teetered for a second, and then slowly fell to the floor on a glistening string of slime.

Cam gagged on the sulfurous odor. He scratched his head, having never seen anything so weird. "What do you think it is?"

"I have no idea, but it's amazing!" Lindsay gushed.

Orville gripped his gun, his eyes darting between the rock and the door to the workshop. "That thing's from another planet, and you should've left it in the lake! It was safe and quiet for 20 years. Now look what's happened! Who knows what its evil purpose is? It could be infectious, an invading alien army, or some kind of sinister weapon!"

"Grandpa, calm down!" Lindsay ordered. "It's just a geologic oddity."

Patrick pinched his nose. "And it smells like puke!"

Lindsay looked around the workshop. "I'll take a sample to school and show Mr. Russell. Maybe he can figure out what it is. Do you have a bucket or something I can borrow, Grandpa?"

Orville begrudgingly stuck his gun into his waistband. "Damn scientists are always getting in the way." He reached under a workbench and pulled out an old bucket and handed it to her. "I suppose you want some tongs or something, too?"

"That would be helpful," Lindsay said.

Orville went to a drawer and fished out an old serving spoon and gave it to her. Bucket and spoon in hand, Lindsay approached the split rock. She took the spoon and scooped up one of the oil-smeared spheres and dropped it into the bucket. Spaghetti strings of oil trailed behind as she did so. She cut the black ribbons with the side of the spoon as if she were a waitress serving a slice of cheese pizza. She turned back to face her friends. "I want to examine this scientifically. I'm sure Mr. Russell will let me use the chem lab. Does anyone want to join me?"

Brian rolled his eyes. "Oh, come on, Linz. We just spent all afternoon at school."

"Have it your way, then," she said, glancing from Brian to Cam.

Cam smiled. "I'll come with you. I have to get my bike anyway."

With a shrug, Brian headed for the door. "Come on, Pat. The show's over. We just watched a rock take a crap."

"Yeah, we were hoping for some *real* excitement," Patrick sneered as he followed behind.

Brian stopped at the door and looked back. "Don't get so wrapped up in your silly lab work that you forget to go to the festival. It starts tomorrow night."

"Don't worry," Lindsay said. "We won't miss it."

"See ya then," Brian said as he and Patrick left the workshop.

They listened to the Mustang drive away, crunching gravel under its wide tires.

Orville snorted. "I hate those two punks." He put his hands on his hips and looked at the black crud all over the table and floor. "Look at this mess!"

"Just leave it for now," Lindsay said. "It may have scientific value. I'll let you know what I find out."

"I can't stand the smell," Orville grumbled. "I'm going fishing." He walked out the door, a black cloud seeming to hover over his head.

Cam wondered if the old man was disappointed. For twenty years he had told his story about seeing a UFO sink into Lake Tecumseh. He had fervently believed there were aliens inside. Now they had discovered the truth. There were no aliens—just black sludge, strange round balls, and an offensive odor.

Cam rubbed his temples again. If he didn't have such a terrible headache, he would have felt sorry for Crazy Old Orville.

*   *   *

Wearing thick rubber gloves and a pair of safety goggles, Lindsay delicately dried the small sphere with a paper towel as Cam hovered behind her in the science lab of Lake Tecumseh High School. Cleaned of its coating of oil, the sphere was as black as a lump of coal.

"What do you think it is?" he asked, his voice tittering with excitement in spite of the nagging headache that just would not go away.

"Not a clue," she answered limply. "What do you think, Mr. Russell?"

Mr. Russell was sitting at his desk at the front of the chem lab, rifling through papers and not paying much attention to them.

"Mr. Russell?" Lindsay repeated.

The distracted teacher didn't glance up. "Beats me, Lindsay."

Mr. Russell was stumped, which Cam found refreshing. Teachers always acted like they knew everything, yet he was as clueless as everyone else.

Cam glanced around the science lab, noting its shiny black bench tops, shelves full of chemicals, and glass-fronted cabinets holding arrays of test tubes, beakers, and flasks. He felt rather out of place. Back in Chicago, science had been one of his worst subjects. He had no interest in the parts of the cell, the elements of the periodic table, or the order of the planets. Those topics were for the nerds. And they were too difficult for him, anyway.

But unexpectedly, here in Lake Tecumseh partnering with Lindsay, he was suddenly more interested in science. His attention was riveted on the strange sphere they had transported from Orville's workshop. One of many that had disgorged in a flow of black oil from their recovered rock. Neither plausible explanation—a glacial erratic or a meteorite—could account for its existence.

Cam was fascinated as he and Lindsay explored the unknown together. They were being scientists, and he didn't feel like a nerd at all. He wondered how his science teachers back in Chicago had been able to suck all the excitement out of the subject, turning it into mindless memorization, dull experiments, and an overriding sense of everyday uselessness.

Lindsay was the missing component. She made science exciting. She was enthusiastic and explained things simply and completely. She could give lessons to teachers on technique.

And she was beautiful.

Cam was entranced.

Noticing the ball wasn't smooth, he asked, "Are those markings?"

Lindsay squinted. "I don't know." She positioned the examination lamp with its large magnifying lens and switched it on. She then pivoted the magnifying glass, which was about as wide as a dinner plate, in front of the sphere.

They both leaned in to look at the enlarged sphere through the lens. What was only the size of a golf ball was now hugely magnified, its image completely filling up the lens like the moon. Its surface was divided by little ridges into an interlocking, hexagonal pattern.

Lindsay slowly rotated the ball to check both hemispheres. Beneath the magnifier, each of her gloved fingers appeared as large as a giant's.

"They're little hexagons, like a beehive," she said. "It's very orderly."

"You're right. Is it heavy?"

"Not at all. It might be hollow."

"Should we crack it open?" Cam asked. "There are lots of them. It wouldn't matter if we damaged one, would it?"

"Probably not." She pursed her lips into a tight line of

concentration. "We should wait. I don't want to do anything rash."

She set the ball into a glass jar and sealed it with a lid. "Let's look at the black liquid under the microscope."

"Cool."

Shuffling through papers at his desk, Mr. Russell noticed Lindsay positioning the large microscope next to the beaker holding the black sludge. "Be careful with that," he said.

"I will," Lindsay said. "I know it's expensive."

Using an eye dropper, she siphoned some of the liquid and squeezed it onto a glass slide. She then placed the slide in the microscope and studied it through the eyepiece.

Mr. Russell glanced at his watch. "I lost track of time, kids. I need to get to Indy for the conference."

Lindsay looked up from the microscope and frowned. "Just a few more minutes. I've several other tests yet."

Mr. Russell began collecting papers and stuffing them into his briefcase. "Make it quick. I need to close up in a few minutes."

"But you won't be back till Saturday! I don't want my research to wait that long!"

"You can't use the lab in my absence," the teacher said firmly. "Besides, that rock isn't going anywhere. So finish up quickly so I can get out of here."

Cam remembered the chores Uncle Gary and Aunt Ellen had assigned him that afternoon. They wouldn't be happy if they didn't get done. "I have to go, too. Chores."

Lindsay was disappointed. "I guess science will have to wait due to chores and conferences."

"But we have the festival, remember?" Cam said.

Her face brightened. "Are we still going tonight?"

"I wouldn't miss it for the world!"

Mr. Russell smirked, watching the two grinning kids out of the corner of his eye.

Cam said good-bye, grabbed his backpack, and headed for the

door. He glanced back before he exited, catching Lindsay watching him over the microscope with a coy smile. He smiled back, eager to spend time with her again.

A couple of aspirin from Aunt Ellen and his headache would be gone before the evening festival.

* * *

Cam arrived at the festival grounds after dinner, just before sunset. He wondered what Lindsay had learned about the little balls from the meteorite during his absence. If anyone could figure it out, he knew she certainly could. She was the smartest girl he had ever met.

Although the scientific investigation was interesting, it took a back seat in his mind as he looked forward to some fun with Lindsay at UFO Days.

In the waning light of the long summer day, Cam took in the sights of the celebration as he got his bearings of the fairgrounds. Sweaty people shuffled in a crowd, inspecting the booths selling food, trinkets, and novelties. Long lines of kids snaked from each of the thrill rides, eagerly waiting their turn. Couples streamed between the gauntlets of game booths, where each passing man was challenged to win a prize for his date.

Noise was everywhere: conversing people, screaming children, shouting hawkers, clanking rides, and music blaring from speakers. The intensity assaulted his ears, but the energy infused his body, and he quickened his step. He wanted to find Lindsay and enjoy the spectacle with her.

Near the food booths, the heavy summer air was laden with a stew of powerful odors: buttered popcorn, sugary cotton candy, and tangy barbecued chicken. Cam spied Lindsay next to a stall selling roasted peanuts. She wore a brown T-shirt with the logo for the *Lake Tecumseh UFO Museum* on it. She handed the seller some money and took a bag of peanuts just as Cam arrived by her side.

She smiled and her eyebrows shot up. "Hi, Cam. How's it going?"

His expression was just as animated. "Great! I'm glad I found you. This place is a lot more crowded than I expected."

"It gets more popular every year." She held the bag out to him. "Want some peanuts?"

They shared the peanuts as they walked the fairgrounds. Lindsay ignored the surrounding commotion while she bubbled with excitement about her research on the strange sphere. "It's really quite amazing!" she said breathlessly. "I couldn't find anything on the Internet about it."

"But everything's on the Internet," Cam said.

"Nothing about this! The sphere's hexagonal features look like they were *manufactured*. Like it was molded or stamped out of a factory press."

"But how could that be? It was inside a rock."

"Beats me. But they don't look natural."

"And the black goop?"

She popped the last handful of peanuts into her mouth. When she had finished chewing, she said, "It's a hydrocarbon, like crude oil. It's flammable and has a similar viscosity."

"Viscosity?"

She nodded. "You know . . . *thickness*."

He liked the way she explained things without making him feel stupid. "So what's the next step?"

"Probably do what you said—crack it open."

"You see, I know the scientific method just as well as you do!"

She chuckled. "You're right! We shouldn't have bothered with microscopes and experiments at all!"

The walked past booths selling trinkets and cotton candy.

"My dreams may help provide answers about the sphere," Cam said, somewhat cautiously.

"Answers? From dreams?" She gave a tight-lipped smile. "That's not the scientific method, Cam."

He shrugged. "I know, but hear me out."

"Are you going to tell me about alien landscapes and multi-legged creatures again? You should be a science fiction writer with an imagination like yours."

He was disappointed she was needling him. "The last dream was different. It was more vivid, like I was watching an unfolding story. I wasn't even in it, I was just an observer."

She stopped and fixed him in her gaze. "What are saying?"

"It's like the meteorite is personally telling me its story."

"And that is?"

Cam swallowed, not sure if he wanted to share more. But he had opened the door and now he needed to walk through it. She might think he was crazy. But he couldn't back out now. "In the dream I experienced the object drifting in space for hundreds of millions of years. I could feel its journey through deep space . . . the endless light-years, flying by unknown stars, and the utter sense of loneliness. It seemed to go on forever, as if there was no hope of ever arriving at a new home. Then finally I saw its descent to Earth and crash into Lake Tecumseh."

"You think the meteorite is communicating with you? ESP? It's a lifeless rock! You saw what came out of it. Just inanimate spheres and oil. There are no aliens."

"I know, but the feelings are even stronger now. So strong I get these headaches all the time." He rubbed his forehead, wishing the dull ache would disappear. "Now it's like someone's trying to enter my mind when I'm awake. There's a mental presence knocking to get in."

She stopped and touched him on the arm. "A mental presence? Oh, come on, Cam."

"I tell you, that's what it feels like!"

She watched him with a concerned, almost pitiful expression.

"Maybe you should see a doctor. If the headache's not going away, it could be a sign of a serious medical condition."

"I hope not."

"I'll mention it to my mom. She's a nurse, and she may have an idea what might be causing your headaches. In the meantime, I think you're letting your imagination run away."

He sighed, trying to formulate a more powerful response, but he came up empty handed. "I know it sounds silly but—"

"Let's see the rest of the festival." She smiled warmly and took his hand.

He was comforted by her touch. He decided he would try to forget about his theories and his discomfort for now, in order to enjoy the time with her.

Walking side by side as a couple, the hawkers of the game booths targeted Cam. "Hey buddy!" a rotund man with a handlebar mustache yelled. "How about shooting some hoops for the little lady? She shouldn't be walking around empty handed!" The man spun a rubber ball in his hand, pointing to a net covering the mouth of a roaring lion. Behind him was a wall of glass-eyed stuffed animals.

"No thanks!' Cam yelled back, knowing all the games were rigged.

"C'mon, it's easy! Win your sweetheart a teddy bear!"

Cam flushed as he looked at Lindsay. Was she his *sweetheart?* The term was old fashioned, but he liked the sound of it. Yet he was embarrassed to have it barked by a stranger.

Lindsay shrugged. "Oh, go for it! It'll be fun!"

Cam stepped up to the booth and purchased a toss. The man handed him the ball and stepped back and folded his arms across his chest to watch.

Cam carefully judged the weight of the ball and the distance to the little fabric net over the lion's mouth. He didn't want to disappoint Lindsay.

"Good luck!" she said, leaning over the railing, eyeing the

potential prizes.

He threw the ball, which unfortunately bounced off the rim. He wasn't surprised. The ball was probably heavier on one side or the lion's mouth was smaller than it appeared.

"Sorry, kid," the man said with a crooked smile. "You gotta warm up a little. Wanna try again?"

Cam fished in his pocket for more money. "One more time."

The man handed Cam another ball. This time, he knew what to expect. He tossed the ball and it funneled straight into the net, striking a bell.

Cam pumped his fist.

The operator scowled. "Good shot, kid."

Lindsay clapped her hands and jumped, and then gave Cam a big hug. "You're a winner!" Her eyes sparkled.

Cam smiled, proud of himself. "You gotta pick your prize."

"What do you want little lady?" the man grumbled. "A kitten? A teddy bear?"

She pointed to a large, stuffed rhinoceros. Its horn protruded over the edge of the shelf like a gray, fabric sword. "The rhino!"

The man smiled crookedly. "The rhino?"

"Yeah, the rhino. They're cool. They've survived for millions of years but are going extinct because poachers want their horn. It's only made of keratin."

"Keratin?" the befuddled man said as he handed her the large, gray rhino.

"You know, like fingernails." She grabbed the toy and gave it a motherly hug. She turned to Cam and gave him a kiss. "Isn't it cute? Thanks, Cam!"

He was happy she was excited.

They left the row of game booths and crossed to the end of the concourse where the song *I Want to Hold Your Hand* overpowered the other noises of the festival. A mop-haired, four-man band was playing on a stage bedecked with a large banner that read: *Welcome to*

Lake Tecumseh UFO Days.

The appreciative audience danced and sang along to the familiar music.

"That's the Roaches!" Lindsay gushed, clutching her stuffed rhino. "A Beatles knock-off! C'mon!" She grabbed his hand and pulled him into the crowd. They squeezed between the people to get closer to the stage.

Once they had shoe-horned themselves into position, they danced to the music in the style of the 1960s, as they had seen on You-Tube. The Roaches cycled through hit after hit: *Can't Buy Me Love*, *A Hard Day's Night*, and *Eight Days a Week*, and more.

Amid the gyrating crowd, Cam and Lindsay were pressed closely together, and she touched him frequently as they danced.

He loved being with her.

Life was wonderful.

A final guitar riff signaled the end of the Roaches' performance, and the crowd applauded appreciatively to the young men on the stage impersonating John, Paul, George, and Ringo. Cam thought the Roaches were a mediocre band, but it didn't matter because they were working with good material that everyone loved anyway.

The emcee announced the next act would be an acoustic band playing folk music. Neither Cam nor Lindsay cared to stick around. They moved away from the stage, shuffling through the mass of people, and rejoined the rest of the festival.

As the night got later, the composition of the fairgoers changed. The families with children went home, replaced by teen-agers and couples on dates.

Lindsay ran into some friends, and Cam was forced to tolerate local school talk as the girls chatted. They were excited about Saturday's Space Queen Competition and the UFO Dance. They also loved Lindsay's stuffed rhino and gazed at Cam admirably for his prowess in winning the prize for her.

Some of the girls acted as if the rhino was stuffed with jewels.

Leaving the cluck of girlfriends behind, Cam and Lindsay retreated to a quieter corner of Grissom Park to rest their feet and sip their sodas. They sat on a park bench beneath a large maple. She placed her rhino by her side like an accompanying child.

The stars sparkled overhead. Noise thumped through the trees, almost drowning out the see-sawing scratches of the myriad crickets. He was thankful they had found a respite from the shrillness of UFO Days, although their location was far from secluded. Even now, in one of the darkest and quietest pockets of the large park, couples passed by at regular intervals.

Neither Cam nor Lindsay spoke for several moments as they held hands and relished each other's touch.

Eventually he scooted closer and wrapped his arm around her back. "I love being with you."

She smiled; the streetlight glowing in her eyes. "I feel the same about you."

They were drawn together like magnets, and they kissed passionately. His lips explored hers while his hands roamed, tracing every sensuous curve and every warm crease of her body. He pulled her closer to him, not wanting any distance between them. His heart was pounding like a drum in his chest. He had never experienced anything so wonderful. He wanted the moment to go on forever.

They were interrupted by the noisy approach of two people. Looking over Lindsay's shoulder, Cam recognized the familiar silhouettes on the shadowy path: Brian and Patrick.

Lindsay turned and saw them as well. "Oh, God," she said, pulling away from Cam and adjusting her blouse nervously.

Brian and Patrick each held a giant plastic cup of soda from a convenience store. They strutted up and stopped in front of the bench. "Hey, what are you guys doing?" Brian asked before taking a sip from his straw.

"We needed a break from the crowd," Lindsay ad-libbed quickly.

Brian was wearing a tight yellow tank top that showed off his muscular arms and torso. "I knew we'd see you guys sooner or later. Everyone's here tonight."

Patrick sipped his soda. "I told you I saw them dancing."

Cam wished Brian and Patrick would just continue their stroll and leave him and Lindsay alone.

"We're out to have a good time tonight," Brian said. "Hang out with us."

Lindsay shook her head. "Sounds like fun, but we're probably going to leave soon."

"Ah, c'mon. It's early. Don't be such a stick in the mud," Brian taunted. "Let's have some fun and go on rides." He pointed to Cam. "It's his first time here. We need to show him a good time!"

"What are you, the Lake Tecumseh Chamber of Commerce?" Cam joked.

"You gotta cut loose every once in a while, Sport," Brian said. "UFO Days only comes once a year." He stuck his thumb into his pocket and let his jaw slacken. "The rest of the time us country folk are bored silly," he drawled in a fake hillbilly accent. "Nothin' to do but eat hog rinds and watch the paint peel on our trailers."

Cam couldn't help but smile at Brian's bad acting.

"We're gonna stand here till you join us," Brian said, crossing his arms.

Lindsay sighed. "Okay, we'll stay for a while, but not too long."

"Great!" Brian said, reaching out and pulling her to her feet. "Have you gone on the Ferris Wheel yet?"

"Not yet," Lindsay said, smoothing her clothes.

Cam stood up. He preferred to spend the evening alone with her, but that didn't seem to be an option at the moment. Brian and Patrick were insistent, and the fun and excitement of the UFO festival still beckoned.

As they walked back to the fairgrounds, Patrick reached into the pocket of his baggy trousers and pulled out a half empty bottle of Jim Beam and presented it to the others. "Pour some of this into your drinks to get into the party mood."

Lindsay blanched. "You're drinking?"

Brian raised his cup into the air and shrugged. "So? What's the harm?"

"You're not of legal age, for one thing!" Lindsay said.

"Who cares?" Brian said. "Everyone else is doing it."

Patrick held the bottle of whiskey in front of Cam like a challenge. Cam nervously glanced around the park to see if anyone was in sight.

"C'mon, don't be such a wuss," Brian said.

The dare hung in the air like the smell of frying oil wafting from the festival.

Cam took the bottle reluctantly and watched the amber liquid slosh inside. It reminded him of his father's old booze he had brought to the party in Chicago. He had thought it would be fun and would make him popular. It had, for a time. He and his friends passed the bottles around, doing shots and playing games, while they huddled on the back porch having a wonderful time. The girls were so friendly that night, hanging all over the boys, and things were going well, until—

Cam shook his head slightly. *That* situation was different. He had been foolish then. Now he knew better. He was in Indiana, and on his own for the first time. His mother was in Europe. Uncle Gary and Aunt Ellen had probably been in bed for hours already. He didn't have to drive, and he didn't have to be anywhere. Why not have a little fun? They were at a festival after all. Brian was right, everyone was drinking. Cam had counted at least three beer tents already. What harm would there be?

Cam poured whiskey into his soda. He felt Lindsay watching his every move.

"I don't think that's such a good idea, Cam," she said.

"Just a little," Cam said with a smile. He presented the bottle to her. "Want some?"

"No, thanks," she said flatly.

Cam handed the bottle back to Patrick, who concealed the Jim Beam with an approving smirk.

Brian grinned and hooked his thumb back toward the lights and noise of the festival grounds. "C'mon, let's go!"

Cam took a sip of his drink. The taste of the whiskey mixed smoothly with his Coke, and he felt a quick rush to his head. He looked over at Lindsay, thankful to have met her. He couldn't wait to have more fun with her.

The four of them arrived back at the festival and made their way through the crowd, their drink cups in hand. Cam was amazed how many people Brian, Patrick, and Lindsay knew. Around every corner they would run into friends, and there would be quick introductions. It was a small town, after all, and like Brian had said, *everyone* was at the festival.

Cam was in a great mood, especially sharing the fun with Lindsay. He admitted he even enjoyed being with Brian and Patrick for a change. The two football jocks were a lot more fun than he would have predicted. They cracked jokes about everything and everyone, often sending Cam into fits of teary-eyed laughter. It was as if the two of them were on stage, competing to see who could make the audience laugh the loudest.

Cam was getting quite a buzz from the alcohol, which made their jokes even funnier and intensified the bombardment of noise and energy around him.

"Let's get in line for *The Predator*," Brian said excitedly to Cam. "That's the best ride at the festival. Guaranteed to make you puke. Think you can handle it?"

"Sure! I'm game," Cam said. He glanced at Lindsay, who had been awfully quiet since they left the park.

"I don't like rides that go upside down," Lindsay said.

"It'll be fun," Cam said.

"I'll pass," she said, hugging her stuffed rhino.

Cam took another sip of his drink. He didn't know why Lindsay was suddenly acting so bored. Girls' moods could change as quickly as the weather.

He was having a good time he thought as the three boys got in line for the thrill ride.

The Predator didn't live up to its reputation, as no one vomited after going on its wild, spinning loops. After the ride, Cam and Brian stumbled dizzily down the ramp laughing together. "That was wicked!" Brian said. "I thought I'd blow chunks!"

"I almost lost it, too!" Cam said, exhilarated by the adrenalin pumped into his system by the fear and motion.

Patrick followed behind them, unsteady on his feet and looking rather pale.

"Are you all right, Pat?" Brian asked as he reached for the drink cup he had placed on top of the trash can. He took a long sip. "You don't look so hot."

Patrick leaned against the fence and bowed his head. "I-I'm fine. I just need a drink."

As Patrick refilled whiskey into their cups, Lindsay stood with her arms crossed, watching disapprovingly. "Did you guys like the ride?"

"It was cool," Cam said. "You should've gone." He drank some more. Except for a few rapidly disappearing ice cubes, it was almost straight whiskey now.

"It's late," Lindsay said. "I'm going home."

"Ah, c'mon," Cam said. "The fun's just starting."

"Yeah," Brian said. "Stay with us."

She turned away. "Not while you guys are getting sloppy drunk!"

"Oh, Linz!" Brian said. "We're just having fun. No need to get all huffy."

"Yeah," Patrick said, regaining his color but swaying slightly. "We're not sloppy."

"You are, too!" Lindsay said.

Cam reached out and gently turned Lindsay around. "Please, stay. I won't drink anymore if you stay."

She looked down at the cup he was holding in his free hand. "I thought I knew you, Cameron Meyer! Is this how you act back in Chicago the rest of the year?"

"No, of course not! I'm just having some fun."

"I'm going home," she said firmly as she turned away.

Brian stepped forward. "I'll drive ya."

She turned and glared at him. "Are you crazy? I'm not getting in a car with you when you're drunk!"

"It's just a little buzz! It's not like I'm drunk!" Brian said. "I can drive real fine."

"I think not!" She turned on her heel to march away, but Brian reached out and grabbed her arm and wrenched her around. He squeezed her body next to him. "How about a kiss for the road?" he said as he pressed his lips against hers.

She grimaced and turned her face away and squirmed in his grip. "Let me go!"

Cam was incensed by Brian's manhandling of her and pounced toward the two of them as she struggled in Brian's grip. "Leave her alone!" Cam shouted as he grabbed Brian by the arm and yanked him away from her.

"Are you her bodyguard or what?" Brian demanded angrily. "I can kiss her if I want!"

"She's not your girlfriend anymore, Brian. She's mine!" Cam yelled.

Brian's eyebrow shot up. "Oh, she is, is she? Well, you didn't waste anytime moving in on my territory, Sport. I thought you were my *friend*, and you steal my girl from me?"

"I didn't *steal* her!" Cam yelled. "She *left* you!"

Brian stepped closer, clenching his fists. "So you're the reason she broke up with me! I'll teach you a lesson, Chicago boy!"

Before Cam could react, Brian lunged toward him in a bright yellow blur and punched, catching Cam right above his left cheekbone. Cam felt as though he'd been hit in the face with a hammer, and as his brain reverberated inside his skull, he stumbled back and fell on his rear with a thud.

Cam tried to shake his head clear, the blow still ringing in his ears. He tasted blood in his mouth and his bottom stung from the fall on the gravel. He wondered how he could have been so stupid not to see Brian's right hook coming. Cam jumped to his feet ready to fight back.

"What did you *do*?" Lindsay screamed at Brian, backing away in horror.

Cam lunged at Brian, who was standing ready like a boxer. Brian swung at him again, but this time Cam was ready and pivoted away just in time. Brian's fist struck only air. Cam extended his leg behind Brian and shoved him backward, tripping him. As he fell, Brian grabbed Cam and the two of them tumbled to the ground, punching and kicking in a swirling ball of intertwined arms and legs.

"Fight! Fight!" Patrick shouted, punching the air with his fist.

"Oh, my God!" Lindsay yelled. "Somebody do something!"

Their fists flailing, Cam and Brian wrestled, grunting and spitting curse words. An excited crowd gathered around, chanting encouragement. Brian was larger and stronger, but his size had little advantage since they were now brawling on the ground. All of Cam's energy attempted to keep Brian from moving his arms or kicking his legs, and Brian was doing the same to him. Their fight had stalemated.

Above the chanting, in the distance, Cam could hear a police whistle blowing.

Someone grabbed him from behind and yanked him off Brian and onto his feet. His shoes hardly touched the ground as he was pulled away. Cam kept boxing, kicking, and screaming as if he were having a temper tantrum. He saw a police officer grab Brian and subdue him.

Brian glared at Cam with angry eyes, dirt and blood staining his torn, yellow tank top. "I'll get you!" he yelled at Cam.

"You and what army?" Cam shouted back.

"Settle down, kid!" a stern voice ordered in Cam's ear. "Fight's over!"

Cam's arms were pulled behind his back. He stopped struggling and turned his head to see the police officer restraining him. He recognized the man—Officer Fred.

A sense of déjà vu settled over Cam like an evening fog. He didn't want to be in trouble with the law again. The springtime party in Chicago was so recent, and now he was being manhandled by a cop once again. Where was his luck these days?

Officer Fred held Cam securely and asked, "Now what's this all about?"

His head throbbed as his body ached from the fight. He tried to shake the alcohol-induced gauziness from his thoughts. He took a deep breath as he let his gaze drop to the ground. He didn't want to say anything. Nothing good could come from it.

He was in trouble.

Officer Fred looked at Brian. "Who started it?"

Brian remained silent as well. He stared at Cam across the gulf between them. Patrick and Lindsay stood nearby. Patrick quickly pitched his soda cup into the bushes to hide the evidence they had been drinking. Lindsay remained expressionless, her hand covering her mouth.

Officer Fred let out an exasperated sigh. "I guess you buddies aren't talking, huh?" He slackened his grip on Cam. "I want you to shake hands now."

Cam was in no mood to shake hands with Brian, but the officer pushed them together. They watched each other warily, and then Brian slowly extended his hand. Cam hesitated, for Brian was a bully. He had grabbed Lindsay, forced a kiss on her, and wouldn't let her go. Cam felt justified coming to her defense.

Then Cam looked at Lindsay, who was sobbing. Tears ran down her cheeks.

His heart shriveled inside. He suddenly felt sorry. He hadn't meant to make her cry.

Begrudgingly, he shook Brian's hand.

Brian didn't release his grip immediately. Instead, he leaned closer and said quietly, "You all right, Sport?"

Cam's face throbbed, and he felt something warm running down his chin. He touched his mouth and his finger came back red. He had cut his lip, meaning the splattered blood on Brian's shirt was his. "I think so."

"You have quite a punch," Brian said, rubbing his side.

"You, too," Cam said, wiping his forearm across his bloody lip.

They released their grip and smiled slightly at one another.

Officer Fred cleared his throat. "Friends again?" He didn't wait for an answer before adding, "We don't tolerate behavior like that here. The two of you are banned from the remainder of the festival."

Banned? Can they really do that?

"We're taking you home to your parents now," the officer said.

As they were herded away from the scene toward the police cars with their flashing lights, Cam turned back to Lindsay. She was dabbing her teary eyes with a tissue, watching their removal silently, her lips closed in a tight, disappointed expression.

Was she upset because the cops were ejecting them from the festival, or disappointed because he and Brain had gotten in a fight? Surely she was thankful Cam had come to her rescue. Wouldn't any girl have wanted that?

But a nagging feeling crept up his spine. Despite good intentions, he had somehow screwed up with her tonight. Things had been going well until the end. They'd played games, they'd gone on rides, and they'd passionately kissed under the maple tree. But somehow, he'd blown it.

Was it because he had drunk the whiskey? Had fun laughing and joking with Brian and Patrick? Was it the fight? He wasn't sure why she looked so sad.

Somehow he knew he had ruined everything.

Cam suddenly felt very alone, cast adrift in Lake Tecumseh again, as he was led away by the police.

CHAPTER TEN

"I'm disappointed in you, Cam," Uncle Gary said, drumming his fingers on the kitchen table. "I expected more from you."

Aunt Ellen stood behind her husband, her hands resting supportively on his shoulders. She emitted a weary sigh. "Your mother warned me, but you've given us no trouble till now."

Cam faced his relatives across the Formica table, his eyes cast downward. His head throbbed from the after effects of the alcohol. He rubbed his swollen cheek. "Brian started it," he mumbled. "He grabbed Lindsay."

"It doesn't matter who started it," Uncle Gary said firmly. "You shouldn't be fighting. Now look at what's happened—you're banned from the festival, including that big dance you wanted to go to."

"I don't know what I'm going to tell your mother . . ." Aunt Ellen said, her voice trailing off.

Cam glanced up. "What can *she* do about it? She's in Italy with that jerk."

"She's your mother and deserves to know what happened," Aunt Ellen replied. "And I'm sure Frank's a wonderful man, not a jerk."

Cam pushed back his chair, screeching the metal feet across the floor. "My mom will make it worse by rubbing my nose in it for years like she's done with everything else."

"Now, Cam, that's unfair," his aunt said. "Your mom tries the best she can. It hasn't been easy for her since your dad died."

Cam didn't understand the connection. He crossed his arms against his chest, sealing himself off emotionally. He didn't want to be having this argument.

His uncle stood and leaned over the table. "You really have an attitude, young man."

Cam shrugged. "So?"

Unexpectedly, his uncle grabbed him by the arm and yanked him onto his feet. Cam's chair fell backward and slammed to the floor. "Hey! Hey!" Cam protested.

Aunt Ellen let out a small shriek. Uncle Gary dragged Cam toward the kitchen door.

"What are you doing?" Cam demanded. "Let me go!"

"Outside!" his uncle growled, shoving Cam through the doorway. "For a man-to-man talk."

"Gary! What—?" Aunt Ellen said

Her husband held out a palm to stop her. "It's *tough love*, Ellen!"

"But you're not his parent—"

"Just wait here!"

In the middle of the gravel driveway, spotlighted by the high summer sun as if they were on a stage, Cam's uncle faced him with an angry, red face. "You're in big trouble, and you've got some explaining to do!"

Cam avoided eye contact and let his gaze drift over the side of the house and into the treetops. He would've preferred to be anywhere else at the moment.

"Look at me!" his uncle demanded.

Cam refocused his attention. "It was nothing. There was a fight. *Big deal.* Why is your underwear in a knot over this?"

"You were *drunk*! How did *that* happen?"

Cam didn't know his uncle knew about that part. Again his attention drifted. He watched the treetops swaying in the light breeze. A busy red-headed woodpecker flicked from one trunk to the next.

"Answer me!"

"We were just having a little fun—"

A slight smirk formed on Cam's lips as he recalled the evening.

Uncle Gary suddenly grabbed him by the shoulders and shook him. "This isn't some kind of joke!"

Cam looked at his uncle, noticing the throbbing veins in his neck and temples. The man appeared very angry.

"What's *your* problem?" Cam demanded.

Uncle Gary released him and pushed him back. "Your mother was right! You're just like your father!"

Just like your father.

The phrase struck Cam more powerfully than any of Brian's punches.

His mother thought he was just like his father? His crude, beer-swilling, underachieving father? The guy who had killed himself by falling off a roof?

Was it true?

"And she's right," his uncle added. "You *are* just like your father. Not only are you his spitting image, you sound and act just like him. I should know. He got into drunken brawls, too. Damn! The apple sure doesn't fall far from the tree."

Cam's mind swirled as though it were one of the falling apples: spinning down, down, down.

He never wanted to be like his father. In fact, he thought he was very different. He wasn't surprised his mother would make a comment like that—she was always needling him about something—but Uncle Gary?

Over the past several weeks Cam had grown to respect his uncle. And now he agreed with his mother?

Just like your father.

Cam thought his uncle was overreacting. Just because he looked like his father—he couldn't help the genes he had inherited—didn't mean he was *the same* as his father, did it?

The question must have been painted on his face, for his uncle's expression softened from one of anger to one of resignation and disappointment.

They both stood in silence for several moments, and then Uncle Gary said, "I know it hurts to be compared to your father, but you need to hear that so you can rise above it."

Cam flashed on his father, a man with some good sides but also a very bad side—alcoholism. His old man had really enjoyed his drink, and Cam did, too, for the few times he had done it.

His head still ached from the Jim Beam. Why hadn't he listened to Lindsay? He respected her opinions about everything else, why not the wisdom regarding drinking? Why hadn't he stopped after just a few sips? Why had he kept taking the bottle from Patrick, refilling his cup with whiskey, and ultimately getting head-spinning drunk?

Perhaps he had inherited the same dysfunctional alcoholism genes that had cursed his father. He had never really thought about it before, considering himself too strong to fall into such a trap.

He had gotten drunk. Many kids did that. But he had failed himself, Lindsay, his mother, his aunt and uncle, everyone. He was a big screw-up. Was he heading down the same path as his father?

The man had been gone for three years. Since his death, Cam felt adrift on a raft with no one to guide him through a difficult and unfriendly world.

He missed his dad. He wished he were there at that very moment to hug him and tell him how much he was loved regardless of the many mistakes he had made.

Even *screw-ups* deserved to be loved.

Beyond Cam's ability to contain them, tears pooled in his eyes. His knees, once so powerful and defiant, seemed to collapse under his own bodyweight.

Just like your father.

The words burned through him more intensely than anything anyone had ever said to him, and he knew the reason: he *was* like his father, and he had tried everything to avoid admitting to himself that he was.

Deep down, Cam knew the truth, and it hurt. For years his father had been the bogeyman in his mind, the man who had not only screwed up his own life, but Cam's and his mother's lives, too. The ghost was easy to blame for all their troubles.

The problem was the ghost was not haunting some faraway locale, some forgotten home. The ghost was inside his heart, and he didn't think he could ever exorcize it.

Uncle Gary embraced him just as the tears streaked down Cam's cheeks in salty torrents. The touch was comforting, but Cam wished it were his father holding him instead. He could hardly remember the feel of his father's arms around him. His father's voice was fading from memory as well. Only photos kept his image alive, and Cam found them painful to view.

His emotional eruption came from somewhere deep inside him, from a place in his soul he had left unexplored. Unable to suppress it, an anguished cry emerged from his mouth.

His uncle patted his back gently and whispered, "Let it out, Cam. You miss your father and you need to let yourself grieve."

For three years Cam had avoided grieving, seeing it as an unmanly sign of weakness.

He thought back: He was fourteen again and the sonorous notes of an organ reverberated through the ornate room of the historic funeral home.

He approached the pedestal within the small grove of bouquets. The spectacular flower arrangements were gaudy in their extravagance and impermanence. The polished side of the sleek black casket reflected the image of him and his mother as they slowly neared. The coffin's lid was open like a giant clam, revealing a white, ruffled interior.

His father's body rested inside. Dressed in a pin-striped suit with a red carnation on the lapel, his hair uncharacteristically neatly combed, his father looked oddly at peace.

Like a walking shadow in her black dress, his mother fell over the open casket and sobbed uncontrollably. Cam stood by idly, twisting his fingers together nervously, eager for the conclusion of the morbid ritual.

It seemed cruel to hold such an extended good-bye to someone who had caused them such pain. He waited silently, hoping his mother would pull herself together like he had. He needed to be strong. Crying was not his way. That was for women and babies, and Cam was a man at fourteen. He had to act like one.

Three years later the tears and pain that Cam had submerged inside for so long had finally surfaced. He cried, unable to stifle the upwelling emotions of loss and regret.

Uncle Gary held him tightly and, drawn by the commotion outside, Aunt Ellen emerged from the house and swallowed him up in her arms as well. She started crying, too, and the three of them stood in the driveway in a shared embrace.

"Your father was a good man," Uncle Gary said. "Hold on tightly to the good memories, but cast the bad ones away."

"Like all of us, he was only human," Aunt Ellen added.

After several minutes, they finally broke apart and dried their eyes.

Cam felt drained, and from the looks of his relatives, they were, too. Perhaps they had never fully grieved for their loss as well.

"I'm sorry," Cam choked out, wiping his eyes again. "I miss my dad."

"We all miss him," Uncle Gary said.

"Especially your mother," Aunt Ellen said. "He was the love of her life. The father of her son. Don't be so hard on her. Every time she looks at you she sees him. She can never escape the pain of his absence."

Cam thought of his mother, wondering what she was doing right now on the other side of the world.

Aunt Ellen was right—he *was* hard on her. She was trying to make a new life for herself, and it couldn't have been easy after being married for twenty years.

Uncle Gary put his hand on Cam's shoulder. "I'm sure your dad's watching over you right now, full of love and pride because of the fine young man you've become."

Cam forced a small smile. Although spiritual things had never comforted him, he wanted to believe his dad still protected him.

Truly contrite, Cam said, "I'm sorry about last night. I really screwed up."

"That's okay, honey," Aunt Ellen said. "We love you anyway."

"Do you think I'm an alcoholic like my dad?" Cam asked, barely above a whisper.

Aunt Ellen hugged him. "Of course not! You're young, Cam. You just made some mistakes. You're going to make a lot of mistakes in your life. We all do."

"It doesn't mean you're an alcoholic," Uncle Gary said. "You have your whole life ahead of you. You just need to make the right choices."

Cam took a deep breath and tried to clear his head. "Thanks," he said, honestly. "Thanks for understanding."

"No problem," his uncle said. "Of course we won't be expecting any more visits from the police in the middle of the night."

"No way!" Cam said. "Never again!"

His aunt smiled. "How about apple pie? I have Cool-Whip!"

The three of them smiled and filed inside the house.

Cam felt lighter, for the grinding weight of his internal reservoir of hate and resentment about his father had lessened. He swore he would learn from his mistakes and be a better person. That's what his father would have wanted.

And now he needed to talk to Lindsay, to explain what had happened, and to apologize.

How would she react when he called her?

Would she be as understanding as his relatives?

Would she even want anything to do with him any more?

The phone rang as they were sitting at the kitchen table eating pie. Aunt Ellen grabbed the receiver off its hook. "Hello? Oh, hi, Lindsay. He's right here."

She handed the phone to Cam. Its coiled cord stretched from the wall like a plastic umbilical. He took the phone cautiously, surprised Lindsay had called after everything that had happened the night before.

"Cam, are you okay?" Lindsay asked.

"I'm fine," he answered, not wanting to launch into a description of his bruises, muscle soreness, and pounding headache.

"I was worried so I thought I'd call."

Cam noticed his aunt and uncle were both watching him intently. They acted momentarily embarrassed for eavesdropping.

"Hold on," Cam said as he stood and pulled the phone and its long cord into the back porch to talk with more privacy. "I'm really sorry, Lindsay," he said into the phone, lowering his voice. "I'll never do anything like that again."

"You guys got out of control last night."

"I know, and I apologize. I hope you'll want to see me again."

She did not answer.

Cam hung onto the phone like a life preserver. The silence was drowned out by his thumping heart. How would she respond? Would she dump him?

Finally, she sighed and said, "Sure, I'd like to see you again, Cam."

He exhaled with relief; disaster had been averted.

"Too bad you're banned from the festival," she continued. "There are better bands tonight."

Cam was disappointed about the ban, but ecstatic that she was still interested in him.

The day was looking much brighter already.

After a long heart-to-heart telephone conversation, Cam and Lindsay made plans to meet at the workshop to inspect the meteorite.

She was concerned because her grandfather wanted to tidy up the oil that had spilled from the cracked rock. She didn't want him to contaminate the specimen and ruin its scientific value.

"And once again he's not answering the phone," she had said, frustrated. "What's up about old people and phones?"

Cam asked Uncle Gary for permission to leave the house, fearing he might have been "grounded" for punishment. His mother would have done something like that.

His uncle waved him away with a sly grin. "Go on and see her. Just stay out of trouble and don't try to sneak into the festival."

Thankful for the leniency, he grabbed his bike and pedaled toward Orville Milford's house.

The heat wave still maintained its chokehold on the land, and Cam was dripping sweat by the time he arrived. Lindsay rode up beside him almost simultaneously. Although she had also perspired in the heat, and strands of her brown hair stuck to her cheeks in the high humidity, he thought she looked as beautiful as ever.

He reached out, smoothed back her errant locks, and kissed her. "Good to see you again."

"You, too," she answered. "I like you sober much better!"

He chuckled nervously. "I'm going to stay this way from now on!"

"Good!" She looked past her grandfather's tow truck to the workshop. The building's weather vane was motionless in the still, hot air. "Let's go see the meteorite."

They walked to the workshop. She pounded on the door. "Grandpa! Are you in there?"

There was no answer, but the wooden doors parted slightly.

"That's strange," she said. "He usually locks it."

She pushed open the door.

They stepped into the workshop and caught a whiff of the overpowering petroleum odor.

Their eyes were immediately drawn to the fractured rock on the table. The small crack had widened even further so the rock resembled a tin can lying on its side with its top peeled back. The oil from inside had completely drained out, creating a large black slick that draped over the edge of the table and pooled on the floor like icing dripping from a macabre wedding cake.

And everywhere among the oily residue were the black shards of what had once been the small spheres. They lay scattered about in tiny piles, like crumpled egg shells.

"What's happened?" Lindsay said. "Did he smash all these things? Why would he do that?"

They scanned the workshop. A fluttering overhead caught their attention, and they both looked up simultaneously. There, flittering amid the dusty rafters of the workshop's ceiling and bouncing around the hanging fluorescent lights, were the strangest things Cam had ever seen.

His lips parted in surprise as he stood, dumbfounded.

It was as if the pages from his dream journal had been ripped out and magically summoned to life: pale green creatures, about eight inches tall, perched on the rafters like giant spiders, their spindly legs curling and stretching like the fingers of a hand.

They resembled lollipops with six legs. Their bulbous heads were shaped like polyhedrons, cut into facets like a diamond, and stood atop stick-like bodies. A green glow shined within their heads, pulsing with mysterious inner energy.

The creatures were almost identical to the sculpture Orville had erected in the woods, except only about one-tenth the size.

"What the—?" Cam mumbled.

"I don't believe it!" Lindsay said. "What are those things?"

She stepped forward, but he reached out and stopped her. "Careful, they might be dangerous."

She creased her brow. "You're right." She scanned the broken spheres littering the bench top and concrete floor. "They must've hatched from the meteorite!"

"This is unreal!" Cam said. He counted about three dozen creatures overhead. They were like specters, identical in every way to those he had seen in his dreams and sketched in his journals, but much smaller.

Lindsay gasped and raised a hand to cover her mouth.

Cam followed her gaze and saw what had frightened her: on the far side of the workshop, obscured from their direct observation by crates and woodworking equipment, someone's legs protruded from behind the table. He immediately recognized the dusty jeans and worn army boots as Orville Milford's.

"Oh, my God!" Lindsay sobbed. "Grandpa's in trouble! We've got to get him out of here!"

Her panicked voice agitated the creatures perched on the rafters. The mass fluttered like tree leaves being stirred by an autumn wind.

Cam hushed her. "Don't make any sudden moves. We don't wanna startle them. They might attack us, too."

She looked at him, her sepia eyes welling with tears. "You think they attacked him?"

"I dunno, but we gotta be careful." He had feared the creatures in his dreams, and he figured they were probably dangerous in real life.

He instinctively lowered his head as they crossed cautiously and silently toward where the body lay. He watched the creatures as he gingerly moved forward, afraid they might come swooping down.

The insect-like creatures stayed in the rafters, their strange heads pulsating with light. Their spindly legs curled and unfolded like sinister little vines.

Orville was sprawled on his side atop wood shavings. Cam and Lindsay crouched over him and gently turned him on his back. A large, red welt resembling an insect bite marked his neck.

Lindsay lowered her ear to his mouth. "He's still breathing," she whispered. "Let's drag him out of here."

They grabbed the man's arms and dragged him across the shop floor. He started to regain consciousness and groaned loudly and began thrashing.

The commotion startled the creatures overhead. Their heads glowed brighter, and they strummed their tiny, tube-like feet quicker. The noise sounded like the irritated tapping of hundreds of pencils on a desk top.

They pulled Orville toward the door, through the pool of black oil and the shattered egg shells, which crunched beneath them. Incoherent and mumbling nonsensical syllables, he struggled against them, froth bubbling from his mouth.

"Just a few more feet," Lindsay said.

They nearly got the old man to the threshold when several of the spider-like creatures began flitting about nervously like moths buzzing around candlelight. Several of them pounced from the rafters and glided downward in a swarm, descending silently like a mass of falling green balloons.

"Watch out!" Cam screamed.

When the creatures floated too close to them, Cam let go of Orville and swatted the things away with his hands. They weighed almost nothing; he felt as if he were punching jellyfish.

Lindsay shrieked as the spidery creatures converged on her, too. One of them got tangled in her hair, its little feet clawing her scalp while its polygonal head pulsed with light. "Get it off me!" she screamed hysterically, flailing her arms while trying to dislodge it.

Clubbing the airborne creatures as if they were swirling flies, Cam went to Lindsay and grabbed the writhing creature caught in her hair. Its head was the size of a baseball, and he yanked it free, pulling out a few strands of her hair in the process. He pitched the creature against the wall, where it went splat like a spit ball, leaving a streak of green slime, a deflated head sac, and twitching, pencil-thick legs.

"Let's get out of here!" he yelled.

Several creatures landed on Orville. Cam brushed them away and grabbed the old man's arms and dragged him toward the door as Lindsay swatted the air behind them.

More green creatures dropped from the ceiling just as they pulled Orville outside.

Cam immediately shut the door, sealing the creatures inside the workshop. He and Lindsay propped against it as they caught their breath.

He could not believe what had just happened. Outside it was a bright summer afternoon. Inside, strange alien creatures flitted about like mosquitoes.

"Do you think this'll hold them?" Lindsay asked.

"I think so. They're not very strong. They're like bags of air."

Orville groaned and shook his head back and forth. Lindsay bent down over him. "Grandpa! Grandpa! Are you all right?"

The old man twitched, as if he were having a seizure.

"We gotta get him to the hospital! He's been stung!"

"I'll call 9-1-1!" Cam said, turning on his heel toward the house.

"There's no time for that! Let's take the truck!"

Cam stopped and looked at the tow truck parked in the driveway, with *Milford's UFO Towing Service – You Crash, We Dash,* on the side door. "Are you sure?"

She nodded. "Help me get him inside!"

With difficulty, they manhandled the moaning old man into the passenger seat of the tow truck.

Lindsay climbed in after him and held him in a bear hug. She felt his forehead. "Hurry, Cam! He's burning up!"

The truck's seat cushions were cracked and brittle, revealing yellow foam padding. Cam jumped behind the steering wheel. The keys were in the ignition. He started the engine, which rumbled like an old tractor.

He hesitated, looking at the unfamiliar peddles and levers.

"Do you know how to drive a stick?" she asked.

"Kinda."

"Well, hurry!"

He pushed in the clutch and shifted to reverse. Quickly backing the large tow truck out of the driveway, he scraped the fender against the mailbox. He and Lindsay cringed at the screech of metal on metal.

"Don't worry about that!" she shouted. "Just get us there quick!"

Cam pulled onto the road and sped toward the county hospital.

Next to him, in the passenger seat, Lindsay cradled her grandfather. Sweat beaded on the old man's head. Drool dripped from his half-open mouth. Every minute or so, his body shuddered.

"Hurry!" Lindsay yelled, distraught.

Cam pushed the accelerator to the floor; the truck's engine whined. Black, oily smoke belched from the exhaust stack. They raced toward the hospital, which seemed so far away.

*   *   *

Lindsay paced the hospital waiting room, her arms folded. She waited nervously for news about her grandfather's condition. She looked at Cam and shook her head. "We should've heard something by now."

They had been waiting for over an hour since Orville was admitted to the ER.

Cam sat in a chair, its upholstery frayed from many previous anxious waits. The waiting room was empty except for the nurse at the reception counter. The room smelled vaguely of antiseptic.

Not knowing how to answer, he reached out and squeezed her hand to comfort her.

She smiled weakly before withdrawing and crossing to the nurse's station. "Any word yet?"

The nurse looked over the top of her glasses. "Nothing since the last time you asked five minutes ago. Please have a seat, dear. Your mom will be out shortly."

Lindsay turned on her heel and went back to Cam. "This is my fault!"

"What do you mean?"

"I instigated the retrieval of the meteorite from the lake. If I hadn't pushed everybody, those spider creatures never would've stung Grandpa!"

"You had no idea—none of us did. We didn't know it would be dangerous."

She wrung her hands as she paced. "We should've listened to him! He warned us about it. He said we should leave it alone!"

She started sobbing. Cam stood up and embraced her. "He'll be all right. The doctors will take care of him."

"Oh, Cam, what *are* those things? They must be alien life from outer space! I would be excited if Grandpa wasn't lying in a hospital bed because of them."

Cam held her tightly. "Both he and I saw those creatures in our dreams. They've been communicating with us using ESP."

"But why just you two?"

He shrugged. "I dunno. Maybe our brain waves are similar to theirs or something." He recalled his nightmares. He felt the dull throbbing of the recurring headache that never went away completely. "It's even stronger now that they've hatched."

"Stronger? Can you make any sense of it?"

"No, not really. I can't understand any of it. I just feel it in my head, like listening to a distant storm, or overhearing a party from down the hall."

Lindsay's mother emerged from the double doors wearing blue scrubs and a blue cap. A stethoscope dangled across her breast like a necklace and her ID badge read *Amy Brock, R.N.*

"Mom!" Lindsay cried, running toward her and hugging her. "How is he?"

Her mother smoothed Lindsay's hair. "We're not sure yet. He's got some kind of infection. We're trying to control his fever, and we put in some IV's."

"Can I see him?"

"Not yet. The doctors are still busy with him."

"Is he going to be okay?"

"I'll let you know as soon as I find out anything." Her mother consoled her with another hug and a gentle brush to her cheek.

Lindsay wiped her eyes. "Mom, we know what's wrong with him!"

A shrill announcement over the hospital intercom urgently summoned Nurse Brock back to the ER. "I've got to go," she told Lindsay. "Just stay calm, and everything will be all right."

"But Mom, he was stung by one of the creatures!"

Nurse Brock rushed from the waiting room, shaking her head. "Not now, I've got to go!"

"They're all over his workshop!" Cam shouted to the nurse's back as she pushed through the doors and was gone.

Lindsay clenched her fists. "Why didn't she listen to us?" She went to the nurse at the counter and said, "You've got to tell the doctors that my grandpa was stung by an alien creature!"

The nurse looked over her glasses and narrowed her eyes. "I'm busy, hon. I don't have time to listen to your silly *Star Trek* stories. Please have a seat, and I'll let you know when there's any news."

Lindsay exhaled loudly with exasperation as she turned away. "Nobody wants to listen to us!"

"It does sound pretty farfetched when you think about it," Cam admitted.

Lindsay headed for the door. "Those creatures are dangerous, and they're all over the workshop. We better go to the police."

Cam trailed behind her. "Do you think they'll believe us?"

"I don't know, but we've got to try!"

* * *

Sheriff Little leaned back in his chair and eyed Cam and Lindsay warily as he drummed a yellow pencil on the paper pile on his overcrowded desk. His large belly squeezed against his uniform, and some of the black buttons looked ready to pop off any minute. "You expect me to believe that story?" he asked, his tone gruff and skeptical.

Exasperated, Lindsay shook her head. "Why would we lie about something like this?"

Sheriff Little smacked the desk with his pencil and then tossed it into an old coffee mug full of mismatched pens, pencils, and markers. "Oh, I dunno. For a thrill? A laugh? Who knows?"

Cam looked at Lindsay. They had been no more successful convincing Sheriff Little of the alien menace as the nurse at the hospital.

The Sheriff wasn't buying any of it, as evidenced by the scowl on his face. With a shake of his head, he rose from his chair. "You kids have wasted enough of my time this evening."

"You've got to believe us!" Lindsay insisted, her cheeks reddening. "The creatures are in the workshop, and they're like nothing you've ever seen before."

"And it's just a coincidence this is the weekend of UFO Days," the sheriff said. "You're trying to bamboozle me with some cockamamie story about alien life forms."

"No we're not!" Lindsay said.

"You're probably in cahoots with my opponent in the upcoming election, looking to embarrass me somehow or use this against me in the campaign."

"No, sir," Cam said. "We're telling the truth!"

"You've got to believe us," Lindsay said. "My grandpa's in the ER and the creatures are responsible!"

Sheriff Little grunted. He was an older version of his son, Brian, but with thirty years of extra fat. "Your grandpa's an old man and his hospitalization has nothing to do with getting stung by alien creatures."

"You know me well, sir," Lindsay said, changing tactics. "Would I be making something like this up?"

He glanced suspiciously at Cam. "Normally, I wouldn't think so, Lindsay, but you've been hanging out with the wrong element this summer."

"Cam didn't put me up to this, and he's not the *wrong element*!"

Cam liked that she was defending his reputation, which had gotten trashed after the fight with Brian.

The sheriff's son. No wonder the man was skeptical. Cam wondered if Lindsay would have been more successful if she had met with the authorities alone.

Sheriff Little shuffled through the papers on his desk. "Now please excuse me, I have work to do."

Cam and Lindsay looked at each other with disappointment. Why were they having so much difficulty getting any adults to believe their story?

The sheriff's phone rang, and he picked up the receiver and announced himself. As he listened to the caller, they watched his expression change from weary annoyance to wide-eyed surprise.

"I'll be right there," he said as he hung up the phone, donned his hat, and quickly moved toward the door.

Cam and Lindsay trailed on his heels, barking questions like braying reporters.

"What is it, Sheriff?" Cam asked.

"Is something wrong?" Lindsay asked. "Is it my grandfather?"

"There's a fire," the sheriff answered, pushing out of the door. "At Orville Milford's workshop."

Cam and Lindsay looked at each other. "The creatures!" they said in unison as they raced after him.

CHAPTER ELEVEN

The odor was unmistakable: a pungent mixture of burning wood, shingles, and paint. Cam smelled the building on fire long before he turned the tow truck onto the road heading toward Orville Milford's property.

Lindsay sat in the passenger seat, her right hand resting nervously on the door handle, as if she were willing to jump out to get there faster.

She pointed through the windshield. "Look!"

A black plume boiled into the twilight sky like an erupting volcano. Venus, the Evening Star, twinkled above, periodically blocked by the smoke as the breeze shifted.

"I don't believe it," Lindsay said. "How can Grandpa's shop be on fire?"

"Maybe the creatures did it," Cam said as he slowed the truck.

In the street ahead, at the end of the Milford driveway, police cars and fire trucks blocked their approach, hiding the fire from view. First responders shouted instructions and scrambled around the vehicles, pulling hoses and hauling equipment. The branches of the trees looked ghostly in the flashing emergency lights.

A police officer stood in the roadway and signaled for Cam to stop. Cam braked and leaned out the window to speak to him.

Officer Fred looked them over warily, his hand on his sidearm. "What are you kids doing driving Mr. Milford's tow truck?"

"It was an emergency," Lindsay said. "We used it to take him to the hospital."

"Uh, okay." Officer Fred mumbled upon recognizing her. "You'll have to turn around. Fire up ahead."

"What's going on?" Lindsay asked.

"The workshop's on fire," the officer explained. "They're trying to keep it from spreading to the house." He motioned with his flashlight. "You're blocking emergency vehicles, so back up!"

"But the alien creatures—" Lindsay said.

"Back it up!"

"All right, all right," Cam grumbled as he put the tow truck into reverse and awkwardly turned the vehicle around. He felt as if he were manhandling a barge, as he had never maneuvered a vehicle that size before.

"We can't leave now," Lindsay said, glancing behind them as they drove away. She pointed to an upcoming side road. "We've got to get a closer look. Turn there."

Following her directions, he drove into a heavily wooded area and then pulled onto the narrow gravel shoulder. The sides of the tow truck scraped against overgrown tree branches and bushes. He stopped precariously close to the weed-filled drainage ditch, the vehicle leaning to its side.

She immediately opened her door and slid from the listing cab, climbing through the vegetation. "The police can't stop us. We'll sneak through the woods to see what's going on."

Cam turned off the engine and clicked off the headlights, plunging them into darkness. He followed her into the woods.

Just enough twilight remained to guide their way toward the Milford property. They found a path and followed it past Orville's alien sculpture, which looked ominous standing in the darkness.

Cam blanched; he hated the sculpture as much as the living creatures.

The two of them approached the workshop unobserved, and hid themselves among the trees for a clear view of the chaotic scene.

The workshop was completely consumed by a red-hot fire belching heavy smoke skyward. Patches of the building's exterior walls had burned through, letting yellow flames emerge like writhing tongues flicking defiantly at the surrounding firefighters. Flaming tendrils curled around the eaves, crinkling the roof shingles with their blistering heat.

"Oh my God," Lindsay whispered.

Cam felt the warmth from the conflagration, even though they watched from about twenty yards away. Amid the smoke, he caught a glimpse of the rooster weather vane rotating dizzily in the updraft.

Sparks and ash from the burning shop drifted over Orville's house. The firefighters were spraying water on its roof to prevent the eruption of a secondary fire. The Fire Chief and Sheriff Little surveyed the scene from the side, barking orders at their men.

Cam turned his attention back to the burning workshop. The inferno was so intense he was certain the alien creatures could not have survived. He imagined them inside, hopping through the rafters trying to escape. Their fragile gelatinous bodies offered little protection from such temperatures. He pictured them curling up and melting in the hellish flames like plastic wrappers thrown into a campfire.

"Grandpa's going to be heartbroken," Lindsay said. "All his tools and stuff gone."

"I'm really sorry," Cam said, holding her hand.

After a few more minutes, the fire reached the roof of the workshop. As the flames burned through the rafters, the integrity of the structure was fatally weakened. The walls collapsed upon themselves like a crumbling house of cards. The rooster weather vane vanished amid the crush of debris.

Nourished by the influx of oxygen, the fire roared even stronger, sending glowing embers high into the sky like ascending spirits.

"What could've caused the fire?" Cam asked.

"I bet it was the oil from the meteorite. I tested it in the lab. It was very flammable."

Firefighters manhandled a bucking fire hose, spraying water over the shrinking pyre that had once been the workshop. The water evaporated and sizzled like frying bacon as it struck the hot remains.

After being thoroughly doused, and its fuel nearly exhausted, the fire was eventually extinguished. Smoke rose from the smoldering wreck, and what little wood remaining glowed orange like charcoal briquettes.

Lindsay motioned him farther back into the woods. "Nothing more to see here until everyone leaves."

They waited patiently as the operation wound down. Sheriff Little and the police left first. The firefighters stayed a little longer, joking and laughing as they collected their hoses and gear. The fire was probably welcome excitement for a volunteer fire department in a small town.

Cam and Lindsay held hands, watching from the dark woods. The air was still heavy with the smell of smoke. Crickets chirped in the underbrush. Overhead, Venus was setting and the Milky Way splashed across the sky.

He squeezed her hand and whispered, "You're missing the UFO Festival."

"I don't care. This is more important, and I'd rather be with you anyway."

He smiled, but he didn't think she could see it, so he kissed her cheek.

Finally, the firefighters departed. The scene was suddenly very quiet and dark. All that remained of the workshop was a pyramid of black sticks and twisted metal smoldering in the night.

"Let's take a look," Lindsay said.

They approached the ruin, sloshing in muddy puddles left by the water spray. They poked around the warm debris with sticks, looking for anything recognizable amid the jumbled slag heap. Everything was melted and molded together. Cam saw fragments of Orville's metal tools, softened and twisted into indiscernible shapes.

"Be careful. Everything's still very hot," she cautioned.

He felt the residual heat transfer through his sneakers. "What are we looking for?"

"Evidence of the alien creatures," she said, kicking debris with her foot. "We need proof they really existed." She bent down and inspected a pile of smoking wreckage. She pushed away some of the collapsed boards and frowned. "It's too hot to inspect and too dark to see anything."

"I bet they were fried," Cam said. "They were like balls of jelly. They couldn't withstand the fire."

"But the remains of the meteorite should be here somewhere," Lindsay said. "It was as hard as diamond, and it survived reentry into Earth's atmosphere. It would've survived this."

"We need shovels."

In the stillness of the night, a car approached, driving without headlights. The vehicle slowed at the end of Orville's driveway.

"Quick! Back into the woods!" Lindsay ordered.

They scrambled toward the trees as the shadowy car slowly pulled onto the property. They reached the shelter of the woods just as the mysterious car stopped near Orville's house.

The driver and passenger stepped from the car, their figures momentarily illuminated by the sedan's interior dome light. The two men wore dark suits. Cam wondered if they were insurance adjusters or nosy neighbors, but why no lights? Obviously, they didn't want to be observed.

The two men crossed to the ruin of the workshop. They clicked on flashlights and surveyed the wreckage. The night was quiet and Cam and Lindsay were close enough to overhear them speaking.

"This incident's contained," one of the men said as he kicked up a small cloud of ash.

"Easiest one yet," his partner answered, a tinge of pride in his voice. "HQ will be happy this time."

"You want to drive back tonight or wait till morning?"

"Protocol says to wait. We need to check the local news reports to make sure they're whistling Dixie. After that, we can go."

"You're always a stickler for the rules."

"That's why I'm the boss."

The men switched off their flashlights and returned to their vehicle. They departed the scene just as quickly and invisibly as they had arrived, driving with no lights.

After the car had pulled away, Cam finally allowed himself to exhale. "Who were those guys?"

"I bet it was the government!" Lindsay said.

"The government? You mean like secret agents? Why would they come here?"

"Somehow they found out about the alien creatures! But how?"

Cam shuffled his feet nervously. He had to come clean, and it wasn't going to be easy. "I know how. I discussed the UFO in an Internet chat room. I know we were supposed to keep it secret, but I blabbed all about it. I didn't think it was a real UFO, so I didn't think it would matter."

She rubbed her chin in thought. "I bet the agents were monitoring the chat room. Grandpa wasn't paranoid after all! They have been spying on him!"

"I'm sorry."

She smiled. "Don't worry about it. There's nothing we can do now—the word is out. The agents said they had *contained* the incident. They probably set the workshop on fire to kill the creatures and cover up the evidence of extraterrestrial life!"

"No way!"

"If the government is monitoring UFO chat rooms and

investigating sightings, they must be worried about something. They sounded like they're dealing with these incidents all the time!"

"That explains why that reporter was so interested in the story as well."

Lindsay's eyebrow shot up. "What reporter?"

Cam quickly related the story of his conversation with Megan Conrad from *American Investigator Magazine* and explained she was due to arrive in Lake Tecumseh tomorrow.

Lindsay struck him on the arm with the back of her hand. "How come you didn't tell me this before? The UFO chat room, the nosey reporter?"

He shrugged. "I dunno. It didn't seem important, and I was embarrassed by—"

"Is there anything *else* you're hiding from me?"

"No, nothing!"

"You've got to trust me, Cam, if this is going to work. I don't like secrets."

"I know, I know." He felt awful he had let her down. He had done that more than once lately and wondered if this would be her final straw.

Fortunately, she seemed to give him the benefit of the doubt and said, "It's getting late. There's nothing we can accomplish here now anyway."

"You're right. All the evidence of the aliens is destroyed."

"Except for the sphere in the chem lab!"

"Do you think it's hatched by now?"

"Probably. The lab's locked and it's in a glass jar, so it's safe. Mr. Russell won't be back from his conference until tomorrow. We can get it then. That'll be our evidence."

"I promise I won't tell a soul about it!"

She smiled. "Good. Let's keep it a secret. We don't want those government agents destroying it like they did the others."

"What are we going to do with it?"

"I don't know yet. Maybe it'll help my grandpa. Maybe it can expose the government cover-up of the existence of alien life!"

As they walked back to the truck, Lindsay babbled excitedly about the ramifications of alien life in the universe. Cam looked at the star-strewn sky, wondering which point of light was the home of the strange creatures that had descended on such an inconsequential place as Lake Tecumseh, Indiana. He didn't have a clue, but he knew from his dreams they had come a long way.

Then he realized his lingering headache was gone. His mind was clear for the first time since the meteorite had split open. Was that an unexpected benefit of the destruction of the creatures?

He hoped so.

*   *   *

That night Cam was not bothered by the usual abstract dreams of the alien creatures' home planet, or their lonely, cold journey through space, or their fiery, dramatic descent into Earth's atmosphere.

Instead, he tossed and turned, recalling the creatures flitting about the rafters of Orville Milford's workshop, their heads pulsing with light. He relived their attack on him and Lindsay, and their fluttering spidery legs. He dreamt of burning buildings, sinister government agents, and squeezing his body next to Lindsay's as they rolled together across a grassy hillside in the brilliant summer sun.

Perfectly ordinary dreams.

Cam was confident the creatures had been destroyed in the workshop fire. Their extrasensory influence on him had vanished. His dream diary, stuffed with several weeks of scrawled notes and drawings, rested forlornly on the side table, unused.

He hoped he never touched it again.

It was Saturday and the UFO dance was scheduled that evening. He wasn't able to go, but he didn't worry about that as he biked to the hospital to visit Lindsay and her grandfather. Instead, he thought about the alien creatures. Although they had been hidden in the meteorite beneath Lake Tecumseh for 20 years, he had never mentally felt any connection while living in Chicago, 180 miles away. Only when he came to Indiana was he close enough to sense their presence and experience strange dreams. Their mental transmissions apparently had a limited range.

When the meteorite was brought to the surface, his feelings and dreams had intensified. When the creatures hatched, he was racked by headaches. Now the creatures were destroyed, the headaches were gone, and his dreams were back to normal.

It all made sense.

But did the ESP serve any purpose? Were the creatures trying to communicate or were they just emitting noise? And what was it about him and Orville that made them susceptible to their signals? Shared brain waves? A mutant gene? He would probably never know.

Had the creatures tried to influence people, to convince them to retrieve the meteorite from the bottom of the lake and rescue them from their imprisonment? That wasn't likely. Neither he nor Orville had ever felt compelled to retrieve the meteorite. It had been Lindsay's obsession, and she was not influenced by the aliens' ESP at all.

Cam surmised he had been the recipient of the creatures' collective thoughts and feelings. He had only received general impressions of their experience—what they looked like, how their home appeared, and how long and lonely their journey had been. He had gotten no clear, concise thoughts from them at all. No commands to *come rescue us* or *here we are.*

Why was he attributing intelligence to the alien creatures? What had they ever done to demonstrate it? The little, flimsy things glowed and flitted about like buzzing flies. For all external appearances, they could have had the mental power of an insect. But he had felt their intelligence in his dreams of their strange world, their long space voyage, and their eons of loneliness. Theirs was not like human intelligence—of that he was sure.

However, it didn't matter now, for the creatures' effects on him were gone. Their mysterious signals had abruptly ceased upon their destruction in the conflagration.

When Cam entered the hospital waiting room, Lindsay was flipping the pages of a ragged magazine. She looked up with red, tired eyes and rose to embrace him. Tearfully, she explained that her grandfather's condition had worsened overnight. His fever was dangerously high, his vital signs were deteriorating, and the doctors were very concerned.

"Did you tell them about the alien creatures?" Cam asked as he held her.

She nodded as she sobbed. "They're not taking me seriously. Even if they did, it's not like they have an alien antibiotic to pull off the shelf and give to him."

"Is there anything I can do?"

She pulled away and wiped her eyes with her fingers. "I haven't eaten all day. Why don't you wait here while I get a sandwich in the cafeteria?"

"Sure."

She kissed him on the cheek and disappeared down the hall.

He settled into a chair and glanced at the old magazines and newspapers on the table. Their well-worn pages represented hours of anxiety from those waiting for news about ill loved ones.

Lindsay had only been gone a few minutes when a serious looking doctor in medical scrubs entered the waiting room. Cam stood, expecting to get an update on Orville's condition. Instead the doctor ignored him and marched through the double doors into the patient area. The attending nurse at the reception counter was faced the other way, typing on a computer monitor, and did not see the doctor pass by.

Cam went to the doors and watched through the glass panes as the doctor paused at Room 117. The doctor looked suspiciously down the corridor and then silently entered Orville Milford's room.

Cam noticed the doctor was wearing shiny black dress shoes with his medical scrubs. Something wasn't right.

And then he remembered the two government agents inspecting the ruined workshop the night before. Although it had been dark, the furtive doctor looked suspiciously like one of the agents.

He glanced back at the nurse. She was focused on her computer.

He decided he needed to investigate what was happening in Orville's room. He shoved through the doors and moved unobserved down the aisle, stopping at Room 117.

He pushed the door ajar just enough to peek inside.

Orville lay in the bed hooked to a multitude of electronic monitors and tubes. Several IV bags of fluid were suspended on metal racks around him, feeding various liquids into his veins. He was still, his face red and swollen, his breathing quick and shallow. Sweat coated his forehead and cheeks.

The doctor had his back to the door and was adjusting one of the plastic IV bags. He removed a syringe from his pocket, squirted some of the fluid into the air, and then stabbed the needle into the injection port of the IV line. He pushed the plunger of the syringe all the way down, dispensing its contents.

What was he giving him? Cam thought.

The doctor crossed his arms and watched as the infusion pump delivered the injected liquid into the old man's bloodstream.

Suddenly, Orville's body convulsed. The electronic monitors started beeping loudly.

Watching through the cracked door, Cam gasped with surprise.

The strange doctor started to turn toward the noise.

Cam immediately realized his mistake and closed the door to avoid being seen. Afraid he had been discovered, he bolted back to the waiting room. His heart racing, he plopped into a chair and grabbed an old magazine and tried to look nonchalant.

A second later the strange doctor in dress shoes emerged.

Pretending to read, it took all of Cam's will not to look up as the man passed by, his suspicious gaze boring through him.

Meanwhile, on the intercom, the attending nurse was urgently summoning assistance to Room 117.

Once the mysterious doctor had exited, Cam exhaled and sank into his chair, relieved at his escape.

What had the man injected into Orville's IV line? Had he poisoned Orville?

Since Orville had been stung by the alien creatures, Cam guessed the government was trying to complete their cover-up of the existence of alien life. Was murder part of the *protocol* the agent had mentioned? Were they trying to contain an alien infection by killing or curing him?

Cam feared the worst as the nurses and doctors scrambled toward Room 117.

Lindsay returned a few minutes later, and Cam quickly explained what had happened.

"My God! What if you're right?" she exclaimed.

The two of them ran to the double doors of the patient wing, but they had been locked.

"I'm sorry, visitors are not allowed at the moment," the attending nurse said from the counter as her fingers shielded the access controls.

"You let that bogus doctor get in!" Cam said.

The nurse's eyebrow arched. "I don't know what you're talking about, young man. We have a medical situation. I'll let you know when I can authorize entry."

Through the windows, they could see doctors and nurses racing into Room 117.

Exasperated, Lindsay turned her back and leaned on the doors. She glared at the attending nurse. "Can you page my mother? I've got to see her!"

The nurse checked the computer. "Nurse Brock is busy at the moment—"

"I don't care! My Grandpa's dying!"

"Please settle down," the nurse said sternly. "We're doing everything we can."

Lindsay sighed and grabbed Cam's hand. He led her back to the chairs.

They silently waited, wondering what was happening.

After some time their attention was drawn to a dark-haired woman who entered the room, a cell phone pressed to her ear. She was about forty with a great figure accentuated by tight designer jeans and a sleeveless blouse more appropriate for someone much younger. She was chattering so loudly on her phone that the attending nurse looked up with annoyance.

"It's not Lake *Takota*, it's Lake *Tecumseh*!" the exasperated woman shouted into the phone with a nasal New York accent. "It's in Indiana! I'll call later, Harry. What? I can't hear you! You're breaking up! We're going to get cut—"

Her signal lost, she shook her phone. "Damn! The reception here sucks. I feel like I'm back in the 90's." She put the phone into her handbag and saw the two of them in the waiting area and strode toward them. "Are you Cam Meyer?"

He stood up meekly. "Yeah. Who are you?"

The woman extended her hand. "I'm Megan Conrad, from *American Investigator Magazine*. Your relatives told me you'd be here."

Remembering their telephone conversation, he shook her hand and smiled. "Nice to meet you, Ms. Conrad."

"Please, don't call me Ms. Conrad. That sounds like my mother. Call me Megan."

Cam introduced her to Lindsay, who said, "I can't believe you came all the way from New York."

"Yeah, I know. It was a drag getting here," Megan answered, rolling her eyes. "My flight was delayed by storms at O'Hare, and this town is in the middle of nowhere. I half expected my rental car contract to state that, like travel into Mexico, travel into Indiana was not covered!"

"Lake Tecumseh is *not* that far off the beaten path," Lindsay protested.

Megan put her hands on her hips. "I'm from *New York*, remember? Anything west of the Hudson is off the beaten path for me. And then there was this hullabaloo in town. Some kind of silly festival . . ."

Lindsay explained the UFO Festival, and then asked, "What exactly brings you here, Megan?"

Megan glanced at Cam. "Your girlfriend's all business. I like that because I'm the same way. Please tell me what's happened with the meteorite, and especially about your grandfather. I understand he's ill, and I'm sorry."

The three of them sat down. Megan removed a small tape recorder from her bag. "I'm going to record this, okay?"

Cam and Lindsay nodded in agreement and then quickly explained recent events. The reporter listened, sitting on the edge of her seat, leaning forward attentively.

When they had finished the story, Megan clicked off the tape recorder. "Fascinating."

"You believe us, don't you?" Lindsay asked.

Megan nodded and looked around the room. The attending nurse was typing on the computer and paying no attention to them.

"I've heard similar stories before," the reporter whispered. "The government calls those creatures *xenophages*."

Cam and Lindsay locked gazes upon hearing the strange word.

"Xenophages? What are they?" Lindsay asked.

"Space parasites. They travel through space as spores inside a sturdy receptacle—what you called a meteorite. That shell allows them to survive the fiery reentry through the atmosphere."

"Amazing! My research was pointing to the same conclusions," Lindsay said.

"The xenophages hatch from the spores inside the pod. The oil inside is a protective fluid," Megan explained.

"How do you know so much about these xenophages?" Cam asked.

"There've been other discoveries like yours over the years. I've done many investigations and have pieced together fragments of the true story. Apparently these meteorite-like pods fall to Earth from time to time. Where they come from, nobody knows."

Cam's recent dreams, powered by ESP signals from the xenophages, provided a partial explanation: The spore pods grew on a distant planet, thousands of light-years from Earth. Their home world had two suns: a small yellow sun and a large blue sun. A barren, stark place, with jagged mountains and lakes of oil. Red vines twined around the hillsides.

The spore pods developed on this alien world—he was unsure exactly how—and budded from the planet like grains of flower pollen cast by the wind. They drifted in hibernation through the vacuum of space for untold eons, waiting to be snatched by some fertile planet's gravitational pull. Once deposited on a new planet, the pods split open, releasing the spherical spores, each containing a xenophage.

Cam quickly related this scenario to Lindsay and Megan, who nodded in agreement.

"Your story dovetails well with what I have uncovered from my investigations," Megan said. "Have you ever heard of Kenderabad, India?"

Lindsay shrugged. "No."

"Westboro, Kentucky?"

"No. Should I have?" Lindsay seemed slightly perturbed at being in the dark.

Megan glanced around them and continued in a whisper. "Those are the two best suspected crash sites I know about. Kenderabad, India in 1949. Just after the partition. The place was chaotic with refugees and violence. Per the official account, 300 people were killed in the explosion of a chemical plant, but that wasn't the true cause."

"You think the xenophages killed them?" Lindsay asked.

Megan nodded. "The Indian government razed the town on purpose. They needed to destroy the xenophages before they could spread. The chemical plant explosion was a cover-up."

"What about Westboro, Kentucky?" Cam asked.

"That was a poor mining village in Appalachia. In 1985, according to the government, a train carrying volatile chemicals derailed near the town and exploded. The town was completely destroyed and a dozen residents killed. My investigation showed there was no train derailment or explosion. It was also a cover-up."

Cam was impressed by the reporter's account. "What makes you think xenophages were involved?"

"I pieced together snippets of the story from eyewitnesses, declassified government reports, and news accounts. According to railroad records, there were no trains in the area. Former residents told me about a large meteorite found a few days before the event, and some kind of giant insects had been observed in the town. All this was supposedly reported in the local newspaper. When I searched the archives, all the editions from that period were mysteriously absent. I think the government expunged all the official records. They want to keep the existence of these things secret."

"But why?" he asked.

Megan looked surprised at the question. "Think of the panic that would ensue if the public learned that alien spore pods occasionally drop to Earth, releasing dangerous creatures."

"My grandpa was stung by one of them, and he's very ill," Lindsay said. "Is that why xenophages are dangerous? They're infectious and make people sick?"

Megan shook her head. "I'm not sure. I haven't been able to learn enough about what xenophages do once they hatch out. They appear to be a public security and health menace. In the two occurrences I've investigated the most, separate governments were worried enough to destroy both the xenophages and the affected town in order to contain the outbreak."

"Government agents already destroyed the xenophages here," Lindsay reminded. "They burned them up in the workshop, so Lake Tecumseh is safe."

"You're fortunate they acted so quickly," Megan said. "I bet those men were with the OSS – the Office of Special Security. It's a dark agency, meaning its existence is officially kept secret. Its organization and budget are strictly off the books. No one really knows who they are or what they do, but they investigate a lot of meteorite sightings and UFO reports and other strange occurrences."

"Those OSS men talked like they were investigating incidents of xenophages all the time," Lindsay said. "After the fire they said it was the *easiest one yet*."

"They've obviously learned a lot in the years since Westboro," Megan surmised. "After a meteorite strike, if they wait too long, the xenophages get out of control and it's harder to contain them and the resulting news coverage. It's much easier to nip the problem in the bud. They monitor the news services and Internet just as I do. When something suspicious is discussed, they move in to make observations, and if necessary, take remedial actions."

"I bet they especially monitor your activities since you specialize in reporting on these things," Lindsay said to Megan.

The reporter sighed. "I bet you're right."

"Grandpa talked about the UFO in the lake for twenty years," Lindsay said. "This whole town is a hotbed of alien stories and sightings. I wonder why the OSS didn't investigate earlier if they were so concerned about xenophages."

"Remember, the whole country is awash with UFO sightings,"

Megan explained. "Even secret government agencies like the OSS have to prioritize. I bet they monitored Lake Tecumseh from time to time, to see if anything new developed. But after twenty years, the UFO story was pretty stale. Then Cam talked about it on the Internet, where it caught their—and my—interest."

"But the Lake Tecumseh pod crashed a long time ago," Cam said. "Why didn't the xenophages hatch out earlier? Are they afraid of water?"

"Probably *cold* water," Lindsay said. "They hatched out quickly in Grandpa's hot workshop. They're probably adapted to a warmer climate and remain in hibernation during the long, cold transit through outer space."

"In my dreams their world was really hot," Cam said, recalling how he had often awakened in a sweat from the imagined heat of the alien planet.

Nurse Brock, Lindsay's mother, pushed through the double doors and went to her daughter and hugged her. "We think he's going to be all right."

Lindsay started crying. "Oh, Mom, I'm so happy."

"It was touch and go for a while," Nurse Brock said. "But then his fever suddenly broke and his vitals started to improve. It's like a miracle."

Cam realized the miracle was from the OSS agent in medical scrubs and black dress shoes. An antidote, not a poison, had been injected into Orville's IV line.

"Can I see him?" Lindsay asked.

Her mother nodded. "Just briefly. Come with me."

The two of them departed, leaving Cam and Megan in the waiting area. "That *is* a miracle," Megan said. "The OSS must've developed a medicine against the alien infection. Perhaps they've been studying xenophages in their secret labs in order to develop a therapy."

"If they're so dangerous why would they risk keeping them?" Cam asked.

"Isn't it obvious? The xenophages are from outer space. A new and unusual life form from another planet. Who knows what the OSS could learn from them. Perhaps the military's interested in their weapons potential."

"I hope not. Don't they have enough Weapons of Mass Destruction without adding xenophages to the mix?"

"Unfortunately, that's not how the world works," Megan said forlornly. "And the OSS just got a new batch of xenophages from Mr. Milford's workshop."

"You think they hauled them away instead of destroying them?"

"The fire was just a cover-up. The xenophages are probably on their way to an OSS facility in Nevada or somewhere by now."

Cam swallowed. He preferred thinking that the alien creatures had been burnt to cinders. "Except for one," he blurted, forgetting his promise to Lindsay not to discuss the spore they had removed before the fire.

"What do you mean?" Megan asked, worried.

"There's one the OSS doesn't know about. We brought a spore to the high school chem lab to study. It hadn't hatched yet the last time we looked."

"It probably has now. If the OSS finds out about it, or if it accidentally escapes, we're in big trouble."

"What do you think will happen?"

She retrieved her cell phone and began punching numbers. "The OSS follows a strict protocol in these instances. They'll stop at nothing to contain the menace. They'll order the complete destruction of this town!"

CHAPTER TWELVE

Lindsay was relieved her grandfather's condition was improving. The antidote administered by the OSS agent appeared to be working. By the time she, Cam, and Megan Conrad left the hospital, the sun had already set.

Their attention was now on the last remaining xenophage. They headed for the high school, where the UFO Dance had just begun. Cam and Lindsay sprinted to the entrance while Megan parked her rental car.

"They're locked," Cam said, pulling on the doors. He peeked inside. The school's hallway was eerily dark and quiet. He turned to Lindsay. "What do we do now? How do we get to the science lab?"

She looked toward the gym. Light beaconed from the little rectangular windows of its many doors. A melody danced across the parking lot, which was loaded with cars. "We'll have to get Mr. Russell."

"At the UFO Dance? I can't get in. I was banned, remember?"

"But they can't stop me," she said confidently. "Let's go!"

Megan approached with her cell phone pressed to her ear as if she were holding a compress against a head wound to keep her brain from oozing out of her skull. She was speaking animatedly to her editor in New York. "I tell ya, Harry, I got a big story here. I just need to work out some of the details." As she listened, she rolled her eyes and tapped her foot impatiently. "Yeah, yeah, yeah . . ."

Cam watched, imagining the editor at the *American Investigator*. He pictured a short, bald man busily jumping from one outrageous story to the next, trying to boost the magazine's circulation. The editor would surely like it if Megan delivered a big story about Lake Tecumseh being bombarded by alien parasites from outer space, and the government's attempt to cover it up.

Finally, Megan said, "All right, all right. I'll call ya later." She clicked off her phone and dropped it into her camera bag. "Damn editors," she mumbled.

"What's going on?" Lindsay asked.

"I have to be back in New York tomorrow. Harry's got a new story for me. Says it's a big one." She repositioned her camera bag on her shoulder. "And it's not like a man hasn't told me that lie before."

Beneath the street light, Lindsay blushed.

Megan looked at the closed doors to the high school. "Locked, huh?"

Cam nodded. "We'll have to go through the gym. They're having the annual UFO Dance there."

Megan snickered. "UFO Dance? That sounds like fun!"

"We'll only be passing through to get access to the school rooms," Lindsay said.

The three of them cut across the grassy lawn toward the gym. As they neared the large structure, which was attached to the main school building like an oversized aneurysm, the music grew louder. Above the row of entry doors hung a large banner that read *Welcome to the Tenth Annual UFO Dance.*

Cam said softly to Lindsay, "I wish we could've gone to the dance together."

She turned toward him and smiled. "That would've been nice."

At the gym entrance, the doors parted and music blared from

inside. A giggling couple skittered out, clinging to one another.

Cam, Lindsay, and Megan went inside. The lighting was subdued for a romantic effect, but sparkling mirror balls and colorful spotlights added visual spice. The place was full of students dressed in their best clothes. On the basketball court, beneath the twirling streamers and an inflated alien saucer, couples danced arm in arm. On one side, bored chaperones mingled. On the other, a sunglass-wearing deejay stood behind large speakers, assorted audio equipment, and piles of CD's, bobbing his head to the beat.

Taking in the view, Megan clicked her tongue. "Isn't this nice?"

"Our decorations look great," Lindsay said proudly.

Cam scanned the faces. "I don't see Mr. Russell. We'll have to look around."

As he stepped forward, a big, gray-haired man in an ill-fitting suit stopped him with an outstretched arm. "Wait a minute!" the large man commanded. "You're that kid from Chicago. You're not allowed here."

Surprised, Cam stepped back. "Who says?"

"I'm Coach Barnes, and I know all about you, Cameron Meyer. You're a troublemaker! Now get out."

Cam didn't think he could get around the coach, who looked as if he had once been a defensive lineman on a football team. Cam retreated a couple steps and glanced disappointedly at Lindsay. "You go ahead without me."

She frowned. "No, let's stick together." She turned to the coach and said firmly, "We need to see Mr. Russell. This is very important."

Coach Barnes retained his frozen, unhappy expression. "You can come in, Lindsay, but he can't." He jerked his sausage-like thumb toward Cam with more than a dollop of disdain. The coach then set suspicious eyes on Megan and asked who she was.

In a smooth, fluid motion, Megan confidently reached out and shook his hand. She flipped her hair back and smiled broadly. "I'm

Megan Conrad, a reporter from New York. Everyone in this town is so charming!" she trilled like an actress. "I'm here to cover your UFO Festival, especially this wonderful dance. It should be a great piece of Americana, don't you think, Coach Barnes?"

"Ameri-what?" Coach Barnes said, caught off guard by her glib demeanor.

"Americana," she repeated. "In New York we call it a *fluff* story. A feel-good piece about small-town life. They're wonderful antidotes to all the crime and drug stories readers get fed these days."

"Is that a fact?" the flustered man said, his eyes twinkling at the woman.

Megan gently touched the coach on his forearm. "Don't you think you could help us out? Let us have a look around, talk to a few students, take a few photos?" She unzipped her bag and removed her camera and took a photo of the coach.

The sudden flash caught him off guard, blinking. "You're a reporter?"

"From New York," she said as she grabbed Cam's hand and pulled him past the coach. "Don't worry, we won't be long," she chirped as they waded into the people nearby. Lindsay followed behind.

Cam didn't dare turn around to avoid reminding the befuddled coach who had just breached his security. "You're pretty slick," he said to Megan.

The reporter stowed her camera. "In my business, you can't take *no* for an answer."

Lindsay craned her neck. "I don't see Mr. Russell anywhere."

"He's got to be here," Cam said. "He's a chaperone."

Lindsay's arrival created a small stir in the gym. Her friends surrounded her and bombarded her with questions: Why was she late? Why wasn't she dressed? Was she dating Cam?

Lindsay brushed by the girls with curt responses, like a cornered politician wading through a crowd of reporters.

She headed for the chaperones. The teachers hovered around the refreshment table, looking as if they'd rather be somewhere else. They shouted over the loud music, which they probably found too modern and distasteful. Mr. Russell was not among them.

Unexpectedly, Brian Little stepped in front of Cam. They had not spoken since the night of their fight. Brian wore a trim blue suit, striped tie, and a red carnation on his lapel, looking as if he had slid off the glossy page of a fashion magazine. On his arm was a lovely girl poured into a tight-fitting red dress. She fluttered her long, dark eyelashes at Cam.

"I didn't expect to see you here, Sport" Brian said to Cam with a smirk. "I have to give you credit, you're resourceful."

Cam shrugged. "I have my ways."

Brian smiled at Lindsay. "You're not dressed for the dance."

"We're not here for the dance. How did you get in, anyway? You were banned just like Cam."

Brian grinned, showing gleaming white teeth. "My dad worked it out with Officer Fred. Since I'm likely to be voted Space King, they didn't think it was fair."

"Figures," Cam spat.

"Come on, Sport," Brian said. "No hard feelings, huh?"

Cam nodded in agreement. He had more important things to worry about than a brawl with Brian. Cam now had Lindsay, and she was the most important thing of all. And surely she wanted the two boys to get along with one another.

They made introductions all around; Brian's date was named Amanda. She tugged on his arm, pulling him to the dance floor. "Let's dance," she cooed.

"Have you seen Mr. Russell?" Lindsay asked.

Brian shrugged as he turned his back on them and walked away with his arm around Amanda's narrow waist. "I'm not my teacher's keeper. He's around here somewhere."

As Brian and Amanda started to dance, Lindsay scanned the

crowd. She pointed across the dance floor. "There he is!"

Mr. Russell stood near the bunting-covered stage beneath the Warriors' scoreboard, speaking to a small circle of admiring students who were probably fans from his Science Club.

"That's Mr. Russell?" Megan said, sounding surprised and intrigued by his appearance.

The three of them weaved along the perimeter of the dance floor, which was crowded with couples because a popular song was playing, and approached Mr. Russell.

The science teacher saw them and broke from his admirers. He looked Cam and Lindsay over, noting their casual dress. Then his eyes fell on Megan for a few moments longer than would have been expected. Pulling his eyes from the reporter, he asked, "Lindsay, what's going on? Cam, how did you get in?"

"We'll explain later," Lindsay said, "but first, please meet Megan Conrad. She's a reporter."

Mr. Russell and Megan shook hands. "That's *Jim* Russell," he said with a smile. "You're a reporter for . . .?"

"*American Investigator Magazine*," Megan said, beaming. "Out of New York." She scanned his slim body from head to toe.

"We need to check on the xenophage," Lindsay said, pricking the two adults out of their erotic bubble.

Mr. Russell's brow knitted. "The what?"

"We'll explain on the way. We have to see the specimen. Do you have your keys?" Lindsay asked.

Mr. Russell felt his pocket. "Of course. Can't this wait? We're about to vote on the Space King and Queen, and I have to officiate."

"No, it can't wait," Megan said. "Please, trust us, Jim."

Mr. Russell smiled slightly at the reporter and then sighed. "All right, let's make it quick, because I have to get back." He pulled a large set of keys from his pocket and unlocked the doors to the school. All four of them entered.

Cam looked down the long, dark hall. The safety lights were

illuminated, and a tapestry of shadows fell in strange designs across the highly polished floor and the orderly gauntlet of metal lockers.

Except for the music seeping in from the gym, the school was preternaturally quiet. Their footsteps echoed as they moved down the corridors.

While Mr. Russell led them to the science lab, they quickly explained what had happened in his absence. "Xenophages?" he pondered out loud, "are they similar to bacteriophages?"

Megan nodded. "Remarkably so, just much larger than the microscopic viruses that infect bacteria. Xenophages are from outer space, and they infect much larger life forms."

"Like humans," Mr. Russell said.

"Like my Grandpa," Lindsay said. "Fortunately, he's recovering."

Pausing at the door to the science lab, Mr. Russell said, "It's so incredible, I can't believe it."

Megan reached out and touched his hand. "It's all true, Jim. The proof is inside. If the spore's hatched, we'll find a live xenophage in the jar. Let's be careful."

Mr. Russell unlocked the door and flipped the light switch. The overhead fluorescents hummed to life, momentarily hurting their eyes, which had grown accustomed to the dark hallways. They all stepped inside cautiously.

The room appeared deserted and ordinary. The black bench tops were clear and clean. Experimental apparatus were stowed in their glass-fronted cabinets. The books and manuals were aligned on their orderly shelves.

"Where's the jar?" Megan asked.

Mr. Russell's eyes swept over the bench tops. He crossed to one and stopped. "It was right here. I'm sure of it!"

Lindsay looked around the room. "It's got to be here!"

They fanned out through the lab, searching for the large glass container that had held the spore. After they had examined every square foot of countertop, Lindsay announced, "It's not here!"

Megan crossed her arms. "Are you sure you brought a specimen here?"

Mr. Russell started opening cabinets and looking inside. "Perhaps the cleaning people moved it."

"Or the OSS," Megan said dryly.

"What? Those government agents you told me about?" Mr. Russell said.

She nodded. "I bet they took it, just like the ones from Mr. Milford's workshop. National security, you know."

"That's breaking and entering!" Mr. Russell said.

"The OSS doesn't concern itself with the application of law, Jim," Megan said. "They're big boys, and they do anything they want."

"How could they have known about it?" Cam said.

Lindsay looked at him tautly. "Did you post something about it on the Internet?"

"No!"

Megan sighed loudly. "I'm not surprised the OSS would beat us to the punch. After all, they're professionals. They do this all the time."

Mr. Russell stood with his hands on his hips. "So we have no physical proof that these things—these xenophages—ever really existed, then."

"I took some photos of the meteorite," Lindsay said.

Megan turned toward the door. "Pictures of a rock and eyewitness accounts are not enough for a compelling story. Harry's going to be mad as hell after all the fuss I raised about coming here this weekend."

"I'm sorry you're disappointed," Mr. Russell said to Megan as he moved toward her. The two of them stepped out into the hall to be alone. Cam overheard the teacher ask the reporter where she was staying that evening.

Remaining in the science lab, Cam noticed the intense concentration on Lindsay's face. "What is it?"

"It's a relief it's gone," she answered. "We don't have to worry about Lake Tecumseh being destroyed by the OSS."

"You're right. What would we have done with something so dangerous anyway?" He reached out and took her hand. "Let's get out of here before Coach Barnes comes looking for me. I don't want a scene."

"Maybe we can sneak in a little dance—just the two of us," Lindsay said, coyly looking up at him. "No one will notice if we make it quick."

Cam smiled. "I didn't know you were such a rule breaker."

"It's been a stressful few days. Let's go."

They returned to the gym and waded through the students onto the dance floor. No one paid them much attention.

Cam looked at Lindsay and smiled. He was certain he was going to enjoy the dance. She coyly smiled back at him.

Off to the side he saw Mr. Russell and Megan Conrad chatting near the refreshment tables, holding bottles of water, apparently enamored with one another.

The deejay started a slow, romantic song, and Cam embraced Lindsay tightly, relishing the closeness of her body, the floral smell of her hair, and the warmth of her breath on his cheek as they danced. He let his hand drop to the small of her back, that wonderful delicious place.

The two of them looked completely out of place among the well-dressed teens on the gym floor, but Cam didn't care. While Lindsay was in his arms, he didn't worry about what anyone else thought. She was all that mattered to him.

Brian and Amanda glided by them, looking like the plastic figures on top of a wedding cake. Brian winked at Cam as they passed. Amanda, on the other hand, cast a jealous glare toward Lindsay.

When the hypnotic song concluded, Cam and Lindsay stopped dancing and stood closely, gazing into each others eyes.

He leaned down and kissed her. "That was wonderful."

"I've wanted to do that for a long time."

A tapping over the loudspeakers drew the crowd's attention to the decorated stage where Mr. Russell stood in front of a microphone, pecking it with a finger while holding a sheet of paper. "Your attention, please! The moment you've all been waiting for: the winners of the Space King and Queen competition!"

Cam glanced at Brian, who was beaming confidently.

The science teacher tried to add drama to his voice, but it was clear his heart was not into it. "By a tally of your votes, this year's Space King is Brian Little!"

"Well, that's a big surprise," Lindsay said facetiously.

The crowd cheered as Brian mounted the stage, his arms raised triumphantly in the air. The pair of girls next to Mr. Russell gave Brian a sash that said *Space King* and placed a rhinestone crown on his head.

"Watch the hair," Brian said while adjusting the crown, which elicited a chuckle from the audience.

Cam realized Brian was one of those guys who always had everything fall in place right before them, sailing through life on greased skids. Most guys had to work hard for success, but Brian's came gift wrapped with a greeting card.

Mr. Russell then announced Amanda was the new Space Queen.

Smiling as if she had just won a Miss America pageant and was going to work for World Peace, Amanda joined Brian on the stage and received a sash and crown. The two of them made a handsome couple, and the audience applauded appreciatively.

"Nothing surprising in that vote," Lindsay said as she clapped.

Cam leaned into her. "You'll always be my Space Queen."

She smiled. "And you'll always be my Space King."

The deejay cued another romantic song, and Brian and Amanda, waving like royalty, descended to the cheering throng to begin their spotlight dance as the Space King and Queen.

Lindsay pulled Cam off the dance floor and toward the exit. "I don't feel like sticking around and watching them hold court."

As they headed for the door, Lindsay's friends stopped her with more questions and gossip. Waiting patiently, Cam looked back to see Mr. Russell join Megan at the side of the stage. They chatted and laughed. She touched his forearm for emphasis as she spoke, and he beamed at her.

Then something else caught Cam's eye. In the shadows behind the stage, Patrick Frazier was carrying something in a large plastic shopping bag. He had a devious grin on his face. Whatever was in the bag was rather heavy because its bottom bowed toward the floor.

What's he doing? Cam thought.

Patrick placed the bag on the steps leading to the stage and then uncurled its sides, exposing the item within: a large glass jar with a lid.

The glass jar missing from the Science Lab!

Even from the distance, Cam detected motion in the container—a twittering, a scurrying. Something was inside.

Then, he saw the glow of a faint green light.

Patrick had the xenophage!

The OSS agents hadn't found the last spore. Patrick had taken it! He had stolen it from the lab. But why? Why had he brought it to the dance?

Cam poked Lindsay in the side. "Look!"

Just as Lindsay turned, Patrick removed the lid from the glass jar and lifted the vessel and shook out the xenophage. The creature escaped and flew into the air, perching on the banner above the stage.

"Oh no!" Cam gasped.

The wily xenophage stretched its six long legs while its head blinked with a soft green light.

The creature was free!

Below, under the admiring gazes of their court, King Brian and Queen Amanda slowly danced in the white oval of the spotlight, ignorant of the alien creature watching them from above. Brian looked over Amanda's shoulder at the swooning girls lining the dance floor and winked at them.

Lindsay looked around the stage, obviously not seeing the escaped xenophage. She shook her head at Cam. "What's wrong?"

He pointed at the small, glowing creature on the banner. "Up there! The xenophage! Patrick had it and let it out!"

Her eyes widened. "Oh, my God! Why did he do that?"

"Probably a joke or something. He doesn't know it's dangerous."

"We've got to evacuate the gym!"

Before they could react, the xenophage launched itself from the banner and drifted over the crowd. As it floated down, it resembled an odd, glowing balloon. A few people noticed it and pointed, unsure what it was. A murmur grew among the onlookers.

Brian and Amanda continued dancing dreamily to the romantic ballad, relishing the spotlight and the admiring gazes of their friends.

The xenophage slowly descended toward Amanda's head, alighting on her crown. Its polyhedral head glowed and its spindly legs strummed and tapped against her scalp.

Brian saw the creature and froze. His jaw dropped open as he stepped back from her.

"What are you staring at?" Amanda squawked.

Brian's lips moved silently like a fish, as if he were struggling to form words. Frightened, he pointed at her head.

"What?" she asked, sounding annoyed her magical dance had been interrupted.

"It's on your head," Brian said, his voice quaking.

She reached up to her crown and touched the legs of the writhing xenophage. She immediately screamed. The bone-rattling shriek pierced through the entire gymnasium.

The crowd grew silent. The deejay stopped the music and emerged from behind his equipment to see what had happened.

"Don't panic!" Brian said as he stepped back farther from Amanda.

She didn't listen. She continued to scream, frantically brushing at her hair, her flailing arms merging into one flapping motion. She knocked off her crown, which fell and clanked across the floor, landing at the feet of the line of girls. They jumped back as if the crown was dangerous.

The xenophage jumped off Amanda's head and floated in the air once again, looking like a feather buffeted by a light breeze.

Nearby onlookers saw the creature and screamed. Panicked girls covered their hair with their hands. People backed away from the dance floor.

The xenophage floated for a few seconds and then landed only a couple yards from where Amanda stood, shrieking uncontrollably, her tongue wagging like a lizard's.

Brian regained his bravado and crossed to the resting xenophage. "I'll kill it!" He raised his foot, poised to smash it like an insect. Just as he was about to do so, the creature flitted away again and was airborne. Brian's foot impacted the wooden floor with a loud thud.

The xenophage drifted over the crowd.

The alarm spread and the gym dissolved into chaos. Students screamed and scattered in all directions, overturning tables and knocking people down. Those farther away instinctively moved inward to investigate the commotion, causing a massive jam on the dance floor.

No one was moving anywhere amid the pandemonium.

Suddenly the fire alarm sounded, focusing everyone's attention on escape. Cam spied Lindsay next to the trophy case, her hand on the red lever of the alarm. "We've got to get people out of here!" she yelled.

He admired her quick thinking. Now people knew what to do. They streamed through the exit doors, quickly emptying the gym.

Twirling in the flow of students, Coach Barnes tried to keep the evacuation orderly. "Walk, don't run!" he called. "Walk, don't run!"

As people fled, Cam and Lindsay watched the xenophage hovering like a miniature hot air balloon, or more ominously, a dive bomber. He wondered how it could fly without wings. Maybe a flotation sac inside.

Patrick stopped next to them. "Cool, huh?" he said excitedly, shouting over the loud blare from the fire alarm. "This'll be a dance to remember!"

Cam punched him on the arm. "You idiot! Look what you've done!"

Patrick looked crestfallen. "Oh, come on! Just a little alien excitement for our UFO Dance!"

"That thing's dangerous, you moron!" Cam said. "Now you've let it out!"

"Dangerous? It's just a giant bug or something."

Lindsay shook her head. "There's no time to explain. We've got to get everyone out! Then we have to kill it!"

Mr. Russell and Megan passed by, heading for the exit. She clutched her camera, taking photos of the xenophage as it flew over the heads of the fleeing students. "We can't kill it," Megan said. "It's extraterrestrial life! The proof my story needs!"

Mr. Russell directed them toward the doors. "Let's get out and let the authorities worry about this thing."

Megan tried to stand her ground, getting more photos. "I've got to document this!"

Mr. Russell didn't listen to her and pushed her toward the exit.

The last of the students were passing through the doors. Hysterical, Amanda fled with the mass, clutching her messed up hair with one hand.

Her crown had been crushed in the stampede.

Brian saw Cam and shouted over the din, "What is that thing?"

Apparently Brian was not part of Patrick's joke. Cam didn't have time to explain. He and Lindsay were pushed toward the river of people evacuating the building. He glanced over his shoulder at the confused xenophage flying around the gym like a fly caught in an enclosed automobile.

Then, unexpectedly, it darted toward the exiting students.

"Look out!" Cam shouted. "Here it comes!"

The students in the rear of the fleeing mob looked back and screamed as the xenophage rocketed toward them with a sudden burst of speed.

"Duck!" Lindsay yelled.

They shielded their heads as the xenophage swooped toward them, its little head pulsating with light and its spidery legs twitching. But instead of striking, the xenophage flew over them and escaped through the open doors.

"It's getting away!" Cam shouted.

He grabbed Lindsay and they raced outside, joining Mr. Russell, Megan Conrad, and the throng of agitated students gathered in the parking lot. The shrill fire alarm reverberated through the night. In the distance, emergency vehicles with wailing sirens and flashing lights approached.

"Where did it go?" Mr. Russell asked, scanning the area for the xenophage.

"It could be anywhere!" Lindsay said. "Did you see how fast it can fly?"

"This is serious," Megan said. "If a xenophage is on the loose, the OSS will take drastic action."

Hundreds of people milled about, chattering noisily about what they had seen. Amanda was in tears, yanking at her tresses to make certain the creature was gone. She had lost one shoe in the evacuation, and the other had a broken heel. Lindsay went to her. "Are you okay? Did it sting you?"

Amanda's mascara had bled over her face, giving her the appearance of a sad clown. "No, it didn't sting me," she wailed. She ran her fingers through her hair. "Is it gone? Please tell me it's gone!"

"Don't worry. It's gone," Lindsay said, backing away just as Amanda's girlfriends arrived to console the hysterical Space Queen.

Police cars and fire trucks raced into the parking lot. Sheriff Little used a megaphone to order the students to clear the fire lanes. When the people pulled back, the emergency vehicles parked in front of the gymnasium. Sheriff Little and Officer Fred emerged from their squad cars, and the firefighters spilled from their trucks, sprinting for the gym.

"We've got to find the xenophage!" Megan said as the authorities assessed the situation.

"How are we going to do that?" Cam asked.

That's when he saw it: a faint green glow in a nearby tree on the school lawn, like some kind of Chinese lantern.

The xenophage.

The creature perched on a branch about twenty feet from the ground, a specter observing them.

Cam pointed to the tree. "There it is!"

But he had shouted too loudly, alerting other students. They, too, pointed to the glowing xenophage. Some girls shrieked. Others started to retreat from it.

The murmur of the crowd grew louder, more agitated.

"We've got to capture it!" Mr. Russell said.

Cam looked around for a rope, a box, a bag, anything that might have been helpful. Nothing handy was in sight. Motion in the corner of his eye caught his attention and he turned back to the tree just in time to see Brian and Patrick running toward it.

"We'll get it!" Brian announced proudly.

The two boys picked up rocks and tossed them at the xenophage.

"Stop it!" Lindsay yelled. "You'll drive it away!"

"We're trying to kill it!" Brian shouted back, throwing stones.

Harassed by the shower of rocks, the xenophage jumped from the branch and flew farther away. Invisible except when it glowed, it appeared and disappeared like a floating green globe as it moved.

Brian and Patrick chased after it, whooping like Indians and throwing rocks.

The xenophage landed on another tree, but only for a second before jumping again and fleeing into the darkness.

Brian and Patrick raced around the schoolyard shouting frantically, trying to locate the creature.

The green glow had vanished.

"Those idiots," Cam mumbled.

Sheriff Little waddled up, scowling. "Looks like a false alarm, Jim," he said to Mr. Russell. "Someone pulled the fire alarm as a prank."

Lindsay stepped up. "I did it, but not as a prank, Sheriff. We had to evacuate the gym because a xenophage was on the loose."

The sheriff frowned. "A xenophage? Is that what you're calling the *creatures* in your silly story now? What has gotten into you?"

Mr. Russell grabbed the sheriff's arm and led him to the side. Megan followed behind. "We can explain, Sheriff," Mr. Russell said.

"I certainly hope so!" the sheriff answered. "I've had enough of these pranks."

As the adults talked, Brian and Patrick returned, panting. Brian had lost his crown and his *Space King* sash was ripped. "It got away," he told Cam and Lindsay.

"You mean you drove it away," Cam said.

"We were trying to kill it!" Brian said. "At least we did something while you just stood with your thumb up your butt!"

"We were *thinking,* which is something you don't do a lot of!"

Brian balled his fists. "You take that back!"

Lindsay stepped between them. "Settle down, you two! This is serious!"

"Of course it is!" Brian snarled. "I'm gonna whip his ass!"

Lindsay poked Brian in the chest. "Stop that! This is serious for the whole town! You know what this means?"

Brian lowered his fists and stepped back. "What?"

Lindsay looked toward Mr. Russell, Megan, and the Sheriff conversing several paces away. "It means our town is contaminated, just like Kenderabad, India and Westboro, Kentucky. Those towns were destroyed to keep the contagion from spreading."

"Cool," Patrick said.

Brian smacked Patrick on the back of the head. "You moron! This isn't a joke!"

"I'm sorry," Patrick said, glancing downward.

"How did you get the xenophage out of the lab?" Lindsay asked Patrick.

"Coach Barnes let me in. I told him some of the decorations were left in the lab. I was planning to check up on the sphere, but was surprised when I saw that bug thing in there! I thought it'd be fun to let it lose and scare the kids, so I took it."

"Now look at the situation we're in," Lindsay said.

Sheriff Little addressed the crowd using a megaphone: "I'm sorry, but we need to close the dance early. Everyone go home now. There's nothing to see here."

The crowd groaned as they dispersed toward their cars.

Brian cleared his throat. "I guess the fun's over for tonight, thanks to Patrick!"

"I didn't know this would happen," Patrick said.

"Let's find Amanda," Brian said, walking away. "I hope she's calmed down."

The two football players departed, and Cam was happy to see them go. Patrick's practical joke had turned into a disaster, and then Brian's rash actions had driven the xenophage away.

Now the town was in big trouble.

Mr. Russell and Megan joined Cam and Lindsay. "You should both get home, too. There's nothing more we can do here now," Mr. Russell said.

"What about the xenophage?" Lindsay asked, her hand sweeping the leaf-shrouded shadows on her left, the direction the creature had fled.

"We've convinced Sheriff Little to look for it, but he's skeptical about the whole thing," Mr. Russell said. "It's going to be difficult to find anything tonight. The search will really start tomorrow."

"Can we help?" Lindsay asked.

"That's a job for the authorities," Mr. Russell said.

Lindsay nodded weakly. "Okay, I'm beat, anyway. I need to get home."

"Do you need a ride?" Mr. Russell asked.

Cam and Lindsay nodded.

"I'll follow you," Megan said to Mr. Russell with a playful wink.

The four of them headed for the parking lot, which was jammed with the cars of the departing students. They noticed a white sedan driving toward the gym instead of away from it. The car's contrary direction further exacerbated the traffic jam. As the car passed by, they saw two men wearing dark suits sitting rigidly in the front seat, scanning the crowd suspiciously.

"Uh-oh," Megan said ominously. "It's the OSS! They must've found out about the disturbance on the police radio. Now they'll find out about the missing xenophage."

"Then what?" Mr. Russell asked.

Megan bit her lower lip. "Then we can kiss your quaint little town goodbye."

CHAPTER THIRTEEN

Aunt Ellen yelled up the stairs, calling Cam down for breakfast. He smelled bacon frying.

In a good mood, he kissed her on the cheek when he entered the kitchen, causing her to giggle.

Uncle Gary sat at the table, sipping coffee. The thick Sunday paper rested under his elbow. "You got home pretty late last night," he said in an icy tone.

Cam snatched a piece of bacon from the platter and sat down. So much had happened; he didn't know where to start. Would they believe him if he babbled about OSS agents and alien xenophages on the loose?

"It's a long story," he finally said.

"We're all ears," his uncle said, folding his arms as his wife sat next to him.

The phone rang and Cam jumped up and quickly grabbed the receiver, thankful for the interruption. Anything to free him from the impending cross-examination, even a call from a solicitor, would have been welcome. As he said *hello*, he heard his relatives complain about people calling too early on Sunday mornings.

It was Lindsay. Her voice quaked, sounding worried. "Cam, something's going on!"

"Is it your grandpa?"

"No, he's okay. Mom's with him at the hospital now. But army trucks are rolling into town! There's an evacuation order! Something about a gas leak!"

Confused, Cam stared blankly out the curtained window. "Is it dangerous?"

She clicked her tongue. "It's not *really* a gas leak! It's the missing xenophage! Remember what Megan told us? The government will destroy Lake Tecumseh to stop it!"

The realization struck home. The reporter had warned that Lake Tecumseh could join the list of destroyed towns, like Westboro, Kentucky, and the hard-to-pronounce one in India. "What should we do?"

"Meet me at the railroad trestle! We've got to stop this somehow—"

Suddenly she was cut off and the phone line went dead. Cam stared at the receiver. He depressed the switch hook several times to restore the line, not because he expected it to work, but because that's what he'd seen people do in old movies.

"Was that Lindsay?" Aunt Ellen asked, sounding concerned.

Before he could answer, a siren wailed in the distance and grew louder very quickly. Urgent sounding announcements were being broadcast, their muffled message rising in volume as the vehicle neared.

Uncle Gary stood. "What in the world is happening?"

"Is it a tornado?" Aunt Ellen asked.

The two of them went to the kitchen window to look outside. Cam stepped behind them and glanced over their shoulders at the road. Trees partially blocked his view, but he could see the camouflage colors of army trucks rolling slowly by their property. A loudspeaker announced a mandatory evacuation and implored *all citizens to remain calm.*

Aunt Ellen gasped, her palm covering her heart. "An evacuation!

What's happened?"

"I don't know," Uncle Gary said. "Something serious!"

Cam didn't wait a second longer and sprinted for the back door. He heard his uncle calling after him, but he was already halfway down the rear steps. He raced toward his bike leaning against the garage door. The air was punctuated with whooping sirens to alert the residents to the looping announcement.

An army truck pulled into their gravel driveway and uniformed soldiers poured from its rear bed like a torrent of green and brown khaki. The men held their rifles at the ready as they approached the back porch.

Cam realized they were rounding up citizens for the evacuation, and he didn't want to be taken away. He quickly mounted the bike and pedaled off in the opposite direction, riding behind the garage and into the adjacent woods.

Shielded from view, he paused to look back into the yard. The soldiers shuffled his panicked aunt and uncle from the house toward a waiting truck. His relatives' frantic gestures signaled they were telling the soldiers about his sudden disappearance. He felt guilty seeing them so upset, but didn't wait to see what happened next. He rode off, deeper into the woods, away from the lake and the houses and the soldiers.

He had to link up with Lindsay. Perhaps she had a plan to save the town. If she didn't, maybe together they would be able to think up something.

They didn't have much time to act.

Cam labored as he pedaled his bike over the rough path leading through the woodland surrounding the lake. His bike tires scrabbled over the gnarled roots protruding from the dirt, jarring his bones. He gripped the handlebars until his knuckles were white to keep from being thrown off. The spokes of his wheels gathered up every loose leaf and blade of grass, slowing his progress. Low tree branches and briars of thorns snagged and scratched him as he passed.

His mind reeled. A xenophage was loose. The military was evacuating Lake Tecumseh. His relatives had been spirited away to who-knows-where. He could still hear the distant sirens and loudspeaker announcements.

Lindsay's rendezvous point was the secluded railroad trestle, a place he remembered well. They had shared a romantic kiss there just a few days before all the insanity had erupted.

He came to the edge of the woods. Just across a grassy shoulder was the blacktop that circled the lake. He skidded to a stop and concealed himself behind a large tree. Peeking out, he watched a convoy of military vehicles snake down the road. Bright yellow school buses accompanied them, full of passengers. The townspeople were being evacuated.

His intended route blocked, he needed an alternate path to the railroad trestle. He pictured the layout of the land in his mind, recalling the county map in the UFO Museum. Lake Tecumseh was like an island in a sea of farmland. The town was to the east of his present location. The railroad ran north to south through the town. Once he got to the railroad cut he'd be out of sight, but there was a lot of open farmland to cross before that.

Cam thought about the endless, flat cornfields across northern Indiana. When he had arrived in June, the plants were just small sprouts. Now it was late July. As a city boy, he had no idea how fast corn grew. Would it be tall enough to conceal him so he could cross the fields unobserved?

He had seen the fields almost every day, but had paid little attention to the green background. Now he wished he had.

He had to avoid the roads, which were swarming with armed soldiers, and riding through the cornfields was the only way to do it. He had to take the chance. He turned his bike around and headed toward the adjacent farmland.

The first field was planted with a low-growing crop, probably soybeans. He couldn't ride across it because he'd stick out like a sore thumb and be seen from a mile away.

He kept moving along the edge of the woods, keeping within its leafy border until he came to the next farmer's acreage. Tall, green stalks of corn greeted him like a welcome shield. They were as tall as he was, and he could ride between the rows across the wide-open property and no one could see him.

Cam quickly wheeled out of the woods and into the cornfield. The sharp stalks scratched his skin like large nail files as he rode down the narrow row. The ground was sloppy due to recent rain, and traction was poor. His progress was slow. His tires plodded through mud, kicking up brown speckles of dirt that coated his butt as he pedaled.

The sun climbed higher into the sky, evaporating the soil's moisture into steamy ripples that hovered over the vast greenness.

The cornfield simmered.

Sweat dripped off him as he rode through the prickly sauna, and he was thankful when he finally emerged from the field and passed into the refreshing shade of the bordering scrub trees.

He caught his breath and wiped his face on his shirt before clambering with his bike over the skeletal remnants of an old barbed-wire fence, across a low ridge of grass-strewn rubble, and down into the abandoned railroad cut.

Ahead the train tracks passed through a wooded area that offered better protection from prying eyes. He climbed back on his bike and rode between the rails toward the safety ahead.

A brave ring-necked pheasant ran parallel with him for a few yards, as if challenging his right to be there, and then darted into the underbrush to escape.

In only a few minutes, a bend in the railroad brought Cam to the old trestle bridging Deer Creek. He dismounted, looking around for Lindsay, who was nowhere in sight. He called for her, but there was no answer.

He wondered if she had escaped the evacuation.

Perhaps she had been on one of those yellow school buses he had seen.

He walked onto the trestle and peered over its iron walls into the water. His reflection was on its mirror-like surface, where water striders skated amid the floating lint deposited by the nearby cottonwood trees.

He called for Lindsay again, but the only sounds he heard were the whine of cicadas and the chirps of sparrows.

If Lindsay didn't show up, what would he do?

Cam's shoulders slumped. He had no plan to capture the xenophage or save Lake Tecumseh from destruction. Lindsay had the brains to figure that out. All he could do was help execute her plan. He grew discouraged as he leaned against the metal bridge, longing for her to appear.

Unexpectedly, a great sense of loneliness washed over him. Although he was standing alone on the trestle, the feeling was too intense, too disconnected from his circumstance.

Yes, a lot was happening to him, but this feeling was way out of proportion.

He looked around the empty woods. He was all alone.

But he felt as if he were *the only person in the entire world.*

Then he realized *he* was not the one feeling lonely. The feeling had come from *outside* him, like a coldness coming from a north wind.

His headache had also abruptly returned. He thought it had disappeared for good with the destruction of the xenophages, but now it was back, and it felt differently.

It felt *very close.*

The missing xenophage! *It* was the one feeling lonely. None of its fellow xenophages were around. The alien creature was all by itself now, and it was telegraphing its feelings via ESP!

The thumping of approaching helicopter rotors snapped Cam back to attention. Overhead he saw a pair of army choppers flying toward town. He moved under the canopy of the trees, afraid they were searching for stragglers.

After the chopper had passed, Lindsay arrived on her bicycle. Her face was flushed and her skin glistening. "Cam!" she called excitedly. "I'm so glad you're here!"

They kissed and held each other for a moment, and then slowly pulled apart. He looked her over, relieved at their reunion while admiring her beauty. "I thought maybe you'd been bussed out of town."

She shook her head as she wiped her forehead with her palm. "No way! It was just like Megan's story about Westboro, Kentucky. One moment it was all calm, and then the next, army trucks arrived and they starting forcing people to evacuate! I bet those OSS agents were responsible because they discovered that one of the xenophages was on the loose!"

"You think they'll destroy the town if they can't find it?"

"That's what Megan warned us about. We have to find it first." She rubbed the bridge of her nose. "But we're just two kids by ourselves. How can we do that? The xenophage could be anywhere!"

"Not anywhere, some place close. My headache's back, and I'm getting its ESP signals again!"

"You are? When did that start?"

"Just now, when I got here. The missing xenophage is trying to communicate with me!"

"Or it could just be a normal headache from all the stress," she countered.

"No, it feels different now. Before it was like a loud, off-key heavy metal band playing in my head. I couldn't understand any of it. There were too many individual xenophage signals. Now it sounds softer and clearer because I'm receiving just one signal from one xenophage!"

"Amazing! What are you sensing?"

"Let me clear my mind and focus," Cam said, standing still and closing his eyes. "That might help filter out the distractions."

He took several deep breaths and exhaled slowly to calm himself. He concentrated on simple, peaceful things, like the robin singing in the nearby tree, the sound of the rustling leaves, and the smell of the woods around him. If he were ever going to hear the xenophage, he had to listen carefully for it.

As he tried to concentrate, distracting thoughts kept popping out of mental slots like burnt pieces of toast: the fight at the festival, the xenophages filling Orville's workshop, the ominous announcements from the army's loudspeakers. He fought to control them, to silence them. His internal struggle reminded him of a sleepless night, when life's stresses could not be put to rest regardless how many hours were spent tossing and turning in bed, trying *not* to focus on them.

Then the ESP signals clarified in his mind. He forced himself to experience the telegraphed sensations, not to shrug them away.

He felt lonely and afraid.

Cam was certain the feelings were coming from the xenophage. He received a torrent of images of a place with rocks and boulders, a bright yellow sun in a blue sky, and green, luxurious vegetation. The accompanying feeling was one of strangeness and unfamiliarity, as if the xenophage were thinking: *Where am I?*

But he felt differently about the images streaming into his mind. It wasn't a distant, alien world like the one he had sketched in his dream journal. It was someplace quite familiar and ordinary.

It was Earth.

He was seeing what the xenophage was seeing. The place it was currently hiding.

Somewhere near.

He opened his eyes and blinked.

Lindsay was staring at him expectantly. "What is it? Did you detect its signal?"

He nodded. "Yes. It's lonely and scared."

"They must be communal creatures, communicating with one another via ESP. I'm not surprised this one's lonely and scared, since it's all by itself."

"And it's very close. I saw its surroundings. Somewhere quiet with piles of white rocks and large boulders. Someplace abandoned—overgrown with weeds."

"Like an old gravel pit?"

"Is there one nearby?"

"The old Zimmerman pit! It's not far!"

Cam recalled the images. "Yes, it's a gravel pit. That's where it is! It's hiding there, searching for the other xenophages."

"You act as if this little thing is intelligent."

"They're more than just alien parasites. They're smart."

"They can't have much of a brain, since they're so small and flimsy," Lindsay said. "Perhaps their intelligence is due to working together as a larger organism. Like individual nerve cells comprising a larger brain. Individually, each creature is nothing, but massed together, they have intelligence."

"That makes sense to me. Let's go."

They mounted their bikes and rode across the trestle, heading north along the railroad. Lindsay explained the gravel pit was only about a mile away. Closed years ago, it was seldom visited, except as a secret hideout for the local kids.

From the main track, a spur rail branched off, which they followed into heavy woods. They arrived at the derelict gravel pit, which was surrounded by a tall fence topped with rusted coils of barbed wire. A corroded metal sign hanging cockeyed from one remaining screw identified *Zimmerman Crushed Stone*.

"This is it," Lindsay announced as they braked to a stop.

Cam peered through the gate, which was covered with *Keep Out* and *No Trespassing Signs* obscured by graffiti. Nearby an old guard house stood with a broken window, peeling paint, and warped wallboards. Pigeons cooed from its guano-covered roof, watching the intruders nervously.

"How do we get in?" he asked.

"There's an opening over here." She followed the fence into the thick brush on their right. Trespassers had worn a small path into the ground. Discarded bottles and aluminum cans littered both sides.

Lindsay peeled back a loose flap in the fence as if she were lifting a curtain. "This way," she said, entering through the opening with her bike in tow. Cam followed her onto the property. They traced a dirt trail to a weed-choked, gravel driveway and then remounted their bikes.

Descending a hill as they rode forward, they passed the abandoned relics of old industry: shells of corroding trucks and conveyor equipment coated with red and brown rust, teetering wooden buildings and shacks, and piles of trash and metal junk.

All around the ground had been excavated to reveal the glacial drifts of gravel and stone that lay just below the surface. Some of the stone had been crushed in giant machines and deposited years ago in large conical piles, waiting to be hauled away for road construction. Weeds and small trees sprouted everywhere. A ghostly film of white dust coated everything like atomic fallout.

The main pit was ahead of them. At its bottom, water had pooled into a large pond that looked perfect for a swim. Its surface looked impossibly blue against the white stone and gravel lining its banks. Above, on the hillsides, trees teetered over the edges of the chewed-up banks, their roots holding them precariously as the soil slowly eroded away beneath them.

Cam and Lindsay stopped and looked around. The pit was eerie in its silence. "This place is huge," she said. "Where do we start looking?"

He recalled the images in his mind that had come from the xenophage. "Nothing looks familiar, but if we walk around, maybe I'll see something."

"If we find it, what do we do with it? How do we catch it?"

"I hadn't thought of that."

They started their search of the property on foot. Cam wondered if they were deluding themselves. The site was large and overgrown. A small xenophage could hide anywhere. The alien creature could be sitting on a tree branch, and they'd walk right under it and never know.

"We could cover more ground if we split up," Cam said.

"Are you crazy? With that thing out there?" It's too dangerous."

"You're right. Keep on the lookout."

They walked for several more minutes, around the perimeter of the water-filled pit, by the piles of crushed stone, and down the rutted roads branching through the woodland.

"We're never going to find it," Lindsay said with a sigh. "Have you received any other messages? Is it still here?"

Cam paused, collecting the strange thoughts in his head. "Yes, but I don't know where. Everything looks too similar. Just rocks, boulders, and trees."

His concentration was interrupted by the approaching rotors of another helicopter. He grabbed Lindsay's hand and pulled her under the thick branches of a tree. "We can't let them see us here!"

They watched through the leaves as an army helicopter, painted a camouflage green, flew around the gravel pit like a hawk on a hunting mission. The chopper slowly looped around several times before departing.

"Do you think they're looking for us?" Lindsay asked as they emerged into the sunshine.

"Maybe," Cam said before suddenly freezing.

"What is it?" she asked, turning back to him.

"The helicopter! The xenophage saw it!" He reconstructed the images in his mind: the chopper repeatedly circling the gravel pit, but from a different vantage point from his own. He was seeing it from the xenophage's point of view and receiving thoughts of confusion at the same time. The alien creature had never seen a helicopter before.

"It's somewhere on the other side of the pit," Cam announced as he pointed across the water. "Over there. I can tell by the way the helicopter looked to it."

"Are you sure?"

"Definitely." He raced off in the direction indicated, Lindsay following.

They went by the lip of the pit toward the far side, where they meandered around the derelict heavy equipment and piles of stone looking for the xenophage.

After a few minutes, Cam grew discouraged as his signal, and his confidence, faded. He paused to rest at the edge of the dust-covered woods. "It must be moving around. We can't let it get away. We've got to stop it here, in Lake Tecumseh."

"But how?" Lindsay asked, uncharacteristically out of ideas.

"We need to lure it into the open. We need bait, and the only bait we have is me."

She creased her brow. "That's crazy! You might get stung!" She flung her hands up at him.

"It's the only way!" He surveyed the edge of the woods. "All this time, I've been receiving bits of its thoughts and feelings. Maybe it's a two-way street. Maybe the xenophage can receive my thoughts and feelings, too."

Lindsay shook her head. "I'm not following."

"You said they were communal creatures communicating via ESP. Since its signals affect me, perhaps it thinks I'm one of its alien brothers. Maybe it thinks I'm another xenophage! Maybe I can mentally get its attention and draw it into the open!"

"That sounds pretty risky."

"It's our only hope. I'll try to kill it before it can sting me."

She grabbed him in a bear hug. "Are you sure you want to do this?"

He kissed her, relishing the taste of her lips. He rubbed his hand along her soft cheek and whispered, "I have no choice. I might be the only one who can stop this thing! You'll have to leave me alone to do this."

"Alone? Why?" She pulled away and looked as if she were ready to break into tears.

"It's too dangerous, and I can't be distracted. I need to concentrate and lure the xenophage out. I'm the only one who can halfway communicate with it now. Maybe it'll listen to my thoughts!"

She reached out for him again, and her lips quickly found his. "Oh, Cam! You're so brave!" She held him tightly.

He regretted prying her away, but had a job to do. "Wish me luck."

She watched him with dewy eyes, blinking back tears. Words caught in her throat, and then she murmured, "Good luck. I love you, Cam."

His response was immediate and came from deep inside him: "I love you, too!"

They embraced again, and it was suddenly as if the entire Hoosier summer had finally reached its climax. For weeks Cam had longed to hear those three words from Lindsay, for he had ached to say them himself. But he had been unsure of what he felt, and what she felt in return. Now there were no more doubts. They had both revealed their true feelings for one another, and the joy rushed between them like steam whistling from an overheated tea kettle.

"I'm the luckiest guy in the world," he said, holding her tightly and kissing her, exploring her body with his hands at the same time.

But he had no time to feel lucky. Another alien image jerked into his mind: An image of him and Lindsay in each other's arms!

In Cam's mind, he saw himself holding Lindsay from the perspective of someone observing from the tree tops only a few yards behind them. His breath froze in his lungs. "Uh-oh," he choked out.

She pulled back. "What is it?"

"It's out there," he whispered. "It's watching us right now!"

She spun from his embrace and looking around their surroundings. "Where?"

"Somewhere really close!"

They quickly scanned the vicinity. They were surrounded by piles of crushed stone, gnarly old trees, and the wreck of an old flatbed truck with missing tires. No xenophage was in view, but Cam was certain it was nearby; the signals he was receiving were much stronger.

"It's hunting us," Cam said. "It wants to sting us."

Lindsay's gaze darted about nervously. "It's no longer lonely and scared?"

"Its hunting reflex has taken over."

"Let's get out of here!"

He steadied her arm. "You go, but I've got to stop it."

"I'm not leaving! We're in this together!"

Before Cam could force her to safety, out of the corner of his eye he saw something swoop toward them from a nearby tree.

The xenophage!

Like a gelatinous spider, its green head glowing in spite of the bright sunlight, the creature flew through the air, heading straight for them.

"Look out!" Cam yelled, jumping on Lindsay and shielding her head from the onrushing xenophage. The two of them rolled in the dust as the creature flew over their entwined bodies, just barely missing them.

They quickly regained their feet. Panting from the surprise, they looked back at the alien just a few yards from them. It had landed on its six, spider-like feet. Its polyhedral head flashed a cool green as if a small neon light were screwed inside its translucent shell. The thing had no eyes, ears, or mouth. Although faceless, it seemed to be taunting them, slowly drumming its thin legs on the ground like a matador provoking an angry bull.

"Stay back!" Lindsay cautioned, clutching Cam's arm and standing behind him. "It might pounce again."

Cam was mesmerized by the tiny xenophage. A strange sensation flowed through him, and he realized the xenophage was communicating directly with him. It was as if the creature had learned to connect more readily with his mind. What before had been vague feelings and gauzy, disconnected images, turned clearer and more concrete.

His jaw hanging limply as he concentrated on the thoughts beaming into his brain, Cam watched the xenophage. He felt the mental connection. The conduit was open. The xenophage was communicating with him, but it was all noisy and garbled, and he couldn't figure it out.

Lindsay pulled him back. "Are you under its control?"

He stumbled, unsure what was going on, yet unable to move. He felt locked to the xenophage in some tight, neurological connection.

"We've got to get out of here!" Lindsay cried.

She struggled to pull him away from the xenophage that had frozen him into a trance. He felt her dragging him away, but his muscles were like flimsy noodles. His heavy legs were encased in cement.

He couldn't move.

Then the xenophage crouched onto its legs and pounced upward at an amazing speed like a tight spring suddenly released. It flew directly toward Cam, targeting his head. He saw the movement but was powerless to react. The xenophage's pencil-thick legs twittered as it sailed through the air, pinpointing his face like a bulls-eye. A three-inch long, needle-shaped stinger emerged from the underside of the xenophage's head as it approached.

The stinger was going to pierce him between the eyes.

Lindsay screamed in horror.

Cam couldn't move or even choke out a gasp.

Suddenly the airborne xenophage exploded just inches from his face, splattering him with warm, green bits of slick flesh and shattered body parts that felt like Jell-O thrown at him.

The loud report of a rifle echoed against the walls of the gravel pit.

Cam's mind was abruptly cleared of the alien influence, and he could think and move once again. He instinctively grabbed Lindsay, who was trembling and trying to catch her breath. He wiped the flecks of green goop from her face and removed a twitching alien leg from her hair. Then he kissed her, holding her tightly, trying to console her.

They turned in the direction of the gunshot and saw the two OSS agents approach, holding rifles. Dressed in dark suits and wearing mirrored sunglasses, they stood out like black shadows in the pasty white dust of the gravel pit.

"Cam Meyer and Lindsay Brock?" the lead agent asked as he lowered his weapon and inspected the area.

They nodded, not knowing what to think about the arrival of the government agents.

The other agent kicked a large piece of the splattered xenophage with the toe of his highly polished shoe. "We've got it."

"Thanks for killing that thing," Cam said.

"It's our job," the lead agent said, a trace of pride creeping into his otherwise emotionless words.

"Are you with OSS?" Lindsay asked.

"Who we are is not important. What's important is that you're safe and that thing is destroyed."

"You mean the xenophage, right?" Lindsay asked while looking around at its scattered, shiny remains.

The two agents looked at each other. "You've been talking to that reporter, haven't you?"

Neither Cam not Lindsay answered.

The lead agent shrugged. "It doesn't matter what Megan Conrad reports in her tabloid, no one will believe it anyway. We've had a lot of practice with these situations. Chemical leaks and inadvertent releases of exotic tropical pets happen all the time. More than you would think."

Lindsay put her hands on her hips. "Exotic tropical pets?" She pointed to the green slime on the dirt around them. "That was no exotic tropical pet. That was an alien life form! These things are crashing to Earth all the time!"

"Believe whatever you like, but no one else will," the lead agent said. "Now that the situation's under control, you and the other citizens of this town will be allowed to return home."

The other agent removed a sleek cell phone from his suit pocket and pressed in a number. Although he turned his back to Cam and Lindsay, they overhead him alerting his superiors about the incident.

The lead agent forced a slight smile. "Thank you for leading us to it."

"You had us under surveillance?" Lindsay asked.

The agent nodded. "We suspected you would find it."

Cam was amazed. He didn't think he had been followed. He couldn't believe he'd been tracked by the OSS men all this time.

Slipping his phone back in his pocket and turning toward them, the other agent said, "Tell me one thing. How did you know it would be here, at this gravel pit?"

Cam tilted his head. "Huh?"

"How did you know?" the agent repeated suspiciously. "Were you in communication with it?"

Although their eyes were covered by mirrored sunglasses, Cam could feel their intense gaze locked onto him. He swallowed and glanced quickly at Lindsay and decided he was not going to tell these two mysterious men anything. "Of course not," he answered, scrunching his face as if it were the stupidest question ever asked. "We were just hiding from the evacuation."

"Is that all?" the lead agent challenged. "What was happening when we shot the thing? What were you doing with it?"

"Nothing," Cam said. "It attacked us. We froze, I guess. It was really scary."

The agents watched him warily, as if they disbelieved him.

Cam looked down at the green, wet remains of the tiny creature that had targeted him. It seemed so small and fragile to have caused so much trouble.

Then he glanced at Lindsay and smiled. He stepped toward her, and they kissed, thankful to be safe, relieved they had defeated the alien menace, and overjoyed at being together.

EPILOGUE

Cam's mother leaned against the old Corolla in the driveway, her arms crossed. Her skin still glowed with the Mediterranean sun from her Italian vacation. "We better hit the road, Cam," she said anxiously, glancing at her Gucci watch, which was a gift from her boyfriend, Frank.

"Just a few more minutes," Cam said with a sigh as he gave Lindsay's hand a squeeze. He didn't want to go home and leave his girlfriend behind. This was the most difficult thing he had ever had to do, except for attending his father's funeral.

His mother smiled coyly as she watched her son with his girl. She turned her attention to her sister, Ellen, who was in Uncle Gary's arms. The three adults chatted amicably, thankfully leaving Cam a few more minutes to say farewell to Lindsay.

The dog days of August had arrived at Lake Tecumseh, but it seemed too early for Cam to return to his old life amid the hustle of Chicago and the routines of high school. His inevitable, prolonged good-bye hung in the humid air.

He looked over his beautiful girlfriend, feeling his heartstrings tightly stretched to the breaking point. How could he leave her behind? How could he leave the girl he loved?

Never would he have predicted this was how he would feel when his mother finally returned to take him home. Less than three months before the two of them had driven together to Indiana under a cloud of anger and resentment. Cam had hated the idea of spending the summer in the isolated resort town of Lake Tecumseh. He felt as if he were being punished for his unruly behavior, abandoned so his mother could spend a fabulous summer in Europe with her new boyfriend. His life had seemed to reach a dead end from which he could not just U-turn and escape.

But things had changed, as quickly as the Midwestern weather.

Lindsay waited, her eyes watery. "I love you, Cam," she whispered, her voice wavering. "I'll miss you!"

"I love you, too, and I'll miss you even more. I'll be back as often as I can. I'm going to get a job and a car so I can visit."

"I hope so," she said, wiping her eyes. "What am I going to do? It won't be the same without you."

He hugged her. "I've had a wonderful summer, and all because of you!"

"It was a lot of fun, wasn't it?"

He had never experienced a summer such as this one. In spite of the adventures—retrieving the meteorite from the bottom of the lake, exploring its mysteries, and battling the alien xenophages—what he enjoyed the most was meeting Lindsay, the girl of his dreams, and sharing the summer together.

She had shown him her town and her life, and had opened his eyes to an improved way of looking at the world. The chip on his shoulder was no more than a pebble now, if it still stuck there at all. He had put to rest the demons that tormented him. He still grieved over the death of his father, but he realized now the direction his life needed to take—the direction his father would have wanted.

He had matured over the short span of three months. He wasn't ready to go back to Chicago, but he knew he returned with a positive attitude and renewed strength to avoid troublesome situations and make better decisions.

Everyone turned as an SUV entered the driveway and pulled up behind the Corolla. Mr. Russell climbed out of the driver's seat, and Megan Conrad emerged from the passenger door, grinning.

"What are you doing here?" Cam asked excitedly. Megan had returned to New York after the xenophage incident at UFO Days. He hadn't expected to see her again.

"Just coming to see you off, Cam," Mr. Russell said.

After quick introductions all around, Cam's mother and his relatives returned to their chatting. Cam suspected most of the conversation was about him. From the happy looks on their faces, it was nothing to be worried about. Over all, everything had worked out well.

Megan smiled and hugged Mr. Russell. "I thought it'd be nice to come back," she said, beaming at the teacher. "Now I have a reason to visit Indiana."

"And New York's never been more appealing to me," Mr. Russell said, squeezing the shapely reporter toward him.

Cam was happy the two adults had found love at their age. He looked at Lindsay. Love was something everyone deserved to experience.

"How's your grandfather?" Megan asked Lindsay.

"He's doing well. He's fishing all the time, and he's busy building a new workshop."

Orville Milford had completely recovered from being stung by a xenophage. Cam thought about the hideous little creatures they had battled just a few weeks before. The whole experience with *real aliens* at this summer's UFO Days had been promptly and completely hushed up by the OSS for the sake of national security. They had even stopped publication of Megan's story about the incident in *American Investigator Magazine*.

Fortunately there were no more xenophages in Lake Tecumseh. Cam had received no further alien ESP signals or headaches from them. He had slept peacefully the rest of the summer, his dreams filled not with alien landscapes and voyages through space, but with Lindsay's beautiful face and the sensuous curves of her body.

His dream journal sat unused.

Cam suspected the xenophages were in government storage somewhere. Whether they were alive or pickled in formaldehyde-filled jars, he would never know.

"Are you still reporting on UFOs?" Cam asked Megan.

She nodded. "Of course, but the OSS monitors my every move. If there's a hint of an alien meteorite or xenophage sighting, they're right on top of it. Everything's locked down really tight right now."

Cam's mother came up and reminded him of the time. "Are you still talking about your alien summer? Maybe you can write a novel about it someday!"

Cam chuckled even though he suspected his mother didn't really believe the story about xenophages. "Someday the truth will get out, and maybe I'll be the one to do it!"

"We can do it together!" Lindsay said, squeezing his hand.

We've got to go, dear," Cam's mother said to him. "Traffic's building."

Cam was disappointed to leave. He said good-bye to Mr. Russell and Megan, and then turned back to Lindsay. He hugged and kissed her one final time, pausing to wipe a tear from her velvety, brown eyes. "I'll see you again, soon."

"I hope so," she whispered. "Please come visit."

"I will. Nothing can keep me from coming back." He wanted to sound strong and brave, but inside his heart was breaking. He steeled himself to keep from sobbing. He gave Lindsay a kiss, wishing they would be reunited in person soon. Although they would trade phone calls and e-mail, nothing could substitute for their being together. As he pulled away from her, he felt as if he were leaving a large part of his soul behind. "I love you," he choked out.

"I love you, too," she answered.

He took a deep breath; it was not easy to leave. He turned toward the adults, who watched with amused smiles and tilted heads the dramatic parting of young lovers.

"You're always welcome to stay with us, Cam," Uncle Gary said.

Aunt Ellen smiled and nodded in agreement.

Cam noticed their eyes were watery, too. Cam thanked them for their hospitality. He had certainly learned a lot from them this summer, and he would miss Aunt Ellen's home cooking.

He glanced back at the cottage, blinked at the bright blueness of the lake's water, and inhaled deeply the fresh, wooded air of the countryside. He turned to Lindsay, who stood tearfully in the driveway, and blew her a kiss. She acted as if she caught the kiss and then cradled her palm against her breast.

Cam grabbed his bag and headed for the passenger side of the Corolla. "Hey, Mom," he called as he opened the car door and threw his bag in the rear seat, "Can we swing by Purdue on the way back?"

His mother froze. "Purdue? You mean you're thinking about college?"

He shrugged. "Sure, why not? It'll be fun." He glanced back at Lindsay and grinned. She was going to Purdue, so why shouldn't he? He had to buckle down, study hard, and stay out of trouble, but he had renewed dedication to do that. He couldn't let Lindsay down. He couldn't let himself down, either. He had done that too often over the last few years, especially since his dad had passed away.

His attitude had changed, and he felt as if he had been reborn due to the intense love of a beautiful young woman amid the quiet flatness of rural Indiana.

His mother slid behind the steering wheel and smiled. "Well, I guess it's all worked out for the best this summer. Who would've thought?"

As they drove down State Road 2, heading back to Chicago, Cam watched the cornfields rush by them in an emerald blur. Their stalks were tall in their green glory, golden tassels waving from their tops, tawny lower leaves already turning brown and shriveling for the autumn. Harvest would not be too far away.

He leaned his head against the seat and sighed, picturing Lindsay in his mind, missing her deeply already.

Summer was just never long enough.

ABOUT THE AUTHOR

Stacey S. Thompson grew up in Indiana and currently lives in Wheeling, Illinois, a suburb of Chicago. Trained as a chemist, he is employed at a large pharmaceutical company in regulatory affairs. In his spare time he enjoys reading, weightlifting, bike riding, and long walks. Writing science fiction is a lifelong dream of his.

Alien Summer is his second novel.

www.ingramcontent.com/pod-product-compliance
Lightning Source LLC
Chambersburg PA
CBHW071136260626
47162CB00003B/809

* 9 7 8 0 6 9 2 0 2 6 6 7 0 *